P9-EEU-341

River Forest Public Library
735 Lathrop Avenue
River Forest, IL 60305
708-366-5205
**November** 2021

7m/4c

# YEAR
### OF
### THE
# REAPER

# YEAR
## OF THE
## REAPER

# MAKIIA LUCIER

**CLARION BOOKS**
*AN IMPRINT OF* HARPERCOLLINSPUBLISHERS
BOSTON  NEW YORK

Clarion Books is an imprint of HarperCollins Publishers.

Year of the Reaper

Copyright © 2021 by Makiia Lucier

All rights reserved. No part of this book may be used or reproduced in any manner whatsoever without written permission except in the case of brief quotations embodied in critical articles and reviews. For information address HarperCollins Children's Books, a division of HarperCollins Publishers, 195 Broadway, New York, NY 10007.

clarionbooks.com

The Library of Congress Cataloging-in-Publication Data is on file.

ISBN: 978-0-358-27209-0

The text was set in Minion Pro.

Cover design by Kerry Rubenstein

Interior design by Kaitlin Yang

Manufactured in the United States of America

1 2021

4500837894

First Edition

*Heaven has no rage like love to hatred turned*

*Nor hell a fury like a woman scorned.*

**—William Congreve,** *The Mourning Bride*

THEY RODE FOR HOURS, through the night and into the dawn, stopping for nothing, not even to rest the horses. They knew what hunted them. A threat that could neither be seen nor heard nor felt, until one turned around and there it was. Too late to run then. Plague was spread through the air, you see. Everyone knew this.

Jehan struggled to stay awake on her horse. Weariness dragged her chin to her chest before she caught herself, jerking upright in the saddle. Bleary eyes took in the tall, stately cypress lining their route and the sun rising above the mountains in the east. Ten guards rode before her, ten in back. So few of them remained. The others had been left behind in towns and villages along the way. Her people. Shed like snakeskin.

Dead like snakeskin.

Jehan could not think of them now. If she did, she would scream. On and on forever. And that would not do, here, in front of the others.

Mari was alive. This she could give thanks for. Just then, Mari looked over from her own horse. She wore a traveling cloak the same midnight blue as Jehan's. Her hood had been pushed back, and long dark hair blew free in the wind. The smile she gave Jehan was tired but reassuring. *Not long now,* she mouthed.

Despite everything, Jehan smiled. Mari had been saying the

same for days. *Not long now. Almost there.* Jehan started to tell her so just as one of the guards ahead slid from his horse. He did not wake and catch himself but fell out of the saddle entirely, hitting the earth with a thud and the unmistakable sound of bone cracking.

"Stop!" Jehan shouted.

Dust rose, pebbles flew. The cortege ground to a halt. Without waiting for assistance, Jehan dismounted. She grabbed Mari's hand and they raced to where the Brisan ambassador already knelt by the fallen guard.

The ambassador flung out an arm to ward them off. "Stand back!"

He was normally a mild-mannered man, gray-haired and dignified. The ferocity of his tone stopped them in their tracks. That, and the panic that lay just beneath the surface. They obeyed. Jehan, Mari, the guards, the envoy from Oliveras. The old nurse and the court painter, wringing their hands in dread.

As for the fallen guard, he sprawled on his back, barely conscious. From the way one arm lay on the ground, the angle hideous and unnatural, Jehan knew it was broken. Just as she understood shattered bones were the least of his troubles. Sweat poured off a face that had turned a familiar mottled red. Pity filled her, sorrow too, but not surprise.

"Plague?" Jehan asked quietly. Mari's hand tightened in hers.

"He's feverish." The ambassador busied himself removing the guard's tunic. Rather than yank it over his head and broken arm, he took a dagger from his belt and sliced through leather and wool.

Mari reasoned, "A fever, then. It doesn't mean . . ." She trailed off in dismay as the ambassador pushed aside the guard's tunic, exposing the pit of his arm, where a boil the size of an egg nestled among downy black hairs. A strange gurgling sound emerged from it. The boil shivered and pulsed, as though the blood and pus and poison within were living things struggling to break free.

Sickened, Jehan stepped back. Everyone stepped back. Fear sent shivers racing up her spine and trailing along her limbs. Plumes of smoke rose in the distance. Another village burning its dead. Jehan could almost taste the bitterness of the ash, thick at the base of her throat.

The ambassador remained crouched by the guard's side. He closed his eyes briefly. When he opened them, they settled on her. Red-rimmed from exhaustion, the smudges beneath grown darker with each passing day.

"Princess Jehan. This can go on no longer. You must leave us."

Jehan exchanged a quick, startled glance with Mari. Jehan said, "What are you saying? Leave whom? And go where?" All around them were anxious mutterings.

"We're hindering you." The ambassador stood, knees cracking. "Every one of us is a threat. Go with Lord Ventillas. Take Mari, take the women — and find King Rayan."

"Father, no!" Mari burst out. A look from the ambassador had her swallowing her words.

Jehan had no intention of riding to the capital of Oliveras without him. "And leave you here? Of course I won't go —"

"Princess Jehan." The ambassador spoke with steel in his voice. "How many years have we been at war with Oliveras?"

*A history lesson? Now?* "Why does that matter?"

"How many? Tell me."

Jehan could not remember the precise number. Who could? Everyone watched, waiting, and a mortifying heat spread up her neck. Mari squeezed her hand. Under her breath, for Jehan's ears only, Mari murmured, "Fifty-two."

Jehan squeezed back. One could always depend on Mari. "Fifty-two," she repeated in a louder voice.

"As many years as I've been alive." The look the ambassador gave her and Mari made it clear he had not been fooled. "I've never known a life without war. Countless dead. Your brothers. My sons. This war ends the day you marry the king. You *must* survive this journey, and your odds are greater if you move quickly. If you avoid all threat."

A traveling quarantine of sorts. It made sense. "But why won't you come? You're the head of this delegation. Father sent *you*."

Beside her, a hitch to Mari's breath. She knew the answer to Jehan's question. She saw it on her father's face.

"I cannot." The ambassador pushed aside his collar to show the boil just beneath his ear. Like an overripe berry, wine-colored, ready to burst.

Jehan bit her lip so hard she tasted blood. Mari's hand slipped free of hers, but when her friend stumbled forward, Jehan caught her arm and dragged her back.

The ambassador did not look at his daughter. Instead, he watched Jehan intently to see what she would do. Church bells rang out in the village. Tolling endlessly. A warning to all who heard to keep away. They would find no shelter there. Fighting a rising panic, Jehan thought about what the ambassador's illness meant. For all of them. She *hated* Oliveras, this kingdom where she would be queen. It had brought nothing but pain and death to those she loved. She wanted to go home, to Brisa. But she had promised her father. She had given her word. Very quietly, she asked, "What will you do?"

Approval flickered over the ambassador's expression. He studied the woods beyond the road. "We'll stay here, make camp." Glancing down at the doomed guard, he added, "No one will take us in as we are. If we can, we'll follow."

"*When* you can," Jehan corrected.

"When," the ambassador agreed. Humoring her, she knew. And now he looked past her. "My lord Ventillas."

The sober Oliveran envoy was a younger man, not yet thirty. He stepped forward. "I'll see them safe, Ambassador. You have my word."

"Brisa is indebted to you." The ambassador bowed. "May God grant your honor many years."

"And yours." Lord Ventillas returned the bow, deep and formal.

Within minutes, a much smaller cortege prepared to ride. Mari stopped her mare as close to the ambassador as she dared. "Father."

The ambassador stood with a dying guard at his feet. Jehan heard him say, very softly, "Mari, you are your father's heart. Be brave, my girl, for me."

Jehan could bear to watch no longer. She spurred her horse down the ancient road lined with cypress. Tears blinded her. She did not look back to see those she had left behind. She did not look back to see if her friend would follow. All their lives, where Jehan went, Mari always followed.

1

WHEN IT CAME to the dead, it was best to pretend he did not see them. This Cas had learned the hard way, early on, when the plague had struck and the bodies lay blanketed around him. And as he crossed the bridge, the ghost keeping pace by his side, it became clear he would have to pretend harder. This particular spirit was growing suspicious.

Cas knew him. His name was Izaro. In life, he had guarded the bridge just beyond Cas' ancestral lands. A grizzled toll keeper with a black beard that tumbled down his chest. Nearly as solid as any living creature. So Izaro was gone too. Who was left?

"Boy?" Izaro said, a question spoken hard and rough. He had caught Cas unawares, appearing from behind a tree near the foot of the bridge. Cas had not been able to hide his expression in time, and Izaro had seen something — an awareness, a recognition — that had made him wonder.

A chill hung in the early morning air, accompanied by the blustery winds of autumn. Cas did not alter his stride. He pulled his cloak tighter about him and glanced down into the river with its rapid westward current. His breathing remained even, his expression bland. If his heart beat faster than usual, no one knew but him.

The horse was another matter. She followed behind Cas, led by reins. A pretty white mare with a black star below her right eye, placid enough until Izaro's appearance. Then her steps shied. She tugged at the reins and swung her head in clear agitation. Did she see Izaro? Or merely sense him?

Cas said mildly, "What's the matter, girl? Tired? We're almost home."

"You see me, boy?"

Cas yawned. They had reached the center of the bridge. Izaro stopped even as Cas and the horse continued on. *Good.* The toll keeper had been fooled. Behind him, Cas heard a muttered "Bah. Dumb as a sack full of cats. Just like his mother."

Cas froze. An instant, only. It was enough. Izaro whisked around to stand before Cas. He threw out his arms, triumphant.

"You *do* see me! I knew it!"

Cas snarled, "Get out of my way." He shifted right. The toll keeper blocked his path. He shifted left. The same. Cas would not go through him, though it was possible. He had done so once, would never forget the repugnant feeling of it, like worms twisting around his innards. It had sent him to his knees, retching onto the dirt.

Thwarted, Cas drew himself up to his full height and glared. He was eighteen, away from home these three years past, and in that time he had grown tall enough to meet the toll keeper's gaze full on. They were both startled by it.

"What do you want?" Cas demanded.

"What do I —? *How* can you see me?"

"I don't know."

It was a question Cas had asked himself many times. If others could see spirits, he did not know this, either. It was not something one asked, ever, or freely admitted to if you knew what was good for you. There were places for the mad, none of them pleasant. "Is that all? Then, good day to you, toll keeper." He waited for Izaro to take the hint and move aside.

Izaro did not budge. Now that he had Cas' attention, he appeared uncertain as to what to do next. The wind whipped Cas' black hair up and around in every direction. In contrast, Izaro's beard lay unmoving against his chest. The seconds ticked by. Finally, it was Cas who spoke. He did not want to ask, but he was desperate to know.

"Have you seen my brother?" The tremble in his voice was humiliating.

"No." Something like pity crossed Izaro's features. "Not for a year. Not since the pestilence. No one comes by here anymore."

Cas had not truly expected an answer. He stepped aside. This time Izaro let him pass, much to the horse's relief, but moments later, Cas heard him speak quietly.

"Will you bury me?"

Cas stopped. He spoke without turning. "You insult my mother's memory, and you expect me to do this for you?"

"Bah. I only said it to chafe you —"

Cas shot a look over his shoulder. "Well, it worked."

"Lord Cassiapeus . . ." Cas grimaced upon hearing his birth name. Izaro did not notice. He was looking to the opposite end of the bridge, where a stone cottage stood off to one side. For centuries, it had served as a place where the toll keepers worked and slept. "No one has been to tend to me. The animals have come."

His words produced a grisly assortment of images in Cas' mind. Reluctantly, he eyed the cottage. Part of the thatched roof had fallen in. Something that would never have occurred had Izaro been alive.

The door stood wide open, knocked free of its upper hinges so that it hung askew from its lower.

*The animals have come.*

"Please," Izaro added.

Cas inspected his hands. Scarred, callused. Hands accustomed to burying the dead. He had hoped to be done with it. "You have a shovel?"

The relief on Izaro's face shamed him. Cas turned away and pretended he did not see.

***

Izaro had been dead for many months. Long enough that the worst of the smell had gone, along with most of his flesh and innards, gnawed away by forest creatures.

From the doorway, Cas surveyed the chamber. An abacus and ledger sat on a table covered in dust. Part of the ledger had been chewed away. Animal droppings littered the floor, the rug, the windowsill. Rats and birds by the look of them. A bed and chair had been placed in a corner. Izaro walked past Cas to collapse onto the chair, and they both stared at the body on the bed. Cas had seen worse. He guessed Izaro had not.

"The shovel?" Cas prompted quietly.

"Out back."

"Where" — Cas gestured toward the bed — "is your preference? The village?"

"Too far," Izaro replied, unable to take his eyes off what was left of him. "Anywhere. Just . . ." His voice broke. "Not here."

With quick, efficient moves, Cas untucked the bedclothes and wrapped the body in them. His actions sent a wave of shiny yellow beetles scuttling off the corpse in every direction. The insects piled into a mound by Cas' boot. The sounds they made, *click, click, click,* grew louder as they formed a single queue and trailed across the chamber, up to the open window, and out of the cottage. The clicking faded away. Izaro, still in the chair, turned a curious shade of green. Cas had not realized it was possible for a ghost to feel queasy.

"Don't look," Cas advised. It was easier to breathe through his mouth. The worst of the smell might have gone but not all of it. Grunting, he tossed the shrouded Izaro over his shoulder and staggered out the door. The body, though heavy, was little more than bone and hair, held together by tendon and rotting wool. It rattled and clacked as Cas rounded the cottage, past a small fenced yard that he remembered had once held chickens. A rusted shovel lay on the ground by the back wall. He grabbed it, then clambered up the embankment, Izaro following close behind.

***

"Here?" Cas asked.

They stood in a grove full of wild olive trees and dense pine. A good place, he thought, to bury a man who had prized his solitude. At Izaro's nod, Cas tossed the shovel onto the ground and laid the body beside it. His heavy cloak followed.

The morning sun offered little heat, and the wind remained brisk, but the work more than made up for it. Cas had already gone to the river twice to refill his flask. As for Izaro, he sat with his back against a nearby olive tree. Quiet at first until Cas, shirt sticking unpleasantly to his skin, tugged it over his head and left it by the cloak. At the sound of Izaro's hiss, Cas went still.

*Idiot.* How could he have forgotten the scars? Cas looked at Izaro, whose eyes were filled with shock and horror, and saw what he saw.

Scarring that covered his back and chest. The long line of a whip, from left shoulder to right hipbone. The crescents formed by a steel-toed boot. Deep purple bands at his wrists where iron cuffs had rubbed the skin raw. Cas had lost any hope the vivid, angry markings would ever fade away.

"Who did this to —?" Izaro broke off. Whatever it was he saw on Cas' face silenced him.

Without speaking, Cas reached for his shirt and put it on. Humiliation rose like bile in his throat.

He grabbed the shovel and dug.

Deeper.

And he remembered.

The last of his beatings had come a year ago, a memory that never strayed far from his thoughts.

"Get up."

The guard's kick had caught him in the ribs as he bent to lift another stone. Flinching, Cas did as he was told. In the years since his capture and imprisonment, he had sprouted upward and outward, though this guard continued to loom over him. "Get your slop," the guard ordered. He marched off, kicking and barking his way past the other prisoners.

Cas had never been so far from home. Only feet away, Brisa's grandest bridge lay in ruins. Destroyed in the ongoing war between Oliveras, the land of his birth, and Brisa, this wretched kingdom in the north. Cas had been among the prisoners sent here to help rebuild the bridge. Stone by stone. He joined the others in the queue waiting for their share of kettle slop. Turnips and cat meat likely, if there was meat at all. At least it would be hot. He had woken with a vicious chill and a discovery that he had spoken of to no one. For he was surrounded by his enemies, and there was no one here to tell.

The shove at his back was expected. Almost perfunctory. Cas ignored it, which only earned him another. This time he shifted and smiled pleasantly at a gray-toothed man named Mendo.

"What are you looking at, Oliveran?" Mendo demanded. "I'll beat that ugly face of yours in, you keep looking at me."

Mendo alone was no threat, but he had friends. Fellow Brisans. Not for the first time, Cas wished his brother were here. For his protection and for his counsel. What would Ventillas do in his place? And as he thought of his brother, the answer became clear. Cas replied, "Ugly? That's not what your sister said."

That was all it took. It was as simple and as pitiful as that. Mendo's eyes widened in outrage and his face purpled as the other prisoners heard and laughed. Cas braced himself. *Here it starts.* Seconds later, he was in the mud, kicked and pummeled by Mendo and anyone else who could get a fist or a foot in. His lip split open. The blows to his stomach had him coughing up blood. A single kick or a thousand. One would think he would become resigned to the beatings after years of imprisonment, able to bear them more easily. It was not so. They never became easier. Every indignity made him feel more like a dog and less like the boy his family had loved. Though terror and pain filled him, Cas fought none of it. Did not even attempt to shield his face as the blows rained down. *Touch me all you want, you mules. As much as you want, today.*

More shouting came from afar. Cas' abusers were hauled off. He squinted through swollen eyes to see the same guard glaring down at him.

"Oy! What's this, then?" the guard demanded.

"The Oliveran started it," one prisoner offered. "Said bad things about Mendo's sister."

It was not the guard who answered but his captain, who stepped into Cas' line of sight. A man not much older than Cas with a weak chin and a crisp uniform. He regarded the situation with mild interest. "Ah. The old sister provocation. Only you don't have a sister, Mendo."

"He didn't know that," Mendo protested. "Can't have a filthy Oliveran insulting our women."

"True." The captain surveyed the prisoners with their bloodied knuckles, then turned to Cas, who had pulled himself to his knees. "What's wrong with you today, Oliveran? You usually fight back."

Cas spat blood onto the ground. "One against thirty?" His voice came out hoarse. It hurt to speak. "To what end?"

"That never stopped you before," the captain pointed out. "I wouldn't be so eager to die if I were in your place. We all know where you're off to next."

Mendo, who didn't have a sister, said, "To hell, you basta —"

"Yes, Mendo, I think he understood. On your feet, Oliveran." The captain turned to the guard, who pulled a whip from his belt. "Fighting is not tolerated in my camp. Someone must be punished. It might as well be you."

Cas swayed to his feet, every inch of him screaming in agony. He shivered. It was so terribly cold.

The guard stepped forward. "Your shirt."

With difficulty, Cas pulled his shirt, stained and torn even before the beating, over his head. A stunned silence fell, followed by a mad rush as everyone — prisoners, guard, captain — backed away from him.

Cas glanced down. He had discovered the boils that morning. One below his collarbone, the other by his hip. They had not been there the night before. And now they had burst open, punctured by kicks and punches. He knew what the boils meant, had heard the rumors from the city, of overrun hospitals and bodies left in the street. He had seen the uneasy watchfulness among the guards.

*This* was what his brother would do. If escape was impossible and death imminent, Ventillas would take his enemies with him. As many as he could. Though it hurt tremendously, Cas grinned, teeth slick with blood as he looked at the men with their bleeding knuckles and panicked eyes.

"Going to hell, am I?" He barely recognized his voice. "I'll take you with me."

But Cas had not died that day, or any day since. Of all the men by the bridge, he had been the only one to survive the plague.

***

"You've done this before."

Izaro's voice recalled him to the present. The toll keeper pointed at the shovel. "Grave digging. This is not your first time."

Cas turned away. "No."

"Where were you?"

"North." Cas shoveled more dirt onto the growing mound. The grave could not be a shallow one. Six feet at least. Otherwise the animals would come sniffing and dig it up again.

"Where north?" Izaro prodded.

Cas did not answer. He wrestled a large rock free and set it aside.

There was a small silence before Izaro observed, "You used to talk more."

"And you less."

A snort. What might have been a laugh. "You never told your brother what I did to you."

"There was nothing to tell."

"No?" Izaro returned with deep skepticism. "A toll keeper beating Lord Ventillas' younger brother? I could have lost my life for that."

The shovel hit another rock. Cas dug it out and tossed it away. "I might have deserved it."

"Bah," Izaro said, amused. "That you did."

When Cas was eight or nine, as a prank, he'd unlocked the pen by Izaro's cottage and set his chickens loose. Cas giggled behind tree cover as the toll keeper scrambled and swore, trying to catch his birds. Unfortunately, a number of chickens vanished into the woods and were lost forever. Cas had not considered that outcome. He had felt badly about it. Neither had he considered his clothing. The red tunic was easily spotted among the wild olive and pine. Izaro had chased him down in no time at all and tossed him over a knee. Cas had been forced to walk home, teary-eyed, for he had not been able to sit his horse. He had also kept the whole mortifying incident to himself.

Cas thought back to Izaro's cottage. The small pen had been latched, the yard empty. "What happened to your chickens?"

Izaro muttered something incomprehensible.

Cas looked over his shoulder. "What?"

"A man came by. He took the toll. He took my chickens."

Cas stopped digging. He turned around fully to stare at Izaro. "Were you . . . ?" He gestured at the open grave.

"Dead?" Izaro's lips twisted. "Not yet. He came in long enough to hunt down the coin. Didn't say a word to me. Wouldn't give me water when I asked. Took my axe, too. Heard him tell his girl to gather up the birds."

A picture came to Cas, of Izaro lying sick and helpless while looters took their fill. "Who was it?" he asked abruptly.

Izaro told him. A name Cas knew. He lived in Palmerin, if he still lived.

"Where did you keep the toll?" Cas asked.

"Under the floorboards."

"How much was there?"

The amount he named made Cas' eye twitch. These lands belonged to Lord Ruben, a neighbor, and Cas could think of only one reason why no one had come to look in on Izaro. To collect the tolls if nothing else. A hot, bitter lump curdled his gut. He asked a question he already knew the answer to. "Where is Lord Ruben?"

Izaro only shook his head.

"The family?"

"All gone."

For so long the dead had been strangers. Or enemies. Lord Ruben had been neither. And if plague had reached its bony, black-ened fingers this far into the mountains, what did that mean for his brother? Cas went back to digging. But after a time he looked at Izaro, gazing morosely down into the deepening pit, and asked, "Can you leave this place?"

"No. I have to stay near the river."

"You've tried to go farther?"

A nod.

"What happens?"

"It starts to hurt here." Izaro placed a hand over his heart. He glanced past Cas and said curiously, "Do you see her?"

Cas looked over to where Izaro indicated. There was nothing but a path leading to the river. The hairs stood up along his arms. "No."

He resumed digging. When he had dug deep enough, he tossed the shovel aside and climbed out. Izaro watched him pull the body, still shrouded, to the very edge of the grave. Cas jumped back in, then carefully eased the corpse into his arms. His nostrils flared in protest. He set Izaro down as gently as he could, climbed out, and filled the hole. Neither of them spoke until Cas was done. He grabbed the shovel, said, "Well, goodbye," and picked up his empty flask.

Izaro looked astonished. "What? Wait!" He hurried after Cas. "What about a prayer?"

Cas kept walking. He tucked the flask into his belt. "What about it?"

"Lord Cassiapeus —"

"Prayers are beyond me." Cas looked straight ahead. He could hear the anxiousness in Izaro's voice. He did not need to see the proof of it in his eyes. "I hope . . . I hope you can sleep now, Izaro. I'm sorry for what I did to your chickens."

But Izaro did not appear to care about his long-lost birds. "Don't you believe in prayer?"

"Not anymore."

"But —"

Cas turned on him so suddenly Izaro stumbled back. "Look where you are! Where we all are, and tell me you believe there's someone watching over us." So many dead. What good had prayer done for them? He flung the shovel to the ground.

Izaro's arms hung by his sides. Subdued, he said, "If I don't believe, what will happen to me?"

"I don't know. I can't help you."

Before Cas turned away, Izaro asked, in a different voice, "Do you see *her*?" They had reached the embankment. Above the bridge and the cottage, where he had left his horse.

"No, I said —" Cas stopped. Because there was someone by the mare.

From this distance, Cas saw a scrawny boy, twelve or thirteen, holding the reins with one boot already in the stirrup and watching Cas with wary eyes. Cas recognized the livery. The stranger wore the blue tunic and gray leggings of a royal messenger, along with a cap perched at a jaunty angle.

But Izaro had said *her*.

"A girl?" Cas asked the ghost, full of doubt.

"I'm dead and I can see it."

The stranger called out, "Who are you talking to?"

"No one," Cas answered. Izaro had seen what he had not, for the voice belonged to a lady. *Not* a twelve-year-old but someone of an age closer to his. Seventeen or eighteen. Her accent held no trace of the mountains, as his did. Her smooth, measured words brought to mind the capital city in the east. She was from Elvira. Cas crossed his arms and marveled at her nerve. She was *stealing* his horse. "Do you know what happens to horse thieves in this kingdom?"

"I do indeed." She swung onto the horse, graceful in her

movements, and did not appear worried Cas would catch her. They both knew he was too far away to give chase. He'd have to pick his way down the embankment to start. By then, she'd have ridden off in the other direction. "But I'm not stealing your horse, sir. I'm borrowing her. You may retrieve her at Palmerin, at the stables by the keep. I assume there is one. Do you know it?"

His family's keep. His family's stables. Yet he did not recognize her. "Borrowing means you asked permission."

"Ah." She held up a finger, like a tutor making a point. "It also means 'to take with the pledge to return.' Which I have just done. Therefore we are both in the right."

"Who says?" Cas demanded.

She lifted a shoulder. "A book I read."

Izaro made a disapproving sound in his throat. "Beware the clever ones," he warned.

Cas ignored him. "Where's your horse?"

"Stolen." Ignoring the look he gave her, she tossed his saddlebag onto the ground, then fished a coin from the pouch at her belt and flipped it into the air. It landed on the bag. "For your troubles. There'll be more when you reach the city."

Cas looked at the coin, then at his sweat-stained clothing, brown and green, nothing to distinguish him from any other dirty, weary traveler. He *was* weary. Walking the rest of the way would add hours to his journey.

He could simply tell her who he was. She would believe him eventually. He imagined what would come next. He could not leave her here, which meant they would have to share the horse. No. He would rather walk. It had been a long time since he had felt at ease in the company of others. Solitude had come to fit him like a glove.

"Fine," he conceded. "You may borrow her. I meant to check her hooves for bruising before we left. I'll do it now."

"Good try." Her smile was genuine. "My apologies, truly, but I need this horse more than you do. I am so terribly late."

*For what?* he wanted to ask, but she was already gone. Cas watched her race away, down the road to Palmerin. Outrage warred with admiration. A horse thief, yes, but she could ride. He turned to admit the same to Izaro, but the toll keeper was no longer by his side. He had trudged back toward his grave, without prayer, unmourned, leaving Cas by the trees and the riverbank, with nothing but his guilt for company.

# 2

H OURS LATER, Cas found his horse. Or, rather, his horse
found him.

He walked along an empty road, a path he had not seen in years.
In the time since he had been robbed by the girl, he had bathed in
the frigid river — thankfully no one had been around to hear his
yelps and gasps — and changed his clothing. A black wool tunic and
trousers beneath a hooded cloak. Tall black boots. All of fine qual-
ity. A doctor's widow had offered them as payment for digging two
graves. One for her husband and one for her son. Cas was grateful.
He had not wanted to return home in old clothing and worn shoe
leather. He had his pride. Even now, after all that had come to pass.

Palmerin's great aqueduct rose high on his left, soaring double
arches and ancient, weathered stone. The old builders had not used
mortar between the granite blocks. They had been fitted together
like the pieces of a giant puzzle. That the aqueduct remained
standing a thousand years after construction was an engineering
marvel. A small copse of trees stood to the right. Most of the leaves
remained green, but some had turned, oranges and golds, and as
he watched them drift to the ground, a white horse bolted from the
copse. His mare. She veered onto the road toward Cas, who, startled, dropped his saddlebag. He kept his arms extended in front of
him, palms out, calling, "Whoa! Whoa! It's me. Whoa!" The horse
galloped on. He was afraid she would not stop. But, seconds away

from trampling him into the dust, she came to a halt. Breathing hard. Just as he was.

"Come now. You're all right." He kept his voice low and soothing, stroking her mane and eventually earning a nuzzled ear in response. He scooped up his bag and made quick work of tying it to the saddle. "What happened?" he asked the horse. "Where is she?" Cas scanned the area. A lone vulture circled overhead, bearded and ominous. A lammergeier. The wind had picked up and there was nothing to be heard but the rustling of leaves and the swaying of grass, tall as his knees.

Until there was.

"Wretched beast! Shoo! Go away!"

Cas spun. There. A voice from the copse. Female, panicked, quite definitely his horse thief. A howling followed her cries. Like a barn cat, but bigger and meaner. Recognizing it, he snatched up the reins and fast-stepped the horse to a tree where she would not be easily seen by passing travelers. And then he ran.

The closer he came to the howling, the more cautious he grew. He navigated around the oak and the pine, the elm and the juniper, stepping over branches and sliding past dry, crumbling leaves to mask his footsteps. A saddlebag lay abandoned in the dirt. So did a messenger's cap. The copse gave way to a small clearing. Cas peered out from behind an elm.

Across the clearing was his horse thief. He could see her boots high up on the branch of a lone flame tree. Just the boots. Bright red tree cover shielded the rest of her. Directly beneath, a mountain lynx pawed at the trunk and hissed. The cat was the size of a large dog. Smaller than the ones that lived at Palmerin Keep. Still a terrible threat. Even from this distance, he could tell something was wrong with it. Lynx were prized among the nobility, their distinct fur — black spots on white — often sewn onto collars and cuffs and into the lining of expensive winter cloaks. This lynx would not be lining any cloaks. Its fur was sparse and mangy. Patches had fallen off, or been chewed off, leaving the skin beneath raw and exposed.

The thief continued to hurl down abuse. A steady stream of vivid curses and threats. Cas crept closer, careful to stay hidden. He was fifty feet away when the howling stopped. The lynx whipped around, hackles rising. It had caught his scent.

Cas retrieved the slingshot at his belt. He reached into his pouch and withdrew an iron ball the size of a plum and covered in spikes. He had learned to keep several on hand for when a simple rock would not do.

All the while, the lynx searched the tree line. It bared its teeth. Cas had been spotted.

"When I come down from this tree you'll regret it . . . Where are you going now, you wretched —?"

Cas stepped out into the open. Hissing, the lynx abandoned the tree and raced toward him on paws that skimmed the grass. As it drew closer, Cas saw the foam that covered its mouth and drenched its beard. Its eyes were horrible. Blood-filled, dripping from the corners. Careful not to pierce himself, he placed the ball in the sling, raised the shot, and waited. His heart thundered in his chest. He dared not miss. He could not risk a bite from this animal, not one scratch. Not with its foaming mouth and bleeding eyes. Only when it launched itself in the air did Cas send the ball flying.

"I am sorry," he said.

The ball lodged deep in one eye and the lynx fell down dead at his feet. A final hiss marked its passing. Cas shoved the slingshot in his belt and ran.

The thief stood on a thick branch of the flame tree, a very high place to have climbed without the help of notches and footholds. He did not see any. With her cap missing, a long dark braid had been freed. Her eyes widened in recognition when she saw him.

"You!"

"Are you hurt?" he called up urgently.

"No! Are *you*? Where is that awful cat?"

"Dead. Your hand is bleeding." Cas could see it from where he stood. If she had been bitten, the day would not end well for her.

"What?" She held up both hands for inspection. "It's from the tree bark," she explained. "Just scratches. It did not touch me. Have you seen my horse?"

Her question silenced him for a full five seconds. "*My* horse is by the road."

"Oh. Excellent. Is she safe?"

Cas felt a little more charitable toward her, seeing her concern for his horse. "It wasn't horse meat it had a taste for."

The thief grimaced, understanding. Lynx normally fed on rabbit or duck. Sometimes fawn. But in the past year, animals had been tempted by the human corpses that lay unburied, or not buried deep enough. The results were that all sorts of beasts — dogs, pigs, goats, cats — were left with bloody eyes and foaming mouths. Animals that must be avoided when necessary, killed when possible, and always, always burned.

With her back against the trunk, the thief slid down onto the branch, legs stretched out before her. "I don't know how I'm up here," she confessed. "I've never climbed a tree before. Not even a tree stump."

Fear could do that, Cas supposed. Have you racing across a clearing and up a tree like a squirrel, death nipping at your heels. "Can you climb back down?"

She gauged the distance from her branch to his boots. "No" was her definite response. She closed her eyes and leaned her head back against the trunk.

Cas pointed out what was obvious. "You can't stay up there forever."

"I'm aware." Her eyes remained closed. "What do you propose?"

*Huh.* Cas considered. He could climb up the tree, but then what? He would not be able to climb down again, not without footholds, not with the thief hanging from his neck. Only one solution presented itself. Sighing, he held out his arms. "Jump," he ordered.

Her eyes snapped open. She looked down at him, appalled. "You're mad. I will not."

"Fine." Cas kept his arms out. His words were testy. They would not be in this predicament if she had not stolen his horse. "What do *you* propose?"

"A ladder . . ." She stopped, immediately realizing the absurdity of her request. They were far from any village, any farm, any ladder.

Cas let it pass. "Come on, then. Jump."

She did not budge. "Why would you help me? I stole your horse."

"Oh yes? I thought you borrowed her."

Silence followed, accompanied by a sour glance.

Cas was beginning to feel like a fool, holding his arms out, talking to a tree. "Listen," he reasoned, "if there was one lynx here, there might be others. You're lucky its claws had fallen out. They're usually excellent climbers." He let her think about that one, adding, "I'll count to five and then I'm off. And I'm taking my horse with me. One."

His words had her bolting upright. "You'll drop me," she said with unflattering certainty.

"I will not. Two."

A note of panic. "You're not strong enough —"

"How kind. Three."

"Wait, please!"

"Four."

Cas would not call what happened next a jump. She merely scooted off the limb and allowed herself to fall. He caught her. The impact knocked the air from his lungs and sent him staggering backwards, where he tripped over his own feet . . . and dropped her.

Cas landed on his back with a pained grunt. The thief tumbled past to sprawl face-down in the grass. She groaned. Directly overhead, the lammergeier circled, closer than before. It was some time before anyone moved or spoke.

The thief pulled herself to her knees. Cas watched her pluck several blades of grass from her tongue. The royal shield had been embroidered onto her tunic. Black thread on blue, it depicted a snarling bull beside a pomegranate flower in full bloom. "Well," she said, rising gingerly and rubbing her backside. "That is the first and last tree I'll ever climb." She smiled down at him, a dazzling smile full of relief and goodwill, and offered a hand to pull him up.

Cas did not smile back. Rolling to his feet with a grimace, he took her hand in his and turned it palm up so he could inspect the blood and scratches.

Her smile faded. "I told you, it didn't bite me."

"Good." Cas had to be sure. He released her hand, far smaller than his, and reached for the other. This one, her left, was worse off. No bites, but more scratches, more blood, and one nasty-looking sliver embedded deep in her thumb.

Cas lifted his gaze, waited for her to do the same. Her skin was golden, a shade lighter than his, and her eyes were a deep brown, as dark as the innermost part of the woods. *I'm dead and I can see it*, Izaro had said. Yes, Cas could see it now too. "What is your name?"

"Lena. What is — gah!" A yelp silenced the rest. She watched him flick aside the sliver he had pulled from her thumb. A drop of blood bloomed in its place. She yanked her hand away, sucked on the wound, eventually offering a resentful "Thank you?"

His smile startled them both. He tucked it away beneath a frown and said, "We need to burn the cat." Cas pointed to the lammergeier. The vulture had landed high up on a juniper, waiting patiently for them to depart before it began feasting. No good could come from eating something so rotten. The thief, Lena, spotted the bird and made a face. "I'll do it."

The lynx had died on the far side of the clearing. She ran past it into the copse and returned with her cap and saddlebag. From the latter, she retrieved stones to strike a spark. Within minutes, the lynx was burning, flame and smoke drifting toward the sun. They stayed well back and watched. She did not see what Cas did, for in the smoke there were human faces. Ten or so swirling about, their features indistinct, leaving behind the impression of wide, frightened eyes and gaping mouths before dispersing into the wind. Lena might have been one of them, if the day had turned out differently. He glanced at her and found her studying him with a frown.

"Your face just lost all its color," she noted. "Do you feel faint? Here, lean on my arm —"

Cas walked away to fetch the mare. He could hear Lena hurrying to catch up.

She offered his back, "I'm very sorry about your horse."

"Not enough to return her." Cas spoke without turning or stopping.

A pause. "Yes, well . . ."

Cas halted. When she drew up beside him, he said, "How do you know I didn't have urgent business of my own? Hm? Visiting my sick grandmother, maybe, before it's too late?"

She blanched. "Is that where you're going? To see your dying grandmother?"

"No." Cas had never known his grandmothers. They had died before his birth. But she did not know that. He continued on.

She said something he did not hear, probably for the best.

Neither spoke as he untethered the mare and climbed on. A glance in Lena's direction painted a forlorn picture. Saddlebag hanging from one hand, cap in the other, head bowed. Bits of grass stuck out from her braid. Much as he wished to, he could not leave her here. He had meant what he said about the lynx. There could be more about.

He leaned down and held out a hand. His words were brusque. "Are you coming or not?"

Her head came up. Hope lit her eyes. "You'll take me with you?"

"I just said I would, didn't I?"

"No," she said slowly. "Not precisely . . ."

Cas looked at her, a hairsbreadth from changing his mind. She must have seen this. Hastily, she put her cap on, then took his hand. He hauled her before him so that her back rested against his chest and her cap fit snugly beneath his chin. He wondered at his decision to help her, to have her share his horse, for one thing he had come to understand about himself was this: He no longer cared to be touched. Not in anger, not with affection. Not in any way. Even now he could feel the cuffs at his wrists and ankles, chafing, his skin rubbed bloody. Too many bodies in too small a place, making it hard to breathe.

*Breathe.*

Cas released a long, pent-up breath. Silently, he took her bag and tied it with his own. She did not flinch from the arm he anchored around her waist, but twisted around to look up at him with a smile. "Thank you! This is very kind of you. I don't know your name."

He stared straight over her head. "Cas."

"Caz," she pronounced. "For Caspian?"

"No."

"Caspar?"

"No."

Exasperation tinged her voice. "Well, then, what —?"

"Your clothing is too big for you." He took in the folded-over sleeves of her blue tunic and her gray leggings, so loose he knew no self-respecting tailor would have approved their use. "You're as much a royal messenger as I am. Whose livery are you wearing? It's borrowed too, I suppose."

"I —" Her mouth clamped shut. Her glare held an understanding. He would ask no questions if she would do the same. She faced forward and said no more.

Satisfied, Cas set off on the road to Palmerin. Where he would learn if his brother remained with the living. Or wandered among the dead.

# 3

I T TURNED OUT his horse thief was as fine a traveling companion as he could have asked for; she slept the entire way. If Cas drew a long, shaky breath at his first sight of the keep, if he scrubbed stinging eyes with a fist, she had not been awake to see it or hear it. Small mercies. Slowing the horse to a walk, he savored the sight before him.

The mountain fortress of Palmerin had been built in a valley surrounded by steep, snow-capped ranges. Rose-colored walls protected its inhabitants, the original deep red faded over the centuries. It was the safest city in Oliveras in large part because it was so remote. Narrow passes, inhospitable winters. If that wasn't daunting enough, it was the ancestral home of the celebrated military commander Lord Ventillas. Most gave Palmerin a wide berth, seeking out easier prey.

To enter Palmerin, one first had to pass through the gates and pay a toll. Cas waited at the end of a queue a hundred long. The closer to the city, the more crowded the roads had become, with others flocking in from outlying farms and villages. Men on horseback, families in carts, women with lace headdresses and enormous straw hats, their skirts full and brightly colored. The boy in front of them, six or seven, drove a wagon filled with baby ibex. On his way to the main square, Cas guessed. Today was market day.

It was midafternoon, the sky clear, the air crisp. A beautiful day. But something was not right. The soldiers guarding the gates wore the king's blue, just as Lena did. Where were the soldiers in red? His family's men?

Cas did not bypass the line or skip the toll, though he could have. Palmerin Keep was his home. But today of all days, dread slowed his pace. Truth lay beyond those walls, and part of him did not want to know, with certainty, what had become of his brother. With doubt, at least, there was still hope.

"When were you last home?" Lena asked, making him jump. She glanced around long enough for him to see clear eyes and an alert expression.

"How long have you been awake?" he demanded. His face burned.

One shoulder lifted. "I wasn't asleep. I was contemplating." A pause. "You've been gone for some time, I think."

They had an understanding. No questions. Even so, Cas found himself answering. "Three years."

He felt her surprise. "Do you have family here? A grandmother?"

"My brother. I don't know if he's still here."

"Oh." Lena touched his hand, on the pommel, and Cas snatched it away in startled reflex. She went still. Her spine straightened so that her back no longer rested against him. Even worse, she raised her hands, palms outward. Just as he'd done earlier when trying to calm his frightened horse.

"I'll go now," she said quietly, and swung off the mare, dropping to the ground on light feet. She tried to undo the knot on her saddlebag, fumbling it.

Cas dismounted. She had meant only to comfort him. His reaction was not normal. He was not normal. Words gruff, he said, "I didn't mean to frighten you."

Her head came up. "You startled me. It's not the same."

"Let me." Untying her bag gave him reason to turn away. *Hand her the bag. Send her on her way.* But he wondered at her traveling alone. Wondered how she had lost her horse and had come to be in possession of a royal messenger's uniform. What was so urgent here in Palmerin that she would accept a ride with a complete stranger? He could have been anyone. He *was* anyone.

Cas held out the bag. "Are you in some sort of trouble?"

A small laugh. She took the bag he offered. "Oh yes. But I'm in no danger."

He reached into his own saddlebag and pulled out the gold coin she had left behind when she had stolen his horse. When he offered it to her, she refused.

"It's yours," she said.

"Keep it. For when you need to borrow another horse. Lawfully, next time."

A smile at this, rueful. The coin disappeared into her pouch. She cast a glance to the guards by the gates. "I have to go."

Cas nodded, saying nothing.

Lena slung the bag over a shoulder. "Farewell, Cas, only Cas, with no other name. I hope you find your brother."

She brushed the mare's nose with an affectionate smile, and just like that she was gone, hurrying to the front of the queue. Heads turned as she passed. She had not bothered to tuck her braid back into the cap, and she was quite clearly a pretty girl in men's clothing. A guard stepped forward at the gates. He was too far away for Cas to see his expression, but there was no mistaking how he stopped midstep, as if surprised, and the deep bow that followed. The guard bent his head, listening as Lena spoke. In no time at all, two horses were produced. Lena and the guard mounted them and rode through the gates, leaving Cas to wonder just who he had escorted to his city.

Two baby ibex poked their heads from the wagon's slats, bobbing their noses at Cas, who smiled. He led the horse forward, listening as the fees were called out:

*One civet for a man on foot!*
*One lynx for a horseman!*
*Half a lynx for a packhorse!*
*Two stoats for a cart!*

The tolls had gone up. No surprises there. They never went down. The line moved briskly and before long it was his turn.

"One lynx," the toll keeper informed him, a small man wearing the king's blue. His wispy mustache drooped and his voice carried the high, nasal twang of the southern border towns.

Cas eyed the blue tunic. "Where are the city guards?"

"Nowhere you need to know." The toll keeper thrust out an open palm. "One lynx. Pay the toll or piss off."

"Ass."

It was not Cas who had voiced the insult. Mere feet away, a soldier leaned against the outer wall, ankles crossed, head bent as he inspected his fingernails.

A soldier in red.

Cas' relieved grin fell away as quickly as it had come. The soldier's name was Thiago. He had guarded the walls of Palmerin as long as Cas had known him. Cas could see every inch of stone behind him, stone that would have been invisible behind any normal living thing. Just as Thiago lifted his head, Cas turned away.

Cas fumbled with his pouch and tossed a silver lynx at the irritated toll keeper. Hurrying through the gates, he did not turn back once. Not even when he heard Thiago call his name. "Lord Cassia? Is that you? But how . . . *Lord Cassia!*"

***

Cas headed home. Up the warren of streets, some so narrow he could spread his arms and touch the walls with his fingertips. Pomegranate flowers bloomed everywhere, deep orange, hanging from baskets and bursting from clay pots. They would bloom until frost and again in the spring. He found himself stopping several times just to look about in wonder. Overwhelmed by all familiar things.

Others brushed by and hurried in the direction of the main square, where the sounds of cheering could be heard. Curious, he followed, leading the mare behind him. The closer he came to the square, the louder the cheering grew, and when he stepped into the plaza, packed tight with onlookers, he saw why.

An old stone church rose to his left. A procession made its way out the doors. The guards first, dressed in polished chain mail and royal blue. Following were the lords and ladies of Oliveras. Lady Rondilla, High Councilor Amador, Lady Sol. Faces he knew. Cas searched them in vain. There was no sign of Ventillas. His brother was not among them.

Directly after the nobles came a woman holding an infant. She wore the plain white robes and matching wimple of a nurse. The baby was dressed far more elaborately in a gown made of cream-colored lace that trailed inches above the ground.

Was this a baptism? Who was the child? As far as he knew, the last baptism to draw such a spectacle here had been his own, eighteen years ago. Peering over hats and heads, Cas turned back to the open doors of the church and found his answer.

Two figures stepped over the threshold. A man and a woman. Cas would recognize King Rayan anywhere, dressed in formal robes the deepest shade of blue. He was the same age as Ventillas, ten years older than Cas, broad and muscular with brown hair and a trim, pointed beard. His skin, bronze in the summer, less so in the winter, had been passed down from his late mother, born and raised on the eastern archipelago. Beside the king was his queen, whom Cas had never met. At this distance, only her cream-colored robes and furred white hood were visible. Cas did not know her face. But even he, so far away at the time, knew her story.

A year ago, Princess Jehan of Brisa had sailed to Oliveras to marry her father's enemy, young King Rayan. A sizable entourage had accompanied her. Soldiers to guard her. Musicians to amuse her. Diplomats to offer wise counsel. Months of preparation had preceded the journey, and all had gone according to plan.

Until plague struck.

When Princess Jehan arrived in the capital city of Elvira, it was in the dead of night with no ceremony. Frightened, bedraggled, accompanied by a handful of people, no more. Everyone else had died or fled along the way. The marriage had taken place immediately. More important, a treaty had been signed, ending a half century of war between the two kingdoms. Cas had heard nothing of what came after. Had not heard about the birth of this prince or princess. That was who the child must be. And now the royal family was here, in Palmerin. Why?

At the sight of the queen, Cas felt a change come over the

spectators. Still cheering, but beneath it a watchfulness. Curiosity mixed with resentment.

"So that's her," a man beside Cas muttered. "Jehan, the foreign witch."

Cas stiffened. He had no love for her either, or anyone else who came from that hellish kingdom beyond the mountains. If the whole of Brisa were to fall into the sea, or burn to its roots, he would not shed a single tear. But King Rayan was a different matter. Cas would not see his bride insulted, no matter who she was. He turned a frown on the man who had spoken. He was tall but spindly, the whites of his eyes a peculiar shade of yellow. The woman with him might have been a sister.

Cas said quietly, "I would watch my words among strangers."

"Or else what?" The man sneered at Cas, then peered closer, brows knit in confusion. "Do I know you?"

"Do you want to?"

"Be quiet, you fool!" The woman grabbed his arm, hissing, "He looks like he could snap you in two. Come on!" The man grumbled as he was pulled away, disappearing into the mass.

The procession headed toward an ornamental lake. Cas led the mare to the water's edge. From this vantage point, he would have a better view as the procession crossed the bridge. Next to him was a man dressed in black, his stiff white collar crushed by the little girl who sat on his shoulders, gripping his hair with two fists.

"What is happening?" Cas asked him. "Is this a baptism?"

The stranger eyed Cas incredulously. He was a stout, clean-shaven fellow, five or so years older than Cas. The picture of a sober government official if not for the small child causing havoc with his hair. "What do you mean? Have you been living in the hills?"

"Farther." Cas craned his neck for a better view.

The man looked from Cas to his horse and back. Shaking his head, he explained, "That's the little prince."

Cas took his eyes off the bridge. "A boy?"

"Three months old." The stranger's smile turned to a wince. "Let go of Papa's hair now. Too tight," he said to the girl before informing Cas, "Today's his naming day."

A naming ceremony, not a baptism. Cas did not understand. Why was the ceremony being held here in Palmerin and not in the capital? He asked.

"Where else would they have it? The king and queen live here. They have for a year, since the wedding."

Cas stared. A very bad feeling came upon him. "What?"

"Well, the queen lives here anyway," the man amended. "The king comes and goes. It's safer in Palmerin. Elvira was hit hard."

Cas tried to take it all in. "We weren't?"

A familiar bleakness shifted over the man's expression. He tightened his grip around the little girl's boots. "Oh, it didn't spare us, that's for certain. But most were lucky. Palmerin is isolated. And clean. There are more people than rats here. Unlike Elvira."

Bewildered, Cas asked, "What do rats have to do with anything?" Plague was spread through the air. Everyone knew this.

The question provoked a strong reaction from the stranger. The man lifted his daughter's leg and pointed a small boot directly at Cas. "*Rats,*" he said with hard emphasis, "are *everything.*"

And then suddenly the rats did not matter to Cas. A terrible suspicion caused him to ask, "*Where* do the king and queen live?"

"At the keep, where else? Plenty of room there with the family gone, God rest them — whoa! Ho! Are you all right?"

Cas could no longer see clearly. The man's face had blurred, and his voice came from far away. *The family gone, God rest them. Ventillas, my brother.* Cas' world tilted; he would have fallen if his mare hadn't bumped against him just then, forcefully, keeping him upright. He gripped her withers. The man and the girl watched him with identical looks of concern. "Are you all right?" the stranger asked again. Cas nodded. He could not speak.

"Tell the truth. You don't look so good . . ." The man glanced away, distracted by the nurse, who had stepped onto the bridge, the prince in her arms. "Look, my girl! Here they come!"

Cas swallowed the grief that crept up his throat. He turned away from the bridge. Across the lake, shops and homes lined the shore. Rose-colored stone, three stories tall. A flash of green stopped his eye. He settled on the green, his mind slowly comprehending what it was he saw. There, framed in a high window. A figure cloaked in the color of the forest, holding a bow and arrow, aimed at the bridge.

Even as his heart seized, Cas heard himself yelling, *"Archer!"* so loudly the man beside him startled and nearly dropped his daughter. The mare sidled away in reproof. Cas pointed at the window. *"Archer!"*

The guards on the bridge were well trained. Instantly, they surrounded the royal family and raised their shields, but the warning had come too late. In horror, Cas watched as the arrow flew through the air and struck the nurse. She cried out, spinning once before tumbling over the bridge and into the lake, taking the baby with her.

The screaming began in earnest.

*"My God,"* the man beside Cas said, before fumbling for the reins Cas threw at him.

Cas yanked off his cloak and boots and dove into the frigid

water. Silt had churned up from the lakebed, making it difficult to see. But he thought he remembered where the nurse had fallen in. He swam in that direction. Shocked faces watched him from the bridge. Guards tried with clumsy hands to remove their chain mail. When Cas came upon a white wimple floating on the surface, he dove. Hands grasping blindly, deeper and deeper still, and when it felt as though he could hold his breath no longer, he touched something solid. An arm? He grabbed hold.

Cas and the nurse surfaced, sputtering. An arrow protruded from her shoulder. But the baby . . . the prince was nowhere to be seen. Cas swiped water from stinging eyes, then raised a hand to fend off the frantic woman who beat at his face and shoulders, screaming for him to leave her, *leave her be,* he had to find the child.

"I'll take her!" A soldier had jumped into the water. He was nearly upon them. Cas shoved the nurse his way and dove.

*Where could he be?* The gown would have dragged the prince straight to the bottom of the lake. Cas swam farther down, and though he no longer believed in prayer, he found himself thinking, *Please, he's only a baby.*

Just ahead came a flash of cream-colored lace. He snatched at the dress and felt the prince within. When he reached the surface this time, a wild cheering erupted.

But for Cas, there was only terror. The prince did not make a sound. His eyes were closed. His lips were blue.

Cas tucked him tight against his side. His frantic, one-armed swim ended when hands reached out and pulled him onto dry land. He knelt on the pebbled shore, the air like ice on his skin. Voices babbled around him.

"Is he alive?"

"Poor little babe!"

"Is he breathing?"

"Give him here!" This from a guard, still in full chain mail.

Ignoring him, Cas put his ear to the baby's lips and heard nothing.

"He's not breathing!" someone whispered.

A stunned silence. Then, loud and shrill: "*He's not breathing! The prince is dead! The prince —*"

"Shut up, you!" Cas snapped. He flipped the baby over, chest and body supported by Cas' forearm, and slapped him twice on the back.

"*Cassia?*"

Cas knew that voice. Dazed, he lifted his head. There was his brother, Ventillas. Alive. Standing two feet away, white-faced with astonishment and wearing the deep blood-red coat of a man of Palmerin. The little prince coughed. His small body shuddered, and as Cas fell back onto the ground in relief, the baby let out a cry, one full of fright and indignation, the most welcome sound of all.

# 4

CAS HELD HIMSELF together, just. There was no privacy to be had here. They were out in the open, watched by many. Only years of keeping his feelings hidden — by necessity, for survival — prevented him from clutching his brother and weeping. The way he used to when he was a small boy suffering from some hurt or another, and Ventillas had always been there.

Uncomprehending, Ventillas dropped to his knees and hauled Cas up by his shoulders, the prince between them. "Cassia . . . how . . . where —?"

Almost it was like looking at his reflection in the rippling waters of a river. They took after their father, a man stern in appearance though he had been kind, the angles of his face sharp and narrow, a nose described as noble by his admirers and beaklike by his enemies. The kingdom's finest military engineer until he had been killed in the war against Brisa.

"Brother" was all Cas managed. Because the baby's shrieks pierced his ears. And the onlookers pressed closer, voices loud, hands reaching. Cas jerked the prince away. Who could be certain that the archer had acted alone? The prince was not out of danger yet.

Ventillas realized this. He rose, barking orders at nearby soldiers. Men dressed in red and blue. An intermingling of royal soldiers and the city guard. At once, the crowds were pushed back.

A perimeter surrounded Cas, Ventillas, and the baby, who was as heavy as a stone, weighed down by his water-soaked dress. The soldiers held their shields outward, overlapping. Cas heard the clink of metal on metal as he tried to comfort the prince, bouncing him around in his arms because what did he know about infants? He held the wet prince against his wet shoulder and flinched when the baby screamed directly into his ear.

Cas sympathized. "It's no great fun being wet, I know," he said soothingly, teeth chattering. "I'm as miserable as you. But we are brave men, Rayan's son, Prince . . . Prince . . . What did they name you?"

One of the soldiers guarding the perimeter laughed. An older man, craggy-faced and burly, dressed in red. Captain Lorenz was his brother's second-in-command. He called out, "His name is Ventillas! The next king of Oliveras will be named for your brother. Lord Cassia, you are a sight for these old eyes!"

Ventillas produced a cloak out of nowhere and flung it over Cas' shoulders. In a low voice, barely heard over the screaming, he said, "Three years, Cassia. I hardly recognized you . . . *Where have you been?*"

His answer would have to wait. There came the rattle of a carriage, the clomp and neigh of horses. King Rayan and his queen rushed through an opening in the perimeter, with more guards, and all was chaos. Without a word, Cas held the baby out to Queen Jehan. She gathered her son close and turned into her husband's arms. Not a glance was spared toward Cas.

It was his first good look at her. Queen Jehan was not much older than he. A furred hood covered most of her dark hair. What he would remember, always, were her eyes. Tear-filled and full of rage.

She looked how a mother would look — his mother, any mother — if someone had tried to harm her child.

King Rayan pressed a kiss to his queen's head, then his son's. He ushered his family into the waiting carriage, a lavish chariot drawn by four horses. Waving away a hovering servant, he removed his formal robes and passed it through the door. The prince would need the dry warmth of it. When King Rayan spun around, all gentleness had vanished. If the queen's anger had been quiet, his was not.

"I want those gates barred! I want that building searched! I want him found and I want his head on the wall before this day is done. Ventillas, with me!"

"Your Grace." Ventillas' words were muted. Something in his tone caused the king to pause mid-tirade. He turned to Cas, standing there soaking wet and shivering beneath the borrowed cloak.

"Friend," the king said to Cas, making an effort to rein in his fury, "how do we thank you? We are in your debt . . ." He trailed off, peering closer, then goggled. *Little Cassia?* he said with such astonishment that Ventillas laughed.

Cas bowed. "Your Grace."

"But where . . . how . . . ?" King Rayan looked to Ventillas, who threw his hands up. He, too, was in the dark.

Ventillas said to Cas, "We'll speak later. You'll go home? Find Jacomel?" His reluctance was apparent. He did not want to leave Cas behind, moments after they had been reunited, as if Ventillas was afraid Cas would vanish once again.

The king, impatient but not without understanding, said, "Cassia, get in the carriage." He gestured toward the open door. Before Cas knew it, he had climbed into a beautifully appointed but extremely small carriage and was sitting opposite a startled queen, a second nurse, and an angry prince who wailed in his mother's arms.

The king poked his head in long enough to say, "Jehan, a friend." The door shut. An order was given and the carriage rolled away.

Cas shifted uncomfortably. His presence could not be welcome. He was a hulking ape in a cramped space, making it smaller. Lake water dripped from him onto exquisite upholstery, crushed velvet piped with silk, the color of the night sky.

Quickly, it became apparent that no one cared he was there, ruining the furniture or otherwise. Queen Jehan clutched her son, which made it difficult for the nurse to unbutton the prince's elaborate dress. No fewer than a hundred pearl buttons marched along his back, beginning at the nape of his neck and ending at the hem, which puddled, sad and ruined, by Cas' boots.

"Tear it off," Queen Jehan ordered softly.

The nurse was elderly, cheeks splotchy, nose red. She wore a white wimple. "My dear, please," she protested. "The gown is two hundred years old —"

"Let me." Cas reached over. He started with a small rent at the top of the dress, followed by a larger one straight down, buttons popping off and falling where they may, until the opening was large enough to remove the prince. Her expression pained, the nurse held up the king's cloak. It was lined with lynx fur. The queen wrapped the prince in the warm, dry clothing. Instantly, he stopped screaming.

Queen Jehan regarded Cas over her son's head. Her furred hood had fallen away, revealing hair black and sleek, not a curl in sight. A diamond circlet sat above her brows. Her face was round without being plump, no sharp cheekbones or angles. Pretty, Cas admitted grudgingly, even with reddened eyes and tears drying on her cheeks. She said, "I'm not certain we can ever repay our debt to you."

"There's no need." His eyes met hers, then fell away. Absently, he rubbed at the scar on his wrist, hidden beneath cloth. "I was the faster swimmer, that's all."

"There's every need. What is your name?" She spoke formal, perfect Oliveran.

"Cas, Your Grace. Lord Ventillas is my brother."

Two pairs of eyes widened. A glance exchanged between the women. Queen Jehan said doubtfully, "*You* are Little Cassia?"

Cas held back a sigh. He hoped the childhood name would go away, as he now stood shoulder to shoulder with his brother and half a head taller than his king. A strange thought. "Just Cas, Your Grace."

"I don't understand," Queen Jehan said. "Lord Cassiapeus of Palmerin was killed three years ago, along with his entire party. How can this be?"

Quietly, he answered, "My friends were killed. Death would have been preferable to where I've been, maybe. But I am who I say."

The carriage hit a bump in the road, rocking slightly before resuming a smooth, steady pace. Cas pulled the cloak tighter around him. He felt the cold to his bones.

"I don't disbelieve you," Queen Jehan said. "How could I? You are the image of your brother. Ventillas!" she exclaimed suddenly. "What a state he must be in! Can you imagine, Faustina? And how wretched you must be feeling," she said to Cas with a smile. "Do not worry. You'll be at the keep very soon, and we will take good care of you."

Cas felt a sudden, bristling resentment. She spoke as though it were her keep and he the visitor. The words were out before he could stop them. "I can take care of myself in my own home. Don't trouble yourself, Your Grace."

Silence.

The nurse sputtered, "Why, you impertinent —!"

"Let him be, Faustina."

Cas scowled at the upholstery. He told himself it was not hurt he had seen in Queen Jehan's eyes, or confusion at his rudeness.

"He cannot speak to you this way. How dare he! The king —"

"Owes Lord Cassiapeus a debt, as I do." Queen Jehan's eyes met his. Whatever warmth he had imagined there had gone. "Today, he can do no wrong." She looked away and cuddled the prince closer, inhaling his scent. "Tomorrow is a different story."

A warning. Cas understood. He said no more.

Curtains had been tied back from the windows. The screen allowed him to see without being seen. Cas watched the city pass them by. Crowds gathered to wave, flinging wreaths of flowers in their path. Too late, he remembered his horse, abandoned by the lake. He groaned inwardly. He had lost her twice in one day.

For the remainder of their brief journey, the queen and the nurse ignored him, speaking among themselves in Brisan. A language Cas understood as well as his own. The nurse, Faustina, said, "That poor girl. It should have been me carrying the boy. This wretched leg of mine."

"I'm glad it was not you, dear heart," Queen Jehan answered. "I could not bear to see you hurt." Then, very, very quietly, "I will find who did this, and I will kill him."

Faustina rolled the ruined dress into a ball. "I will help."

Cas was quiet. He relived the moments before the younger nurse was struck by the arrow. He had not seen the archer clearly. A glimpse of a profile, an arm extended along bow and arrow. The distance across the lake was not inconsiderable. And yet he could not help thinking that the person in the window who had tried to murder the prince had not been a man, but a woman.

## 5

THE DOOR SWUNG OPEN the moment the carriage stopped, and a man appeared, white-faced and anxious.

"Your Grace, the child —?"

"Is not harmed," Queen Jehan assured him, "but he is dreadfully chilled, master steward."

"Not for long. Please, allow me." He helped her down from the carriage, unaware of Cas, who watched him intently. Jacomel, master steward of Palmerin, was in his late middle years, with a soldier's muscled build despite his long retirement, eyebrows as dark and heavy as his mustache, twirled at the tips. He was impeccably dressed in black. At his belt hung a ring of keys in all shapes and sizes. Growing up, Cas had never failed to be aware of his approach, preceded as it was by the clank and jingle of iron.

The old nurse followed the queen. Before she did, Faustina made sure she had Cas' attention. She tapped the corner of her eye, then pointed at his, the message clear: she was watching him. Cas was careful to keep any trace of amusement from his expression. He knew something about self-preservation.

Cas sat alone in the carriage. It was quiet here. Outside there was chaos. Guards clamoring around the queen. Servants rushing about. The rough mewling of the household lynx. Through the door, he caught his first glimpse of Palmerin Keep, a sprawling structure with the same rose-colored walls that distinguished the city. Shallow steps led to doors studded with iron bolts. Directly above the doors was a splendid window, three times the height of a man and carved into a delicate, twelve-petaled rosetta.

Queen Jehan paused at the foot of the steps and turned to the steward. "We know the way by now, Master Jacomel. No escort is needed. There's another who requires your attention."

A brief, baffled silence. "Another, Your Grace? Forgive me, but who —?"

Queen Jehan directed her gaze at the carriage. *Will you hide in there forever?* her expression said to Cas. *Get out now.* Taking a deep breath, he stepped down, out of the shadows and into the light.

The steward's questioning gaze fell on Cas. Recognition was instantaneous. Master Jacomel's eyes widened, and widened some more. He clutched his heart as though the shock caused a physical pain. *"Cassia?"*

"Master Jac." Cas could not help the catch in his voice. A dozen steps brought him to the steward, who took Cas' face in both hands. Cas went rigid at his touch, until he realized the steward's hands were trembling. He forced himself not to flinch, as he had with Lena, for this was a man who loved him.

"How are you here? Where have you *been?* My God, you're a giant! We thought —!"

"I'll tell you everything, I swear it, in exchange for a bath." Cas covered the steward's hands with his. "I've forgotten how cold the lake can be."

"Lake?" For the first time, Master Jacomel realized Cas was soaking wet beneath his cloak. "*You* saved the prince. How — oh, never mind that now! Come with me!"

Queen Jehan had disappeared into the keep. Cas and Master

Jacomel followed. Halfway up the steps, a pair of lynx watched their reunion with disinterest. They were nothing like the lynx that had chased Lena into the copse. These were sleek, beautiful, healthy cats. Big cats. As Cas passed one, he ran a hand through its fur. Standing on all fours, its back was level with his hip.

Cas did not make it far into the great hall. Members of the household staff converged on him, and everyone spoke at once. There were new faces, servants he did not recognize hovering at the back of the crowd. But most Cas had known all his life. He was happy to see them, he was. He smiled. The words he spoke did not sound foolish. He had practiced them. Outwardly, all was well. But inside? Here within he fought a crushing sense of claustrophobia, of the world closing in. It had always felt crowded in his cell. Even the air he had breathed belonged to others. Never his alone. Mercifully, Master Jacomel shooed everyone back to their posts, but not before ordering that a tub and hot water be brought up immediately, along with food.

The crowd reluctantly dispersed just as a man Cas' own age approached. Of average height and weight with dark, close-cropped hair, he held a tray piled high with scrolls. Cas recognized Faro, his brother's private secretary. Faro glanced up at the sound of keys, an affable smile on his face. Then he saw Cas.

As though he had walked straight into a wall, Faro stopped. His mouth opened and closed like a fish's, and he dropped the tray. It hit the stones with a horrendous clatter. The scrolls bounced in every direction, causing others in the great hall to laugh. Faro did not notice.

"Oh, for pity's sake," Master Jacomel said as they passed the secretary without stopping and headed up the staircase. "Help him," he instructed a nearby chambermaid.

Over his shoulder, Cas offered, "It's good to see you, Faro."

The secretary found his voice. "And you, Lord Cassia! Welcome home! But where have you —?"

"The scrolls, Master Faro," the steward reminded him. "Quickly now. You'll see more of that, I'm afraid," he warned Cas as they climbed the stairs. The keys jingled. "And who can blame them? What a day this has been. Terrible! Wonderful!"

Upstairs, more servants rushed in and out of Ventillas' chambers. But when Cas glanced through the open doorway, he saw the queen sitting by a fire with the prince. A silver-robed man he thought might be a physician hovered over them.

"Lord Ventillas gave them the use of his chambers," Master Jacomel explained at Cas' questioning look. "He's in your rooms, so you'll have to share until all is sorted. We are filled to the rooftops here."

The corridor was lit, not with torchlight but with the last of the summer's fireflies. Each wall niche held a glass ball set on an iron stand. Within each glass were thousands of sparking, blazing insects, darting here and there and giving off enough light to rival the outdoors. Cas and Master Jacomel traveled down the corridor and to the right, where the keep's second-largest set of chambers, Cas' old rooms, were located. Master Jacomel closed the doors behind them.

Cas stood in the center of the room. He turned slowly. "It looks the same."

A fire blazed pleasantly in the hearth. Tapestries decorated the walls and kept the heat in. Another door led to a darkened bed-chamber. Above the hearth, on the mantel, was a miniature of the Palmerin aqueduct that he had built a lifetime ago, as a young boy.

"I cannot say the same for you." There were tears in Master Jacomel's eyes. "I thought it was your father standing outside that carriage. Does your brother know you're here?"

A nod. "I saw him by the lake."

"Did you tell him where . . . ?"

"There was no time."

Master Jacomel pulled a handkerchief from his sleeve and wiped his eyes. "Then don't tell me. I should not be the first to hear. Child, how we mourned for you."

Cas touched the steward's shoulder, then dropped his hand. It was the only comfort he could offer. "I would not have stayed away if I could have helped it, Master Jac."

The steward crumpled the handkerchief in a fist. "I'm not going to like this tale of yours, am I?"

The scars on Cas' back pulled at him. "No."

There came a knock at the door.

Two male servants hauled in a large tub, which they set before the fire. Six chambermaids followed, each carrying a bucket of steaming water. Another brought towels. Yet another produced a cake of soap and a bottle of fragrant oil. Cas stopped her from pouring the oil into the tub. He refused to reek of jasmine or whatever that terrible smell was.

"Ten of you to draw a bath?" Master Jacomel's handkerchief had disappeared up his sleeve. If the servants noticed his reddened eyes, no one dared show it. "Lord Cassia is near dead with cold. Out, out!" He pointed to the door and sent everyone scurrying.

When they had gone, Master Jacomel knelt before a chest set against the wall. He opened the lid and rifled through clothing. Cas laid the cloak over the back of a chair, then went to stand by the hearth. "The queen has lived here a year, I heard."

"Yes." Master Jacomel held up one of Ventillas' tunics for inspection before tossing it aside. "Your brother was part of Princess Jehan's cortege. He brought her to the king in Elvira, but it was no longer safe there with the plague. Lord Ventillas offered them sanctuary here. The other guests have not been in Palmerin as long. Most have come for the naming ceremony."

"I didn't know Ventillas was part of her cortege." That meant he had traveled to Brisa. Cas and his brother had been in the same kingdom without either of them knowing it.

"He volunteered to go. It was hard for him to be here after . . . well. Distraction has been good for him."

After Cas had vanished, was what Master Jacomel meant. "There've been no reports of plague for months, anywhere. Besides the occasional animal. Why is she still here?"

Master Jacomel had been examining the cuffs on a jacket. At Cas' question, he looked over with a frown. Cas knew his words were mean-spirited, ungenerous. He would not apologize for them.

"Because of the child," Master Jacomel said simply. "Queen Jehan learned she carried the prince after they arrived here. She wanted to stay until the babe was born."

"And Ventillas agreed?" His brother, who hated the northern kingdom even more than Cas did. At least he had, once.

"Could you say no? To a woman with child?"

"She's a Brisan princess," Cas said, his tone flat.

"She's the queen of Oliveras," Master Jacomel corrected. "Our queen now."

Cas stepped closer to the fire, as close as he could get without being burned.

"Cassia." Master Jacomel shook out the jacket and laid it across his arm. He came to stand beside him. "I'm beginning to harbor a terrible suspicion as to where you've been these last three years." Cas did not look away from the flames. He could feel the weight of Master Jacomel's knowing. "But the war is over. Hear me when I tell you Queen Jehan is not without influence. She has the might of the king behind her. He loves her. Do not make faces at me, it's true," he added at Cas' expression. "You saved her son's life today. Do not destroy that goodwill by saying something foolish in her presence."

Cas thought of the carriage ride with the queen and her nurse. *I can take care of myself in my own home. Don't trouble yourself, Your Grace.* Huh. *Too late for that.*

"When will she go?"

"A week, maybe less. The prince is old enough to travel safely. They will all go. The packing has already begun."

A knock on the door once again. More servants brought in trays of food. But just as they slipped from the chamber, another figure appeared in the doorway.

Sorne.

"Cassia." Her smile was wide, her color high. As though she had been running. She wore a leather apron over her red dress, gloves and shears peeping from pockets, and a red kerchief in her hair. "When I heard — I dared not believe — but you are alive, and oh, you are here!"

She rushed across the chamber, threw her arms around him, and wept noisily, sobbing into his neck. Cas did not move. His arms hung at his sides. Sorne's father had served his faithfully in the war. Orphaned as a young girl, she had come to live at the keep as his father's ward and then, upon his death, as Ventillas'. She had been a childhood companion, and before Cas had left home, a boy of fifteen, he had tucked a flower in her hair and kissed her, and promised to return by summer's end. He barely remembered that boy. Helplessly, Cas looked over her head. To Master Jacomel.

"Come, Sorne. There'll be time to speak to him later." Gently, the steward took her by the elbow and guided her to the door, ignoring her protests. "Those clothes will not fit perfectly," he said to Cas. "They will have to do for now. Eat. Rest. No one will disturb you here." He left with Sorne, closing the door behind them.

***

Cas could not remember the last time he had washed in hot water. The bath nearly scalded him, but he did not care. Delighted, he scrubbed his skin until all traces of the lake's grime had gone. He dressed in his brother's trousers and found that the length was fine, but they were loose, riding low on his hips. He left the shirt and jacket where Master Jacomel had placed them. There was no one here to see the scars, puckered and hideous, that marred his chest and back.

A rumble reminded him of how much time had passed since his last meal. It had been this morning, before he had buried Izaro and killed the lynx and discovered his horse thief up in a tree. He sat on a rug by the fire and made quick work of the food. There was enough here for three. Goose with pears and duck with turnips.

A mushroom soup. Bread and wine and fresh goat's cheese drizzled with honey. He ate every morsel, licking his fingers and barely restraining himself from licking the plates. Nothing was wasted. He had learned to eat what he could, when he could. Who was to say when his next meal would come? There were no certainties in life except that life was uncertain. And reminding himself of this, he changed his mind. Deliberately and with great pleasure, he lifted each plate, each bowl, and licked them clean.

Master Jacomel kept his word. No one came to the door.

The hour was not late. Early evening, yet weariness had him yawning widely and eyeing the darkened bedchamber. When was the last time he had slept in a real bed? A few minutes to rest. That was all he needed before he faced his brother and his king and told a story no one would be pleased to hear.

He crossed the chamber. Shirtless. Barefoot. He spread his arms wide and fell face-first onto the bed. *A short rest only,* he said to himself as darkness took over.

A few minutes.

No more.

***

When Cas woke, night had fallen completely. A glass ball had been placed on the windowsill. The fireflies within cut through the gloom of the bedchamber. His brother sat in a chair by the bedside, watching him, his expression unreadable.

Bleary-eyed, Cas propped himself on an elbow. He was famished. Odd. He had just eaten. "The prince. Is he —?"

"He eats, he sleeps, he wets himself. He is well," Ventillas said.

That was good news. "Did you find the archer?"

"Not a trace. Whoever he is, he's gone."

There was something wrong with his brother's face. Cas looked closer. An ugly bruise purpled beneath Ventillas' right eye. It had not been there earlier. "Who hit you?"

"You did."

"What?" Cas sat up. Flattened pillows littered the enormous bed. Blankets lay tossed and rumpled. The fur coverlet had been kicked to the floor. Every inch of the bed had been slept in. His side, his brother's. Ventillas had slumbered beside him and Cas had no recollection of it. "I didn't . . . What hour is it?"

"You came home yesterday," Ventillas said as Cas gaped at him in astonishment. "You've slept the night and day away, Brother. Though I would not call what I saw sleep." In the room lit by fireflies, Ventillas' gaze dropped to the scars on Cas' chest.

Ventillas was no stranger to injuries. He knew the damage caused by whiplash.

Within Cas rose a familiar, bone-deep humiliation. "I'm sorry," he said quietly, though he was not certain what he apologized for. Allowing himself to be captured? Losing his brother's men?

"Don't." Violence simmered just beneath the surface of his brother's calm. A pitcher and cup sat on a nearby table. Ventillas rose, poured water into the cup, and thrust it at Cas. "It's just the two of us here, Cassia. I want to know where you've been. Don't leave anything out."

First, Cas drank every drop of water. And then he told Ventillas everything. From the day he was captured three years ago by Brisan soldiers to the day he walked free. Well. Almost everything. He did not mention the ghosts.

A knock came at the door.

"*Leave us,*" Ventillas snapped.

The door was opened by the only person who dared. Master Jacomel was there with a summons from below. The king would like a word.

# 6

WE WERE BEGINNING to worry, Cassia."

King Rayan addressed Cas from the high table in a chair normally reserved for the lord of the keep. A giant lynx slept at his feet. Everyone else had fallen silent the moment Cas appeared. The household and its guests, hundreds gathered for supper around long wooden trestles. An eerie quiet among so many.

Standing beside Cas, Ventillas murmured, "You're among friends here. Keep your head high." The bruise on his brother's face appeared more ominous in the fully lit hall. There were firefly globes on every surface and torches on the walls. His brother strode off to take his place beside the king.

Who waited for Ventillas to be seated before continuing with a smile. "But our good doctor has assured us there was nothing wrong with you that rest wouldn't cure."

Startled, Cas found the silver-robed physician at a table, the same man he had seen tending the queen in Ventillas' chambers. Had he examined Cas while he slept? But of course the royal family would want to make sure he suffered from nothing more than exhaustion. He had held the prince after all, and shared a carriage with the queen. His face warmed. What else had happened as he slept? Who else had come through his bedchamber, poking and prodding? He strongly suspected Master Jacomel. Cas had been given a different set of Ventillas' clothing for supper, black wool with silver thread-ing, only these fit perfectly. He pictured the steward leaning over him with his measuring strings, muttering widths and lengths to a nearby tailor. How could he have slept through it all?

Cas approached the high table, walking across a floor strewn with dried hyssop and mountain savory. He stopped twenty feet away. There was Sorne to his right, sitting beside Faro, Ventillas' private secretary. Sorne wore a wreath of pomegranate flowers in her hair and smiled brightly at Cas, then frowned at something Faro whispered in her ear. Cas looked away. It helped to focus on the king and queen, and Ventillas. It made it easier to pretend he wasn't being watched by all the rest. He bowed, then said, "Forgive me, Your Grace. I didn't mean to sleep the days away."

"One could say you've earned your rest." These words from Queen Jehan, who wore a dress of forest velvet, the cuffs trimmed with black fur. Gracious, he was forced to admit, given his rudeness yesterday. Cas bowed a second time, murmuring, "Your Grace."

King Rayan sent a smile her way. "My queen reminds me that however dark today may feel with an assassin in the wind, there is much to be grateful for." He rose, waited past the scrape of chairs and benches as everyone followed suit. "Our son is out of harm's way, and a boy . . . a *man* we had thought lost to us has returned." He raised his cup. "We are in your debt, Lord Cassiapeus of Palmerin. Welcome home."

*Welcome home, Lord Cassiapeus. Welcome home.* The words echoed throughout the chamber. Cas desperately wished he could flee and suspected Ventillas knew it. His brother's smile was strained. He alone knew where Cas had spent these last years.

Where.

And how.

It was for him that Cas summoned a smile. He bowed once again, in thanks. Before he straightened completely, he caught a glimpse of red. A girl at the high table, standing near the end. Recognition coursed through him. She wore a gown of wine-colored silk, a gold circlet on dark hair that fell loose around her shoulders. A far cry from the ill-fitting messenger's uniform she had worn the day before. Lena, his horse thief. He had known she was no courier. But who was she to be sitting at the high table, beside an empty chair, one he was certain was meant for him?

Their eyes met. Smiling slightly, she lifted her cup and mouthed one word. *Cassiapeus.* Not Caspian, or Caspar. Suddenly, his smile no longer felt so false. Until King Rayan returned to his chair and said, "Joyful as we are, grateful as we are, we must ask you, Cassia . . . Where, in the name of all wretched things, have you been these past three years?"

*Best to get it over with.* "In prison, at first. In Brisa."

Silence fell. King Rayan glanced quickly at Ventillas, who dipped his head in grim confirmation. The look he exchanged with his queen was harder to decipher. No longer smiling, he said, "How?"

Cas fought to keep his voice even. "I was sent to inspect the aqueducts, beginning in Palmerin and ending at the northern border. I, along with three others." If the aqueducts were not maintained properly, there was a risk the water would be blocked by debris or siphoned off by thieves for personal use. He had traveled with three soldiers as his personal guard, friends, all of them lost. "It should have taken us months only to travel there and back, visiting neighbors along the way. We were ambushed by Brisan soldiers near the Cevalles Pass."

More silence. All color had left the queen's face. Then, "On whose side of the pass?" King Rayan demanded.

Cas knew the importance of his answer. The royal marriage was a new one. The treaty between the two kingdoms was as fragile as the parchment it was written on. To learn that Cas, a member of one of the oldest, most powerful families in Oliveras, had been abducted *in his own kingdom* and imprisoned abroad would do nothing to strengthen diplomatic relations. But Cas could not lie to his king.

"On our side, Your Grace."

An angry buzzing filled the hall. The stares sent the queen's way were unfriendly, the same looks he had witnessed yesterday after the naming ceremony. Resentment had risen like a stink in the air.

"Yes?" King Rayan said to no one in particular. He covered Queen Jehan's hand with his. "Does someone wish to speak?"

No one did. The voices subsided. Ventillas gripped his cup, his knuckles white against the silver.

King Rayan said, "What happened, Cassia?"

"I was kept in a prison near the border. I don't know for how long. Later, they sent some of us to the capital. A bridge had been destroyed, and they needed prisoners to repair it. I was put on as a diver, to lay the foundation, because I knew how to swim." Cas had not minded the work. What he had not been able to bear were the nights in his cell, chained to the wall like an animal. He found himself looking at Lena, whose smile had vanished entirely.

"Cassia. How did you escape?" King Rayan asked. Beneath the table, the lynx had woken. It lay with its head on its paws, watching Cas with yellow eyes.

"I didn't. Not really. I caught the plague."

The uproar lasted mere moments, before his brother's fist came down on the table, demanding silence.

Cas said, "All I remember is that I fell ill by the bridge. A year ago. I woke up in a hospital six weeks later. I was told that . . . the other prisoners and guards had also been brought in."

*Going to hell, am I? I'll take you with me.*

"They were not as fortunate as you," King Rayan guessed.

"No. There were so many dying, or dead. No one cared when I stood up, found some clothes, and walked out."

"Why has it taken you so long to return?" King Rayan asked, perplexed. "You could have found a ship and been home months ago."

Ventillas lifted his cup and drank deeply.

"I could not pay for passage," Cas said simply. There had been no Oliveran countinghouses in Brisa. No place to borrow against his family's fortune. "Even if I did, the harbor was impassable. The cemeteries were full. They were burning bodies in the fields. And still, they could not keep up. One of the bishops consecrated the waters."

Queen Jehan pressed a hand against her throat. Cas felt her horror. She had not heard. None of them had, even so many months later. The bishop, in desperation, had blessed the waters so that the bodies could be buried at sea. They had not been weighed down. There were too many of them. Cas wondered if he had considered how grisly a sight would result from his actions. Corpses bobbing among the cogs and galleys. Or that it would make sailing from the harbor an impossibility. The few ships that still had crews to sail them had not been able to maneuver around the dead.

More than one person pushed aside their supper plate, their appetites lost.

Cas said, "So I headed inland. I took work where I could until I earned enough to buy a horse" — another glance at Lena, whose expression was suffused with guilt — "and then I came home the same way I left."

"Through the Cevalles Pass," King Rayan said.

"Yes."

*We searched everywhere, Cassia,* Ventillas had said. *For all of you. We thought you had been attacked by bandits in the forest. Your bodies thrown into the river, the horses stolen. We found no trace of you.*

The next question came from Queen Jehan. "Why did you not tell the guards who you were when you were first captured? Surely you knew your brother would have paid any ransom for your safe return."

"I did tell them, Your Grace," Cas said to her. "The four of us were separated from the other prisoners and treated well, relatively. I was told a messenger had been dispatched here. When the courier returned . . . he brought a letter stating that both lords of Palmerin were at home, and that whoever I was, I was an imposter. The men with me were killed immediately."

Cas was trembling. It felt as if he were telling someone else's story. He hardly knew that younger Cas, who had been so foolish, certain his family name would be enough to guarantee their safety.

"They were killed," King Rayan said, his voice heavy. "But not you."

"No, Your Grace. I don't know why."

"Did you see this letter?"

"I did not."

Ventillas spoke for the first time, his tone flat. "There was no ransom demanded. Any courier would have been received by me or, if I was not here, by my secretary. They lied."

But Cas was no longer listening. A movement to the right had him turning his head. He saw Faro by Sorne's side, sweat beading his forehead. Faro, Ventillas' private secretary, who would have received the ransom demand in his lord's absence. Faro, who suddenly looked pale and terrified.

Cas took a step toward him. Goose flesh prickled along his arms. "Faro?" he said in disbelief.

Faro did not look at Cas, instead smoothing some imagined wrinkle from his black tunic. He sat at the end of a long table. By this time, Ventillas had risen slowly from his chair. Eyes on his secretary.

"Faro?" Ventillas, too, had seen the sweat and the terror.

Faro jumped to his feet. "My lord Ventillas?" Sorne remained seated, a hand on Faro's sleeve, confusion on her face.

Ventillas' words were drawn out, deliberate. "Three years ago, did a Brisan courier deliver a ransom demand from the Cevalles Pass?"

Faro mumbled something incoherent.

Ventillas snarled, "Speak up!"

The entire hall jumped, Cas included. The only exception was King Rayan, who leaned back in his chair, hand propped on his chin.

Faro stammered, "Yes. Yes!"

"What did you do with it?"

Faro turned frantically to the chamber entrance, where two guards stood by. There was nowhere for him to run. He addressed the king. "Your Grace, I —"

"Oh, don't look at me," King Rayan said mildly. "I'm only a guest here. You don't want to know what I would do, if I were Lord Ventillas." His expression hardened. "Answer the question."

"I burned it," Faro confessed.

*"Why?"* This from Cas and Ventillas, spoken in the same breath.

Frightened as he was, the look Faro — cheerful, scholarly, *gentle* Faro — leveled at Cas was full of venom. "She would not look at me when he was near," he said. "It was always him, since we were children. I only wanted her to *see* me."

A stillness had gathered about the chamber. Cas could not speak. His eyes met Sorne's horrified ones. Both hands were clamped over her mouth, as though trying to hold back a scream.

"Do you mean to tell me," Ventillas said in a voice more terrifying for how calm it was, "that you allowed three men of Palmerin to be sent to their deaths, condemned my brother to a Brisan prison, because of a *girl?*"

Cas was trying to comprehend the fact that Faro had not simply ignored the demand for ransom. He had taken the time to pen a response, calling Cas a liar. The vindictiveness of it took his breath away.

Ventillas shoved his chair out of the way. It crashed to the floor. He stalked around the high table, past a frozen queen and a wide-eyed horse thief. Before he even stepped from the dais, he yanked his dagger free of his belt. Seeing it, Faro cried out and tried to flee but stumbled and landed on his knees, hard. Those closest to him scattered.

"Please, please don't," Faro begged. Ventillas grabbed him by the collar, exposing his throat. *"Gah —!"*

"Ventillas," Cas said.

Ventillas whipped his head around to glare at Cas, who watched him blink through a haze of fury. Whatever he saw in Cas' expression had him saying, "No. Don't think to ask for mercy after what he's done."

"Not for him." Cas stood alone in the center of the hall. He was barely aware of the onlookers. There was just him and Ventillas and a desperate, weeping Faro. But that was not true either. There were three others who could no longer speak for themselves, who demanded justice. Jorge, Sans, Arias. They had died in the north, afraid, hundreds of miles from home.

Cas walked over until he was standing by his brother and looking down at a kneeling Faro. He said quietly, "I am sick to death of death."

"So are we all." Ventillas was unmoved. "One more won't matter." His dagger pressed against Faro's throat. There was a yelp; a line of blood appeared. Ventillas studied Cas even as rage pulsed at his temples. "What do you propose?" he said abruptly.

His question prompted surprised murmurs. Rarely did Ventillas change his mind once a decision was made.

Faro saw this. He turned to Cas, hopeful. "Please, Lord Cassia, forgive —"

"Be quiet." Cas did not look at him. The keep had a dungeon, but Cas did not want Faro to remain at Palmerin. He just wanted him gone. He said, "Exile."

"No." Ventillas refused outright. *Too lenient,* his expression said. *You will have to do better than that.*

So be it. A more fitting punishment. Something between exile and death. Cas' throat was too dry to swallow. But his words, when they came, were even. "Master Faro, your family has served Palmerin as scribes for the last hundred years. Is that not correct?"

"Yes!" Faro cried. "Faithfully, Lord Cassia! My father and grandfather—"

"In turn," Cas interrupted, "you have been treated well by my family, have you not?"

Faro eyed the dagger hovering an inch from his throat. "Yes . . . ?"

"Compensated generously, given a home, treasures." Cas studied the pin on Faro's tunic. Gold, shaped into two intersecting scrolls. Embedded with a ruby.

"Yes," Faro whispered.

"You are left-handed, Master Faro. I remember." They had been taught by the same tutor. Long ago. They had practiced their penmanship together, sitting side by side in the keep's archives, surrounded by books and ink.

Faro did not answer, only looked mutely from one brother to the other.

"That is the hand you used to deny my ransom," Cas continued. "To call me a liar. To murder my friends. You will not have that power again." He looked at Ventillas, saw the barest flicker of surprise before he nodded acceptance.

"Very well." Ventillas sheathed his dagger. "We'll do it now."

"What do you mean—? Oh no! *No!*" Faro screamed.

Cas made himself watch. It took seconds only. On Ventillas' order, three men stepped forward. One soldier to hold Faro down by the shoulders. Another to grab his left arm and stretch it flat along the table. The last was Jacomel. Master steward of Palmerin.

A soldier in a former life. Expressionless, he unsheathed a sword and brought it down just above the wrist bone, severing the hand cleanly. It lay there, palm up, beside a platter of braised rabbit and a jug of wine, both sprayed with blood.

"And exile," Cas said again, over the cries that erupted. Sorne screaming. Others violently ill. Supper was over.

Cas walked away. He did not look at the head table and he very carefully did not look at Lena. The guards by the door wore red, men of Palmerin. They stepped aside as he passed, wary. As though they no longer recognized him. Cas did not blame them.

Some days, he barely recognized himself.

# 7

C AS FLED TO THE STABLES. He had stopped trembling by the time he pushed open the doors, where the scent of hay and leather filled his nostrils, along with a whiff of horse manure.

"I heard you were back."

The voice came from his left. A man straddled a bench as he mended a leather harness. The sight of him, alive, unharmed, filled Cas with relief. Jon was the keep's stablemaster. Eight years older than Cas, he was five feet tall and curly-haired. The late hour and task meant he had exchanged his more presentable clothing for worn trousers and a frayed shirt. He set the harness aside and stood, eyeing Cas from top to bottom, shaking his head.

Cas said, "Then why do you look surprised to see me?"

"Why? You didn't look like this the last time I saw you." Jon came over and reached out to grab Cas' upper arms where the muscles rippled. He shook them for emphasis before letting go, so quickly Cas did not have time to step away first. "You were like a stick I could snap in half. Like a praying mantis I could step on."

They grinned stupidly at each other. Cas wondered about himself, that he could smile after the carnage he had just left behind at supper. But he had worried Jon would not be here. Jon, who had been a boy himself when he taught Cas how to ride a horse.

Jon's smile dimmed. "I heard you were back. Nothing else, though. The others?"

Cas did not have the heart to repeat the tale. Jon would hear of it from someone else. "Gone."

Jon was quiet. He crossed himself. "My horses?"

"Taken. They would not have been harmed." Not horses like those. Chargers, palfreys. Some animals were more valuable than men. And thinking of horses, Cas said, "Have you seen a white mare, with a black star here?" He tapped below his right eye. "She would have been brought in by a man with a little girl."

The stranger by the lake had seemed an honest sort. Not one to walk away with someone else's horse.

"That would be the city inspector." Jon headed down the nearest aisle and Cas followed. "Gaspar. He came by yesterday." Several horses eyed them over stall doors. Cas was struck once again by a feeling of being in a place both familiar and unfamiliar. They stopped before Cas' mare. She pushed her nose against his, a gentle scolding. *Where did you disappear to?*

"Sorry, girl." Cas opened the door and ran his hand along her side. The name Gaspar was not known to him. "The city inspector, he's new?"

"Been here a year, maybe a little more. He left your saddlebag, too." It hung from a hook on the wall. "He's a competent one. The merchants don't like him, though."

"Why not?"

"Because he's competent." A shrug. "He won't take their bribes, like the old inspector used to. The butchers can't pour blood in the streets anymore. They can't leave pig heads in the alley." Jon leaned against a post and folded his arms. "Your mare's a spoiled one. The lady's been here twice already to brush her down."

*Lady.* That brought Cas' head around. "Lena was here?"

A snort. "Lena to you, maybe. Lady Analena to the rest of us."

Cas considered every noblewoman he had ever met, in Palmerin and beyond. He did not know her. "Who is she?"

"One of the king's historians, or so I heard. I'm not sure if that's true. Aren't historians all old, bearded men?"

"Not all of them." A royal historian, he mused. One who dressed as a boy and traveled alone and trusted strangers far too easily.

Cas unhooked a brush from the wall. The horse did not need to be groomed. Lena had done a fine job. He did it anyway, the repetitive motion distracting him from his thoughts, which kept returning to Faro and his severed hand. *Do you mean to tell me that you allowed three men of Palmerin to be sent to their deaths, condemned my brother to a Brisan prison, because of a* girl?

"What's her name?" Jon asked, eyeing the horse.

Cas had only ever called her *girl.* "She doesn't have one."

Jon gave him a look but held his peace. Perhaps sensing the dark turn Cas' thoughts had taken, he stepped back, prepared to leave him to his own company.

"Jon."

"Hm?"

Cas could hear the grooms working late, saw them here and there with shovels and buckets. But there was no sign of Jon's brother, who also worked in the stables. He asked, "Where's Felix?" and instantly regretted the question when he saw Jon's expression. "I am sorry. So sorry, my friend."

Jon nodded, the way one does when they've been told *I'm sorry* a thousand times. "He went to the horse fair in Elvira in my place. I'd broken my foot the day before. Fell off a horse. Stupid. When he came home . . . he wasn't well. We couldn't let him through the gates."

"Why not?"

"The city inspector. He kept out anyone who was sick. Even if they looked healthy, he made them camp outside the walls until he was sure. The queen was here by then, you see. With child. He's cautious, that one."

Cas was quiet. "Did it help?"

"I think so," Jon admitted. "They're saying Trastamar lost half its people. And Salome close to that. But not here." Saddles lined a shelf behind him. He took one, slung it over his shoulder, and said, "There are bad people out there, Cassia. Cheats, murderers. While my brother lies dead in the ground." He turned away, but not before offering a smile that no longer reached his eyes. "I'm glad to see you back. Welcome home."

*** 

Cas lost track of how long he remained in the stall. At some point he had shut the door and sat in a corner while the horse rested in the other. He told himself he was not hiding.

His thoughts had turned to *what if*s. What if Ventillas had been allowed to pay his ransom? What if Faro had never been born? What if Sorne's parents still lived? Had they been alive, she would never have come to Palmerin as his family's ward. Would never have caught Faro's jealous eye. *What if?* It was a question that could send a person leaping off the city walls in despair, if he allowed it to consume him.

The door creaked open. He glanced up, expecting Jon, but it was

Lena who stood there, looking down at him with his back against the wall, elbows on drawn knees. She wore a black velvet cloak, the hood pushed back. "Here you are. I've been looking everywhere for you."

Cas had wanted to be left alone. Not discovered in a horse stall, sitting like a lump among the hay and oats. Embarrassment turned his voice surly. "I don't want to talk."

"Then we won't." In contrast, her tone was light. She hung the cloak on a hook beside his saddlebag, then helped herself to a brush. Red skirts billowed as she lowered herself to the floor. It was not a large space. The hem of her dress covered his boots. Cas watched her kiss the horse on the nose. She produced a shiny apple from a pocket hidden in her skirts, smiling as the mare made quick work of the treat. True to her word, she did not speak. She pulled the brush through the horse's mane before gathering a section into three equal parts.

Cas guessed her intent. "No braids," he said.

Lena's hands stilled. "But she enjoys them," she protested.

"How can you tell?"

"Just look at her."

He cast a skeptical glance at the horse. The mare *did* look pleased, but he thought the apple might be the real reason. Still, he relented. "Just one."

He watched her work, quiet, efficient, and, to his surprise, her presence was a balm on this wretched night. She wore tiny gold earrings shaped like pomegranate flowers. They were also engraved along the gold circlet on her head, in different stages of bloom. When she began a second braid, and a third, he let her be. Curiosity won out over his desire for silence. "You're a historian."

"Yes. Well, no. Almost." She snuck a sideways glance, self-conscious. "I hope to be."

"You're an apprentice?"

"Sort of." Her hands never stopped braiding. "My grandfather is teaching me . . . was teaching. That's over now."

Cas heard the catch in her voice. He did not ask her to explain.

Halfway through a fourth braid, she said, "May I ask a favor?" She did not wait for him to say yes or no. "Please don't mention our first meeting to anyone. Ever. Or our second, for that matter. It would save me some trouble with my family."

Stealing someone's horse. Nearly mauled by a lynx. He did not doubt it. "I don't know your family."

"Oh, you do," she assured him. "A year ago, I had fifteen brothers and sisters." She glanced over in time to witness Cas' goggle-eyed astonishment. "Half siblings," she clarified. "Most I'd never met. That was before the pestilence. Today, I have one brother only, and he sits at the high table."

"You're King Rayan's *sister?*" There was no great resemblance that he could see, beyond the rich brown hair and dark eyes. Traits shared by most of the kingdom. Nothing like when strangers looked to Ventillas, then to Cas, and saw instantly the blood that bound them.

"Yes." She looked down at the braid as she spoke. "One of the old king's many skeletons."

The former king's indiscretions were infamous. Rayan's mother had despaired until, one bitterly cold night, after learning of yet another child born of her husband's infidelities, she fled the palace and retreated to the nunnery at Salome. Her final years had been spent there, in silence and in solitude.

Cas said, "We all have skeletons."

That brought a small smile. "Oh, I'm aware. I was raised by my grandfather, my mother's father. Historians are experts on skeletons."

"Where is your mother?"

A shadow passed over her face. "I don't know. She brought me to my grandfather's right after I was born. And then she left. No one's heard from her since." Lena reached into her pockets and withdrew a handful of silk ribbons, red to match her dress. She thrust them at him. "Here, guard these, won't you? Otherwise, she'll try to eat them."

Cas took the ribbons. "This is a man's horse," he told her.

"They'll be gone before you ride her again. I promise." She took a ribbon, secured a braid, and began another.

Cas would hold her to it, for he could not ride the mare as she was. Though she did look nice, with her braids and ribbons. He would never say so out loud. Farther down the aisle, Jon reminded someone to fill the oat buckets.

Lena said, "I remember reading your family's history when I was a girl."

"Mine? Why?"

"For fun."

Cas snorted.

"Really." Her mouth turned up at the corners. "Palmerin was founded by two brothers I learned, a thousand years ago. The elder, named Ventillas, was a celebrated military commander and engineer. The younger, Cassiapeus, was also a soldier and engineer, but his main duty was as keeper of Palmerin. While Ventillas defended the kingdom abroad, Cassiapeus remained in the mountains, charged with the safety of the city and its people. You were named for them."

She had reached the end of a braid. Cas offered a ribbon and said, "Ventillas was lucky. His name isn't so awful. But Cassia-peus . . ." What else was there to say? It was the worst. They shared a smile. She did not try to convince him his name was anything other than terrible. He respected her for it.

"You told me your name was Cas, but everyone here calls you Cassia."

"It's an old name." One from his boyhood. "It belongs to some-one else."

"I understand," she said after a moment. "Cas it is."

Time passed as another braid was worked. Lena held out her hand.

Absently, he passed over the ribbon. "Why were you looking for me?"

She looked away. "No particular reason."

"Lena."

A section of mane over another, and another. Expertly plaiting. Her words were quiet. "You gave him a second chance. The scribe. If he chooses to use it. It's more than your brother would have done. My brother too."

She spoke of Faro, who Cas had forgotten completely since her arrival. "He'll starve before he finds other work. I've done him no favors." Cas had only prolonged the inevitable.

"You don't know that."

Cas did not wish to speak of Faro. He asked again, "Why were you looking for me?"

Lena's hands fell away from the unfinished braid. She turned to him, her expression troubled. "Because you haven't seen Palmerin in three years. This is your homecoming, Cas. And you should not be here all alone, sitting in a horse stall."

She could not have painted a more pathetic picture. His voice was low, almost inaudible. "Don't feel sorry for me, horse thief. I don't need your pity."

"I'll feel sorry for you if I want!" She looked as stung as he felt, before glancing past him. Her eyes narrowed.

Cas turned to look. The stall door stopped a foot above the ground. He could see a pair of black boots pressed up against the wall. Someone was standing right there listening to them, he realized, outraged. How much had he heard?

The door was closed but not latched, as the latch was on the outside. Cas placed his palm against the door and shoved it open as hard as he could. There was a satisfying crack, followed by a groan.

"My nose!"

Cas was on his feet and out of the stall. He yanked the eavesdropper around. "What do you want?" he demanded, then let go, surprised. A soldier in blue. He was Cas' age. Just as tall but far thinner, wiry. His ears were uncommonly large. Cas remembered him from the lake. He had jumped into the water and taken the nurse away so that Cas could search for the prince.

The soldier clutched his nose with both hands. "You broke my face!"

"Next time don't creep up on me," Cas snapped.

"Hey! I wasn't *creeping*."

Jon poked his head around the corner, eyebrows raised. *Trouble here?* Cas waved him away.

"What would you call it?" Cas asked. The eavesdropper was

exaggerating, Cas saw when he dropped his hands. Nothing was broken. There was hardly any blood.

Lena came to stand beside Cas. She wore her black cloak. "Bittor, you clod. Serves you right." She thrust a snowy white handkerchief at him.

The soldier snatched it from her without thanks. "Oh, don't look at me like that, Analena," he grumbled. "You were in a horse stall with —" He waved the handkerchief at Cas. "I thought you might need rescuing."

"You thought no such thing."

"What do you want?" Cas said again.

With a hiss, Bittor shoved part of the handkerchief up a nostril. His words were garbled. "The king wants to see you. Now." He turned to Lena. "I'm supposed to find you, too."

Cas said, "Why?"

Bittor glared. "Did I ask? Does it matter?" He stomped off, white lace hanging from his nose, past Jon and a young, wide-eyed groom.

Cas cleared his throat. "Lena," he said, then fell silent when she gave him a look every bit as dark as the one she'd sent the eavesdropper. She lifted her hood and walked off.

And now a summons from the king. *Splendid.*

## 8

C AS WAS LEFT to bide his time out in the quiet, firefly-lit corridor. With Lena, who no longer wished to speak with him. And with that gnat Bittor, who suddenly did.

They stood outside a chamber that had been his mother's sanctuary. A place where she had retired with her ladies to embroider and read, to play music. He had spent his earliest years here along with the other castle infants, until she had died giving birth to a sister. They had been buried together, mother and daughter, and this chamber had remained empty ever since.

"You don't believe in coming home quietly, do you?" Bittor leaned against one wall, Cas directly opposite, each with their arms folded. Lena sat in a chair beside Cas and ignored them both. "You save the prince," Bittor continued. "You expose the treacherous scribe and chop off his hand . . . during supper. That was diabolical, by the way." He shoved the blood-streaked handkerchief up a sleeve, his nose red as harvest peppers. "Remind me not to get on your bad side."

"Too late." Cas eyed him with disfavor. "What is your name again? Bitter?"

"Bih-*tor*," the soldier corrected with indignation. "Bih-*tor*." His expression, aggrieved, spoke to a lifetime of correcting others.

If he had been anyone else, Cas would have sympathized. He

had grown up, after all, with the name Cassiapeus. Wondering what had become of Faro, he asked, "Where did they put him?"

"In your dungeon." It was Lena who spoke. "He'll be taken away as soon as he can travel."

"Alone, as it happens," Bittor added. "His lady love has decided not to marry him after all."

*"Marry?"*

"Next week. Sorne, that's her name, isn't it? I bet she feels like she's escaped the noose. One more week and she would have been exiled with him." Bittor pressed gingerly at his swollen nose. "Was she your girl?"

Lena's head was bent, her hair falling forward, so Cas could not see her expression. She had been tracing the embroidery on the arm of her chair with a fingertip. At Bittor's question, the finger stopped.

"No," Cas said, willing Bittor to silence.

Bittor did not take the hint. "Does she know that? I heard she visits your statue every day."

"What?"

Cas' reaction brought a pleased grin to Bittor's face. "It's in the gardens. A memorial statue. Your brother brought in a sculptor from Elvira." He gave Cas an assessing look. "It's a good likeness."

"Bittor." Lena spoke on a sigh. "Why are you still here?"

The door opened and out came a woman, thin and wan, dressed in unrelieved black.

Lena leaned around Cas to greet her. "Hello, Abril."

Cas did not imagine it. Dismay flitted across the woman's face the instant she spotted Lena. She returned the greeting with little enthusiasm. "Lady Analena, Lord Cassia." There was no hello for Bittor.

Cas bid her good evening. She was not from Palmerin. Her voice, like Lena's, belonged to someone who had grown up in the capital city. Dark circles ringed her eyes, and seeing them, Cas felt a momentary kinship. Here was someone whose sleep was as troubled as his.

Lena said, "I sent a note to your lodgings this morning. The messenger said you received it?"

Abril appeared uncomfortable. "I . . . yes. Forgive me, Lady. The day slipped away from me." She carried a wooden box by its handle. The sort of battered, paint-streaked box used by artists.

Lena smiled. "No matter. Tomorrow, then? I will meet you at midday, in the library."

Abril tightened her grip on the handle. A splotch of green paint covered one knuckle. "I don't think I can be of help to you, Lady. My memory is . . . not what it was."

Lena rose, red skirts brushing by Cas. She took Abril's hand in hers. Her words were gentle. "I don't wish to cause you pain, but the king has asked that I complete my grandfather's history. To do that I must speak with you. It will not take long, I promise."

Abril mumbled, "Of course, Lady. Tomorrow, then." She slipped her hand free of Lena's and hurried down the corridor, shoulders hunched, disappearing around the corner.

"What was that about?" Bittor asked.

Cas wanted to know too, but Ventillas appeared in the open doorway, frowning after Abril. "Cassia. Lady." He waved them in and sent Bittor off with his question unanswered.

Much had changed in his mother's old chambers. A small grouping of chairs remained by the fireplace. The king and queen gathered there. As for the rest of the room . . . all had been cleared.

Her favorite instruments, the bandurrias, the tambours, were gone, along with her spinning wheel and writing desk. In their place, on the stone floor, was the largest tapestry Cas had ever seen. It had been arranged in a coil, like a massive, sleeping serpent. At least two hundred paces if stretched out. And the height? Six feet or so. As tall as he. He could not make out the images from where he stood. Several looms sat in a corner, the threads pulled tight between rollers.

"It's been a strange night," King Rayan said in weary greeting. "Will you eat?" The table beside him was covered with platters and bowls and pitchers. Next to the table, a pair of lynx slumbered.

Cas no longer had an appetite. All he could picture was a different table and a hand without an arm. "No thank you, Your Grace." Ventillas stood by the fire with a cup in his hand. Cas joined him there, glad for the warmth.

Lena also refused. She chose to sit on the rug within reach of Queen Jehan, who touched her hair and said, "Bittor found you. Good. Where did you run off to?"

Lena leaned against the queen's green skirts. "The stables. Not far."

They were sisters by marriage, who clearly cared for each other. It was something Cas had understood when Lena told him who she was, but it was a strange thing for him to see firsthand.

King Rayan said to Cas, "You're wondering why we've asked you here, at so late an hour."

"Yes," Cas admitted. Ventillas, scowling into his cup, had offered no hint that Cas could see.

"We cannot demand reparations from Brisa, Cassia," King Rayan said bluntly. "Not for a crime committed three years ago."

Cas had thought as much. "It does not matter."

There was a sharp clink as Ventillas slapped his glass onto the mantel. "It is not right."

"Ventillas, the terms of the treaty are clear," King Rayan said with the air of a man whose patience had been tried. "You were there. You signed it too. Any violations that occurred before then can't be touched."

Queen Jehan directed her words at Ventillas. Words sharply spoken. "No, it is not right. Was it right when Oliveran soldiers sacked a Brisan village with no provocation? Women, burned. Children, dead—"

Outraged, Ventillas protested, "That is not what happened—"

Cas exchanged a glance with Lena, her uneasiness a reflection of his.

"The story changes daily, depending on who tells it." Angry color slashed the queen's cheekbones. "War is an ugly business, my lord of Palmerin, and it is never one-sided." She stared tightlipped at Ventillas, who glared right back. King Rayan rubbed his temple as though the ache within were tremendous.

The silence lasted long enough for Queen Jehan to take a deep breath and settle back in her chair. The fire crackled. "Ventillas," she said, her voice softening. "My friend."

Ventillas' own words were gruff. "Forgive me."

"There is nothing to forgive. He is your brother and harm was done to him. If I were in your place, I too would want to set the world afire."

One of the lynx woke and stretched. The size of a foal, it padded toward Cas and lowered itself beside him. Lena eyed it, wary. She edged closer to the queen. Cas buried his hand in its fur, scratching behind its ears and feeling its purr ripple along his arm.

"It's a bitter pill to swallow," King Rayan said. "No reparations from Brisa, but you will have them from us. The lords of Palmerin have been good to my family. Cassia, if there is something you wish for that is in our power to grant, you have only to ask."

The king had barely finished speaking before Cas answered. "There is nothing."

A silence. Ventillas cautioned, "Cassia . . ."

"I won't profit from what happened," Cas said flatly. "Accept gold or land, or a new title, because I'm alive and my friends are not." The thought sickened him.

Lena's words were quiet. "That is not why they offer."

"Lena. I can't accept it." Cas remembered himself too late. The familiar use of her name, when they should have only just met, settled into the quiet that followed. Lena winced and avoided looking at her brother, whose eyes had narrowed. Hastily, Cas added, "But I'm grateful for your offer, Your Grace. Your Grace."

Queen Jehan looked from Lena to Cas, eyebrows raised. She said only, "You saved our son's life. Will you not allow us to thank you for it?"

"You have already thanked me."

"Very well," King Rayan said, his tone brisk. "We will consider the matter of Brisa settled. Don't look at me like that, Ventillas. It wasn't I who taught him to be so noble." He wrapped both hands around his mug. "As for our son, my wish is that you make no decision now. You're young, Cassia. There are many years ahead of you. You don't know when you will find yourself in need of a king's favor." When Cas opened his mouth to respond, King Rayan held up one hand. "This is my wish." There was steel behind his words, and this time Cas kept his mouth shut.

Lena rose and changed the topic entirely. "You were eyeing the tapestry earlier," she said to Cas. "Would you like to see it?"

"Yes." Cas gave the lynx one last scratch before following her across the chamber. "Sorry," he muttered when they were far enough away from prying ears.

"*Oh well,*" she said under her breath. "He finds out everything eventually. I don't know why I bother." In a louder voice, she said, "Isn't it lovely? Abril drew the original pattern, but the weavers are all from Palmerin. From your guild."

Enough space had been left between the coils for a person to walk without trampling the tapestry. It was divided into a number of scenes. Cas studied the first one. There were four ships, great bulky carracks with forecastles and aftcastles. Silk threads dyed the deepest blues and greens were used to represent the sea. The ships themselves were threaded with browns and golds and blacks. Lena seemed to be expecting a response.

"It's big," Cas commented. The others had drifted over and were strolling beside the later scenes, speaking among themselves.

Lena said, "There are thirty weavers here every day, along with Abril. Sometimes more. It will go to Elvira when it's finished."

"To the palace?"

"Yes. It will hang in the great hall. It's meant to show gratitude toward the people of your city, who offered sanctuary to a new queen in the darkest, most desperate of times."

Formal words. Pretty words. It sounded as though she had already begun writing that history. Cas pointed to the figures on the ships. "Who are they?"

"Queen Jehan's entourage," Lena said promptly. "Princess Jehan, then. More than a hundred traveled with her. Envoys, soldiers, servants, musicians —"

"Friends." Queen Jehan spoke softly ten feet away.

"And Lady Mari," Lena said quietly. "Princess Jehan's closest companion. There she is, in green."

Cas peered closer. Of the four ships, one sailed slightly ahead of the others. People crowded the main deck, but high up in the forecastle, two figures stood alone. Two women, arm in arm. One dressed in yellow and the other green. He glanced at Lena. She shook her head slightly at his unspoken question. The journey had ended badly for Lady Mari.

"They disembarked in Trastamar" — Lena moved on to the next panel of images — "where they were supposed to rest for several days and prepare for the journey overland. But by then the pestilence had struck the city. Many soldiers died there, along with our royal historian."

There was a hitch to her voice. Royal historian. Now he understood. "Your grandfather?"

"Yes. The last entry in his journal is dated the day they disembarked."

She looked so sad. Cas was no good at comfort, but, surprising himself, he shifted slightly so that his arm touched hers. Lena smiled up at him, a smile that wobbled around the edges. Behind them, Ventillas coughed delicately. Cas stepped away, fast, and heat warmed his ears. He had completely forgotten their audience.

The next minutes were spent following Lena along the coiled landscape. In the port city of Trastamar, a large group of travelers was depicted on horseback and in carriages, making their way south toward the capital. Well-known landmarks showed the route. The ancient bridge at Ollala. The double-steepled church at Salome. The hospital in Gregoria. Unsettled, he saw that the farther the entourage traveled, the smaller it became. By the time they arrived at the gates of Elvira, the group had been reduced to four figures on horseback. The princess and three others.

"So few," Cas said.

"Yes." Queen Jehan appeared beside them. "There is your brother." She pointed to a man with a shield on his back. The flag he held bore the symbol of their kingdom: the head of a snarling bull next to a pomegranate flower in full bloom. "You've met Faustina, my son's nurse." Beside Princess Jehan was a woman wearing white robes and a wimple. The queen added with a fond smile, "She was my nurse too, once upon a time." Her smile faded. "And that is Abril."

The fourth figure was off to one side. Set apart. Alone. A woman dressed in black. Behind her was a wooden box splattered with paint.

Ventillas said, "We traveled together to Brisa, Abril and I. She was good company. The journey home was hard on her."

"Must you meet with her, dearest?" Queen Jehan asked Lena, a small frown settling between her brows. "You've spoken to the rest of us. Surely you have enough for your history?"

Lena hesitated. "Grandfather would have wanted me to speak with her."

"She's right, Jehan." King Rayan smiled at his sister. "He was very thorough with his research, your grandpapa. You're a lot like him."

Lena smiled, as though he had offered her the greatest of compliments. She said, "I won't pester, Jehan."

Queen Jehan placed a hand on Lena's cheek. "The last thing you are is a pest." Her hand fell away. "It's just . . . dear Abril, she's become fragile. She is not the person she used to be."

# 9

"ASSIA."

The voice came from a figure huddled in the gloom by the back stairwell. She sat on the stone with her knees drawn close to her chest.

Sorne.

"I didn't know." Her voice rose just above a whisper. The flower wreath she had worn to supper lay by her slippers, the blooms torn and flattened, as though she had ripped it from her head and flung it against a wall. She was crying. She had been crying a long time.

This was not Sorne's fault. She had not known about the ransom demand, or Faro's deception. In this, she was as blameless as Cas. But seeing her reminded him of the men who had been lost. What Cas knew and what he felt warred with each other. "I know you didn't. It's done."

"*Cassia*. You blame me. Everyone does. You want me to go."

Only a few firefly globes remained. The rest of the keep had gone to their beds, and the corridor was dimly lit. His bedchamber was just there. He could see the door. Turning away from it, he went to the stairwell to crouch before Sorne. His words were low. "We were friends once, you and I."

"More than that." Sorne grabbed his hand. "You kissed me. I know you remember."

He had kissed her. He did remember.

Cas tried to pull his hand away. She only tightened her grip. "Sorne, it was three years ago—"

"Does it matter?" She leaned closer, imploring. "When you went missing, I could not believe you were dead. But one year became two, then three. My heart was broken, Cassia. Then you came back, and it must mean—"

"Stop." Carefully, he peeled her fingers from his. "You must stop. Listen to me. If someone is blaming you for what Faro did, if you are being treated poorly, I will put an end to it. This is your home. No one will make you leave." He rose, feeling like the scum that coated the surface of a cesspool, and forced himself to say the next words. "But if you feel that you must go, start somewhere else . . . in Elvira perhaps, I will help you."

Sorne looked as though he had struck her. "You want me to go."

"I want you to be happy. To live your life."

Her lips twisted. "Far away from you."

"That isn't what I—"

She scrambled to her feet, angrily dashing the tears from her cheeks with a fist, then whirled around and disappeared down the stairwell. She left the wreath behind.

When Cas turned, Bittor was standing in the corridor. Seeing Cas' expression, he held up both hands. "I was heading for the stairs, minding my own business. I was not creeping. Though if you ask me—"

"I didn't." Cas pushed past him toward his bedchamber.

Bittor spoke to his back. "It's a bad business what happened. I would have cut off both his hands."

For once, his words held no trace of mockery. Cas turned, but Bittor was already in the stairwell, footsteps fading into the night.

***

Cas dreamt of rocks and water and woke up flailing. He threw the covers aside and sat up. The chamber appeared the same as yesterday. Fireflies on the windowsill. The bedclothes in disarray. Only this time, Ventillas was at the table by the window, ledger before him, quill in hand. Doubtless trying to complete some important task before his mad brother woke up in a sweat.

Again.

Ventillas had turned in his chair. They regarded each other across the dimly lit room.

"How long?" Cas asked. Had he slept another day away?

"An hour only."

Which was a different sort of misery. Cas flopped onto his back. "I can sleep on the floor."

"If you were disturbing me, I'd tell you." A short silence, followed by "Is it the same dream every time?"

"Yes."

Ventillas set the quill aside. Waiting.

Cas kept his eyes on the ceiling as he spoke. "They had me laying the bridge's foundation. Moving boulders from the riverbank into the water." He did not need to explain this to Ventillas, who, like their father before him, served as the kingdom's chief military engineer. Ventillas was no stranger to building bridges or, when necessary, to burning them down. "I was tamping the stones when they shifted and pinned me. I made it back up eventually, but not before swallowing half the river."

"No one helped you?"

Cas snorted. "I was an Oliveran surrounded by Brisan criminals. No one helped. The dream ... it's of being trapped by the rocks, and taking that first deep breath underwater. I thought that was the end for me."

How many times had he almost died? When had he stopped counting? He could not remember that, either.

Ventillas said, in a voice Cas could not decipher, "Your nightmares are of drowning, and yet you were the first one in that lake when the prince fell in."

Cas sat up. He had gone to bed without a shirt. His brother's expression did not change, but Cas reached for the shirt hanging from a bedpost and pulled it on. "I wouldn't have gone in if I'd stopped to think about it. There was no time." Remembering the assassin in the window, he asked, "How did the archer get into the house? That's Master Gallo's home, isn't it?"

"No, he moved away months ago," Ventillas answered. "Master Dimas lives there now. With his daughter. Do you remember him?"

At the name, Cas felt his eye spasm. "I remember."

Ventillas did not notice. "The archer broke in. It was empty at the time. Everyone had gone to see the procession."

"What about the servants?"

"Dimas gave them the day off. I arrived there just after the family returned home. We found a broken lock on a back door. The archer had used the attic. It was that window that faced the lake."

"A broken lock. Nothing else?"

"No. Whoever he was, he left no trail for us to follow." Ventillas drummed his fingers along the table, scowling. "It's unthinkable, Cassia, that something like this could happen in our city."

A prince nearly murdered. An assassin slipping through their fingers. Cas agreed. "It's humiliating."

The drumming stopped. Drily, Ventillas said, "Yes, that too. Thank you for pointing it out, little brother."

Cas smiled briefly. "Were the neighbors questioned? Maybe —"

"The neighbors, their neighbors. The entire street. No one saw anything." Ventillas lifted a glass from the table and drank deeply. Indicating a cup on the bedside table, he added, "Master Jac left that for you. It will help you sleep."

Cas leaned close to the cup and sniffed. Tea, no longer hot. It smelled faintly of mandrake. "No."

"One drink won't hurt —"

"No." Cas rolled to his feet. Mandrake was a distant cousin to poppy, to opium. He did not want to start down that path. He was afraid he would never be able to step away from it, once he had begun. To distract Ventillas, he said, "What's this about a statue in the gardens?"

A dull flush worked its way up his brother's neck. "I'll have it taken down."

"What does it look like?"

"Not good," Ventillas said, annoyed. "That sculptor was inept and his fee was absurd."

Cas smiled. He had left his boots at the foot of the bed by a large chest. He sat on the lid, grabbed a boot, and tugged it on.

"Where are you going?" Ventillas asked.

"I want to see it."

"You don't." Ventillas sounded certain. Watching Cas pull on a second boot, he said, exasperated, "It's the middle of the night."

"Maybe it will look better in the dark."

A reluctant smile from Ventillas. "I'm telling you, you won't like it." But he grabbed his cloak off another bedpost and followed Cas out the door.

*** 

"What were you thinking?" Cas said, mystified.

Ventillas looked embarrassed. The keep's inner garden was surrounded on all sides by covered walkways two stories high. Sporadic torchlight flickered from wall brackets. Unlike the formal gardens at the front of the keep, with their neat rows of olive and orange trees, this one had a half-wild look to it. Vines climbing the walls, bushy shrubs left to grow as nature intended. Pomegranate flowers bloomed around a small fishpond stocked with pike. The air always smelled of rosemary and saffron and whatever else Cook tended to in a far-off corner. Best of all, the benches underneath the trees were large enough for a growing boy to nap on. It had been one of Cas' favorite places, something Ventillas had not forgotten. Hence the horrible statue.

"Lady Rondilla recommended him. Some famous artist out of Elvira," Ventillas added with remembered annoyance. "The sketches he drew were good, but I wasn't here to see him sculpting it and by the time I came home —" He grimaced. "I just wanted him to be done and go. It's depressing to look at."

Cas held his torch higher. The statue was carved from stone and was life-size, and it had been placed on a pedestal. At that angle, Cas could see clear up its nose. Its enormous stone nose. His nose did not look like that. It was an exaggeration and an insult. The statue was dressed like an old man in formal court wear, with a long robe and a stiff, ruffled collar that rose to its ears. And what was wrong with its ears? He peered closer, saw that they were slightly pointed at the top, like those of an elf in a bedtime story.

Cas turned to his brother in utter bafflement. "My ears."

Suddenly, Ventillas laughed, the sound rumbling into the night. "You're right, it's terrible. Even the cats hate it. Come on."

"Where?"

"To get rid of this cuckoo." Ventillas called to a guard standing beneath an archway. "Get more torches out here. We're going to need the light."

***

Carrying a torch, Cas followed Ventillas down the steep, winding staircase. The original armory had been built in the central keep, as safe as possible in case of a breach to the outer walls. The air was cooler down here. It smelled of metal and leather. At the bottom they came upon a door made of iron.

Ventillas produced a large key, warning, "Mind your head." Cas stooped beneath the door, built for smaller ancestors.

A series of connected chambers made up the armory. The ceiling was low. Stone archways separated each room. There were racks full of swords and walls lined with shields. Round shields. Kite shields. Some made of wood, others covered in boiled leather. There were crossbows and longbows and plenty of arrows for both. A long wall displayed armor, but not the sort currently in use. Those were kept in the main armory near the amphitheater. These were old, going back centuries, some collected from faraway places after foreign wars. Scale armor and mail armor. Armor made from the hide of an animal called a crocodile. There was a bronze cuirass, the front plate molded to resemble a bare-chested, heavily muscled warrior. It was mounted along with its greaves, which protected the legs, and a helmet, arranged so that at first glance it looked as if a warrior stood at attention. The bronze had been polished until it gleamed.

Ventillas gestured wide with his key. "Choose one."

The smile crept up on Cas, along with anticipation. He had rarely been allowed in here as a boy. "Anything?"

"Except for that." Ventillas pointed to a massive warhammer on a wall, spiked at the tip. "That's mine."

Which was fine with Cas. He did not want the hammer. He walked over to the strange crocodile armor and reached above it for the mace on the wall.

A spiked mace made of iron. One hundred and eighteen spikes covered the ball. Cas had counted them long ago. A larger spike jutted out from the tip. The handle was nearly three feet in length, longer than most. Cas tested the weapon's weight. Five or six pounds. A good solid weight. This would destroy an ugly statue, and anything else it came across.

Ventillas strolled over, the warhammer propped on his shoulder. "You've been eyeing that one since you could walk."

"Yes," Cas breathed, his tone reverent.

Amused, Ventillas walked toward the door. "Come on, then. Let's see how you like it."

\*\*\*

By the time they returned to the courtyard, an audience had gathered. As requested, torchlight filled the niches along the passageways. The fireflies were used only indoors. Their brightness did not last as long in the cold. The light had brought curiosity seekers, mainly guards, but others had come from their beds, peering down from the balcony. Men and women and children. Many in long voluminous robes, some with floppy nightcaps still on their heads.

Cas heard the jangle of keys and the crunch of gravel underfoot. "Warhammers? Maces?" Master Jacomel said mildly. "Are we under attack?"

Bemused, Ventillas asked, "What is everyone doing here, Master Jac? All I wanted was some light."

"Where you both go, excitement follows. Shall I send them away?"

"No." Despite the cool night air, Ventillas removed his cloak and shirt and tossed them onto the ground. "We might as well bring out some wine. Keep them warm."

Master Jacomel went off to arrange for the drink. Cas kept his shirt on. A flash of blue in the upper balcony caught his eye. He looked up to see Lena near a pillar, watching him.

She was dressed in one of those voluminous robes. No cap, though. Her hair remained loose, dark and lovely and so long it tumbled out of sight behind the balustrade. She lifted a hand in silent greeting.

"Breathe, Cassia," Ventillas murmured. "You don't want to faint in front of the lady."

Cas *had* been holding his breath. He sent Ventillas a dark look, which only made him laugh. Turning back to Lena, Cas bowed slightly, returning the greeting.

Ventillas swung the hammer onto his shoulder. "You first," he offered.

Cas picked up the mace. He circled the statue once, determining where best to strike, then swung. The spikes slammed into the chin and half the head broke away, including the nose, especially the nose, flying straight up into the night sky. By the time it returned to earth, splashing into the fishpond, the cheering had erupted.

***

In the end, the statue was reduced to rubble. Cas and Ventillas were on their knees, trying to catch their breath. Cas could feel his hair, stiff with sweat, bouncing around his head like a rooster's crown.

A festive atmosphere had taken hold, helped along by flowing barrels of wine. Food had arrived as well, heaped on tables near the shrubbery. Master Jacomel was off by the fishpond, overseeing the removal of Cas' stone head.

Ventillas contemplated their work. "It's an improvement."

"Agreed." All that was left was a stone boot on the pedestal.

Ventillas gave him a sideways glance. "What do you say, little brother? Tired enough to sleep?"

Startled, Cas turned his head, met his brother's eyes. Was this why Ventillas had done it? Trying to tire him to shreds so that his mind sought out nothing but rest? Ventillas, more parent than brother because he had to be. Cas swallowed past the lump in his throat. He nodded, because he could not speak.

"Good." Ventillas' hand came down on Cas' shoulder, using it as leverage to push himself to his feet. He called out, "All right then, the lot of you, the entertainment's over. Off to bed. Master Jac is old and needs his rest."

***

Cas woke to the sounds of thunderous snoring; Ventillas lay facedown beside him. More snoring came from the two pages sprawled on pallets by the window. Cas sat up, yawning, before it came to him. It was well past dawn. He had slept dreamlessly for the first time in three years.

## 10

COOK WEPT when she saw him.

Cas endured the tears soaking his tunic and the kisses peppering his face because he would not hurt her feelings for anything. And because she fed him. Mountain food, food he had dreamt of for years. He would never admit it to a soul, but he had missed Cook and her kitchen even more than he had missed his brother.

"She's hardly left the ovens since she heard you were home," Captain Lorenz remarked, sitting across from Cas with a steaming mug in his hand. "Any other time we are rationed. There's barely enough to keep a grown man standing."

"Oh, hush. You don't look hungry." At the next table, Cook cracked brown eggs into a bowl. Her birth name was Talesa, but no one used it except maybe the captain when no one else was about. Theirs was a relationship of long standing. Like the captain, she was the age Cas' parents would have been, had they lived. She wore a white apron over a red dress. Dark hair had been pulled into a knot high on her head, the shape of it the same as the plump pastry buns lined up on a table, awaiting the ovens. She had always been thin, suspicious for a cook, but doubt never lasted longer than the first bite of her red rice, or her chicken kelaguen, or her bunubunus, sweet and fried, filled with the season's fruit.

A little boy sat beside her on a high stool. Five years old, he cheerfully rolled strips of dough into noodle thinness. He wore short trousers and a loose-fitting tunic. Cas could see right through him to the wall where pots and pans of every size hung from iron hooks.

Cas averted his eyes. When Ventillas was an infant, a fire had broken out in this very kitchen. Two people had perished. A gamekeeper, and Cook's young son, who had been napping in a corner. The spirit had always been there, Cas knew. Sitting beside his mother, longer than Cas had been alive. The only difference was that now Cas could *see* him. A disquieting thought, imagining all the things that had once been hidden from him.

The kitchen was a loud, clamoring space with rough stone walls and a fireplace on each end. Tables scattered about, some for eating, others for the undercooks to knead, chop, and gut. The household staff dined here throughout the day. Servants and guards snatching meals on their way to various tasks. Cas kept company with a handful of soldiers. Bittor was among them, his nose only a little red, along with several women Cas learned were tapestry weavers. No one mentioned Faro or his hand.

Cas finished a bowl of latijas in moments. Closing his eyes on the last spoonful, he savored the taste of custard, cake, and cinnamon on his tongue. *Cinnamon.* The sudden dropping off of conversation had him opening his eyes.

Cook was weeping again. The others, when he turned in their direction, studied their mugs and bowls with great concentration. Self-conscious, Cas set his spoon down. At least he had not licked the bowl. Quietly, he said, "I am perfectly well, Cook."

She flapped a hand at him, sniffling. "Of course you are. It is the spices. They upset my eyes."

"Here, lad." Captain Lorenz's words were gruff. He heaped a

bowl full of frit Palmerin — black Palmerin pig and wild rice cooked with oil and onions — and slid it across to Cas. "Where are you off to today?"

*Whoever the archer was, he left no trail for us to follow.* Ventillas' words came back to him. They were likely true. But Cas could not stop thinking of the window by the lake, and the man who owned the house. What harm could there be in taking a second look? Accepting the bowl from the captain with thanks, he said only, "I'll walk the city, I think. Get my bearings."

Ventillas entered, a ribboned scroll in hand. He wore a brown leather tunic that fit him perfectly. Cas wore an identical tunic, only his stretched tight across the shoulders. He had been careful this morning not to make any sudden movements. Ventillas stopped when he saw the array of dishes before Cas. "You never make latijas for me," he said to Cook.

"Or me," Captain Lorenz added.

A good-natured chorus of agreement rose from the soldiers.

Cook poured batter into a pan. "You have all discovered my secret. Lord Cassia is my favorite."

Ventillas' words were wry. "That has never been a secret." Pushing aside platters and cups, he unrolled the parchment onto the table. "Tell me again where you saw the lynx." Cas had told Ventillas of the cat with the bloodied eyes. He had warned there could be more. Cas took a closer look at the parchment. It was a map of Palmerin, the city proper as well as the surrounding lands all the way to the borders. He traced the aqueduct's path until he saw a familiar copse of trees. "Here. You're going hunting?"

"We can't have these on the roads." Turning to Captain Lorenz, Ventillas said, "We'll need archers."

"They'll be ready to ride when you are," Captain Lorenz said.

Satisfied, Ventillas said to Cas, "You didn't have a bow and arrow with you. How did you kill it?"

Cas took his slingshot from his belt and a spiked ball from his pouch. He placed both beside the map.

Captain Lorenz nudged the ball with the tip of his eating knife. "This would do it. It looks like the devil's marble."

Bittor leaned around the weavers to see. "Where did you get it?"

"A graveyard keeper in Brisa." The irate keeper had used them on any animal caught digging up the plague dead and leaving rotting corpses strewn about for the villagers to discover. Cas did not mention these things. People were eating their custard.

Ventillas picked up the ball carefully. "One shot was enough?"

"If you can hit it in the eye. I'll come with you," Cas offered.

"Ah . . . no." Ventillas returned the ball to him just as a girl appeared in the doorway. She was around twelve and had come to inform Cas that Queen Jehan wished to see him this morning, not this afternoon as had originally been agreed upon.

Cas repeated blankly, "Originally agreed upon?"

"Yes, Lord Cassia."

Frowning, Cas turned to his brother, who shrugged. "Did I not tell you? You're to meet with the queen today. And the tailors."

"Tailors?"

Someone snickered. It sounded like Bittor.

"Yes, tailors," Ventillas said. "It will be . . . what? An hour out of your day? My clothing doesn't fit you, Cassia. You need your own."

Carefully, Cas rolled his shoulders, knowing Ventillas was right. He would be lucky if the tunic lasted until supper without splitting at the seams. Ventillas reached for a stuffed egg and popped the whole thing in his mouth. Resigned, Cas turned to the girl waiting patiently by the door and asked what time he was expected. "I'm to bring you now, Lord Cassia."

Worse and worse. Cas put the slingshot and ball away just as another figure slipped by the girl. The entire kitchen fell silent.

Sorne.

She stopped in the face of so many stares. A terrible mottled heat climbed her neck. Ventillas looked as if he meant to speak, but his mouth was full of egg. She turned to flee.

Cas said, "Sorne."

Slow and uncertain, she turned back.

"I'm just leaving. Here, take my chair." Cas rose and held it out for her.

Guilt sat on his shoulder, arms folded, shaking its head in judgment. Palmerin Keep was her home as much as it was his. And last night he had suggested she leave it. Partly for her sake. Mostly, he admitted, for his.

Sorne approached the chair as though it were coated in arsenic. She sat. "Thank you, Lord Cassia." Her tone was distant. Like a stranger. Which was what they were now. Time and circumstance had turned them into strangers. The thought saddened him.

The chatter picked up again. Ventillas pulled out a chair beside Captain Lorenz and launched into a discussion on how best to hunt rotten lynx, breaking off long enough to tell Cas he would see him tonight.

Reaching past Sorne, Cas helped himself to two more bunubunus, then offered Cook a bow, formal enough for royalty. She laughed. Beside her, the little boy smiled and waved goodbye, his hand covered with flour from another table, another time. As always, Cas averted his eyes and pretended he did not see.

***

For the next three hours, Cas stood on a pedestal, much like his statue had until its destruction the night before. A hundred bolts of fabric passed beneath his nose. For his approval. Or rejection. No part of his body was overlooked. There was linen for his under-drawers and wool for his cloaks. Silk for the trim on his hats. There were hunting gloves, riding gloves, visiting gloves. Leather tunics and embroidered tunics. Robes that trailed and those that did not. A mind-numbing assortment. The master tailor barked orders to his assistants, who spoke around pins and needles clamped between their teeth. Cas had lost count of the times he had said, "Do what you think is best" and "I will not wear that." The thought of Ventillas out hunting diseased lynx filled him with a deep burning jealousy.

"He will need something to wear for supper this evening." Queen Jehan was brisk in the manner of military commanders as she ordered Cas and the tailors about. Only this commander wore blue trimmed with white lace. "That one there," she said. "Every-thing else will keep until the end of the week." And, seeing the tai-lor's agony, she added, "Dear sir, don't despair. We'll find you more help." She circled the pedestal, hands clasped behind her back. "He will need shoes as well. Why, this is charming. Lord Cassiapeus, what do you think of these slippers?"

The shoe she held up for his inspection was made of soft leather dyed the color of mashed peas. The tip was long and pointed. It curled at the very end.

"I will not wear that."

His fitting had become a public spectacle. The tailors and seamstresses had taken over a chamber just off the great hall. Guests strolled in to visit with one another and to offer up their opinions on how Cas should be dressed. Many of the women held fans, delicate, hand-painted, so that the room was filled with the rhythmic *tap tap tap* of fan against collarbone. At a table by the window, Sorne arranged pomegranate flowers into vases. She kept to herself, alone in a crowded room. Several ladies brought embroidery hoops. Others, like the nurse Faustina, held infants, so many that Cas asked the queen in an undertone, "Your Grace, how many babies are in this keep?"

Queen Jehan compared samples of fox fur and sable. Absently, she answered, "There are forty in your old nursery, including Prince Ventillas."

Cas nearly fell off the pedestal. "Forty! Where did they come from?"

That brought her head up. "Where babies usually do, Lord Cassiapeus" was her dry response, provoking giggles from a pair of nearby seamstresses.

Queen Jehan smiled across the chamber at her son. To Cas, she said, "Most of the children were born within months of each other. It is human nature, I think, to want to create life after so much death."

Cas fidgeted. He had no wish to hear about the queen and her need to create life. "I like the fox fur," he said.

Amused, Queen Jehan gave the fur to the master tailor. It would line the earflaps on a new winter hat. For the hundredth time that morning, Cas wondered why she did this. Overseeing his wardrobe was something Master Jacomel could have done. Or Cas himself. He did not need so much. It was a sentiment echoed by Master Jacomel, who came by to ensure there was plenty of food and drink for their guests. Out of the queen's hearing, the steward said, "This is not a task for a queen, Cassia. She does you a great honor. Be sure to tell her so."

"I did not ask her to do it," Cas protested. At the steward's look, full of threat, he added, "*Fine.* I'll tell her so."

"Good." Appeased, Master Jacomel brushed a stray thread off Cas' shoulder. "Lady Analena is in the archives."

"I . . ." Cas had not asked. Before he could inquire further, the steward moved away.

Soon after, a young woman approached, her arm in a sling. The nurse from the lake. Smiling shyly, she thanked him for saving her life. She did not remain long. Her face was drawn, tired, and the queen sent her back to bed.

King Rayan also stopped in briefly, councilors trailing. "You look like you're standing on a hangman's scaffold, not a tailor's block."

"It feels like the same thing."

King Rayan laughed. Bolts of fabric lay strewn about a nearby table. He tapped on one of them. "Perhaps a strong, sturdy wool," he suggested. "For catching young ladies who fall from trees."

Cas winced. King Rayan still smiled, but there was a thread of annoyance in his softly spoken words. "I'm grateful to you, Cassia. You know this. But when my sister places herself in harm's way, I should like to hear about it. Understood?"

"Understood, Your Grace. Apologies."

Satisfied, King Rayan went on his way. There was one unpleasant incident, but Cas had braced himself. He had known it was coming. When instructed by a tailor to remove his tunic and undershirt, he did so. Conversation trailed away as his scars were exposed for all to see. More than one horrified gasp was heard, until Queen Jehan said quietly, "Master tailor," jolting the older man into action. He hurried over with his measuring strings and worked quickly as Cas looked blankly across the room, trying to keep all expression from his face. Only a few minutes passed before he was allowed to dress. By then, Sorne had fled the room in tears.

At last, Queen Jehan told Cas he was no longer needed. He stepped down from the block. Queen Jehan said, for his ears alone, "I wonder how you can bear to have me in your home."

Cas would not shame his brother, or Master Jacomel, by speaking his thoughts aloud. He bowed. "You are our guest, Your Grace. We are pleased to have you here. Thank you for today. Ventillas will be glad to have his clothing to himself again."

It was hard for him to look at her and not think of his time in Brisa. Her expression said she knew this, but all she said was "There are no women in your family, Lord Cassiapeus. No older sisters. It is the queen's pleasure."

He was trying. She was trying. In the end, they could do no more.

# 11

I N THE KEEP'S ARCHIVES, Cas found Lena high up on a ladder, pulling a book off a shelf. There was no one else about in the quiet space with its tables and bookshelves, its globes of every size. Stained-glass windows threw cheerful prisms over her green dress and pretty dark hair. He studied her profile from the doorway. She looked cross.

"What's wrong?" he asked.

The glance she spared him said the last thing she wanted was companionship. "Nothing at all. Today has been a delight."

Very cross. As she climbed down the ladder, the enormous book clutched to her chest, he walked over to a table near the windows. Parchment was spread across the surface, the pages covered in heavy ink. A hurried, masculine scrawl. Before it was a spouted pot with dancing, prancing lynx painted on the sides. He could smell the richness of the drinking chocolate from within. Two delicate cups showed no signs of use. She had hoped to speak to the artist today, he remembered. Abril. The one with the sad eyes.

Cas said, "Your painter did not come."

"No." Lena's response came halfway down the ladder.

"Why not go to her?" Cas felt the chocolate pot. Cold. "You said she's staying in town?"

"At an inn. Lord Ventillas offered her a chamber here while she finished the tapestry, but she refused." Her slippers on solid ground,

Lena came over and flopped into a chair beside him. She set the book on the table. Leather-bound with gold clasps. The title had been written in gold leaf: *The Heraldic Shields of the Kingdom of Oliveras.* "She'll be at supper tonight. I'll speak with her then. And besides, I've just been informed I'm not to leave the keep without a man-at-arms by my side."

*Ah.* Another reason for the cross expression. Cas leaned against the table's edge. Her hair had been arranged into a single intricate braid, emerald pins tucked throughout. "He's your brother. He worries about you."

"My brother, yes. *Not* my keeper." Lena snatched up the pages and tapped them violently against the table even after the edges had lined up. "He thinks I'm still a child." *Tap.* "Man-at-arms, *pfft.* Do I *look* like I need a nursemaid to you?" *Tap.* She turned her face up to him, her expression full of mutiny.

Cas drew back, alarmed. "No."

"Of course I don't." Setting the parchment aside, she propped her chin on one hand, mutiny transformed into gloom. "Why can't he see that I'm perfectly capable of taking care of myself?"

In fairness to the king, her horse had been stolen and Cas had been obliged to rescue her. She might still be up in that tree if he had not come around. Still, best not to say so. "Don't ladies normally have guards, some kind of escort when they travel?"

"I am no lady, Cas!" she cried, her voice echoing in the vast space. "Not like the ladies here. I grew up in my grandfather's house, a small one in the middle of Elvira where the booksellers keep their shops. It could fit into a corner of this archive." A swinging arm encompassed the room. "I could go where I wanted, when I wanted.

And then word comes that I'm the only one of the king's siblings to survive the pestilence. And suddenly I'm important. Everything is different. Now I need a man-at-arms."

She said *man-at-arms* in much the same way another would say *hair in my soup.*

Cas was at a loss. Someone kinder would pat her shoulder or murmur soothing words. *There, there.* Cas was no patter. Seconds ticked by before he reached for the pot and poured the cooled chocolate into a cup. He offered it to her. "The king found out you were traveling alone?"

Lena took the cup with thanks. "Until I met you, yes." Straightening suddenly, she said, "Were you scolded too?"

"Not really."

Lena scowled into her cup.

Cas asked, "What did you tell him exactly?"

"More than I meant to."

Cas poured the rest of the chocolate for himself and waited.

Lena wrapped both hands around her cup. "I went to Trastamar first, before coming here. It was simpler to travel as a boy and go alone than to ask for permission and be told no." She glanced up at him briefly. "I had to. My grandfather died in Trastamar. His words stop there. Which means that, from the day Jehan disembarked to the night she arrived at the palace, there is no official record. What happened to the people in her cortege? Did they all die of plague? *You* survived. Perhaps there were others. What happened to the carriages? And everything on them?"

Cas could hear it in her voice. "You found something."

"Not in Trastamar," she admitted. "The graves were unmarked.

I could not tell who had died, let alone when. And there was no one left to ask." Lena set her cup down, a gleam in her eye. "But I found one of the carriages."

His cup stopped halfway to his lips. "Where?"

"Near Ollala," she said. "A traveling camp found it abandoned in the woods. No horses, no cortege. They added it to their caravan." Her lips curved a little. "You should have seen it, Cas. Twenty-five rickety old wagons, and in the middle of it all was a royal carriage, painted blue and gold, pulled by donkeys."

Traveling camps were common in Oliveras. Extended families moving from town to town to sell goods and services, staying no longer than the passing of a season. The picture Lena painted was a vivid one. Cas could have been sitting beside her on a horse, watching the caravan go by.

He said thoughtfully, "They told you it had been abandoned?"

"Yes. They let me search it too. I looked all over. Above the carriage, beneath the benches, in case there was some sort of hidden compartment." She reached for a battered leather bag on the floor by her chair. Pulling out a sheaf of papers, she said, "I found this in a box strapped behind one of the wheels."

Cas set his cup down with a clatter. "Is that . . . ?"

"Blood? No," she assured him. "I thought so too at first. I think it's tomato soup. See?" She held them out.

Cas took the papers. A huge red stain had marred the top page and seeped into the parchment below so that the sheets had stuck together. He sniffed. It might have been tomato. He could not say for certain. It did not smell like blood. The words along the edges were still readable. He glanced at the stack of parchment on the table, the one Lena had tapped to death earlier. The handwriting, heavy, masculine, was the same.

"This is your grandfather's."

"Yes. He liked to work and eat at the same time, and he wasn't the neatest of men." She smiled briefly. "I don't know why it was separated from the rest of his belongings. I can make out some of it." She pointed to the corners that had escaped the stain. "See here? I think it's his copy of the ships' inventory."

The pages looked well and truly stuck. Cas tried to tug them apart. Lena's warning hiss stopped him. He asked doubtfully, "Can they be separated?"

She whisked the pages away from him. "I'll try steaming them apart tonight. I haven't shown them to Jehan or my brother yet. I wanted to see if I could read it first."

"Did you find anything else?"

A shrug. "A ladies mirror and a pair of spectacles. I left them with the camp. I paid them too, since they were so helpful." Her expression darkened. "Helpful as a bum rash, it turned out."

Cas' brows rose. "What happened?"

"I fell asleep by the river. The same morning I met you. I only meant to take a short nap. I had plenty of time to ride to Palmerin, change, and still be part of the naming ceremony. But when I woke, my horse was gone. Someone in the camp must have followed me."

"How do you know it was one of them?"

Lena was quiet. "I could smell him. Or her. Whoever. The pipes they smoked were distinctive. They smelled like burned lavender."

His mind turned dark, imagining all the ways she could have

been hurt, killed. His words came out brusque. "This is why you have a man-at-arms."

"Don't you start too. Rayan was already quite vocal about it." Subdued, she sipped at her chocolate. "I've spoken to Jehan and Lord Ventillas. Trying to learn what happened once they arrived in Trastamar. But I think they keep things from me. Because they can't bear to speak of it. Or they are trying to spare me. Or . . . they think I will not do their stories justice. I am not my grandfather, after all." Pushing her cup away, she lowered her forehead onto the table. "I'm sorry," she said, her words muffled. "You've come to look for a book or a quiet spot away from all your guests, and instead you're forced to listen to my tale of woe. Tell me to leave. It won't hurt my feelings."

She was a pitiful sight. Face on the table, arms hanging straight down at her sides. A stack of tomato-stained parchment by her head. After a moment, a very long one, Cas said, "I'm a man-at-arms."

Lena lifted her head. "What?"

"Lord Ruben was a neighbor. I was his page when I was a boy, and then my brother's shield bearer. King Rayan knighted me a little over three years ago. Which makes me a man-at-arms."

"That is very informative. Why are you telling me this?"

Cas did not quite know himself. "I need to see to something in town. You, I think, need to get out of this keep. Come with me."

Silence fell, followed by a toneless "You feel sorry for me."

"I'll feel sorry for you if I want."

The corners of her mouth lifted, reluctantly. He had repeated her words back to her. She remembered. "You're going into town?" she asked.

"Yes."

"May I ride your mare?"

Cas looked at her. "Yes," he said finally.

Her smile grew. "Then I accept. I'll meet you in the stables." As if something had just occurred to her, she asked, "Why *did* you come here? Were you looking for a book?"

Ducking his head, Cas headed for the door. It was easier to answer when he did not have to face her. "No. I was looking for you."

# 12

"IS IT JUST ME," Lena asked, "or is this city uncommonly clean?"

Cas had noticed it too. As they made their way through the streets, Lena on his mare, Cas on a much larger palfrey, its coat shiny and black, he saw things he had missed before. Where was the blood puddling outside the barber-surgeon's shop? Where were the swarms of flies? And the horse dung? He had never seen so few steaming piles on the ground. Navigating around them used to require his full concentration. This afternoon, all he had to dodge were the handful of spirits wandering by, their expressions full of confusion and loss.

He said, "We've never been as filthy as Elvira—"

"Insults!"

Cas smiled. She had cheered considerably since leaving the keep. "But I don't remember it being this clean either. We have a new city inspector. I heard he's very particular. This could be his doing."

Their cloaks kept the wind at bay, chillier now that the sun hid behind clouds. They slowed their horses when they reached a square busy with marketers. From their covered booths, merchants sold everything from fresh vegetables and secondhand clothing to pretty songbirds locked in their cages. A fountain stood in the center, water shooting upward from the mouths of four stone lynx.

City dwellers gathered around the fountain's edge. Eating, laughing, minding young children. The aqueduct rose just beyond the square, double arches and ancient, weathered stone.

Lena sat up straighter in her saddle. "What are those?" she exclaimed.

Beside the fountain, three mammoth frying pans had been placed over open fires. Each measured ten feet in diameter, like the cookware of a fairy-tale giant. Three men stirred the contents with wooden spoons large as boat paddles. They wore loose white shirts and rough trousers that stopped below their knees. Despite the cool weather, their feet were sandled. Faded kerchiefs held back long black hair.

"Pika," Cas answered, smiling. "It's a local dish."

"I see the rice." Lena inhaled deeply. "I smell the garlic. What else is there?"

Cas recited from memory. "Saffron, jumping beans, onions, peppers. Rabbit, usually, but sometimes they'll have chicken or snails."

"Oh." Her excitement dimmed considerably. "I hope it's not snails." Then, "What are jumping beans?"

"Look." The horses had brought them close enough to one pan to see the white beans, thousands of them, hopping straight up in the air at least a foot before falling back into the pan. "They grow in the mountains. Nowhere else. The heat makes them jump. So. Jumping beans."

Lena was smiling, delighted. "I should have brought some parchment. I need to write this down."

One of the men stirring the pika happened to look their way. He was the youngest of the three, Cas' age, his face pitted with scars.

Recognition came when he spotted Cas, followed by a wide grin. He waved madly with his free hand, shouting, "Cassiapeus!"

The recognition was mutual. Cas' laugh had Lena turning to stare at him as though he had just sprouted antlers on his head. His hand shot up in greeting. "Cassiapeus!" he shouted back. Heads swiveled in their direction.

It did not take her long. "His name is Cassiapeus too?"

"He was born a week after me," Cas explained. "His mother thought it would be lucky to name him after the lord's new son. So we were both punished."

Lena laughed.

"Are you hungry?" he asked her.

"Yes. I want to see those beans. You?"

Rueful, Cas nudged the palfrey toward their lunch. "Always."

***

They ate their pika on their horses, leaving the market behind and wending their way toward the lake.

Lena was in luck. Today's pika had come with rabbit, no snails. It was served in a bowl made of tightly woven leaves. Their spoons were also leaves, fashioned in some ingenious way into scoops. Both were meant to be thrown away after use. From the way Lena admired hers, Cas suspected they would be returning to Elvira with her as keepsakes.

Cassiapeus the cook would not take his money. "Next time," he had told Cas, his kerchief and hair whipping in the wind. "Today it is welcome" — he offered Lena an extravagant bow, which made her smile — "and welcome home." He placed both hands on Cas' shoulders — Cas managed to control a flinch — then hustled off to tend to the queue that had formed in his absence.

"You are well loved here." Lena had copied the way he dined on a horse. Reins and bowl in one hand, spoon in the other. A useful skill he had learned while traveling long distances. "It isn't just Cassiapeus back there. Lord Ventillas has always been kind to me, but every time I've seen him, he's been so serious, so sad. Last night when you beat up that poor statue" — she glanced over, caught his smile — "it was like looking at someone else. He was happy."

"It's good to be home" was all he said. They rode for a time in silence, until he pointed to her bowl with his spoon. "Do you like it?"

She showed him her empty bowl. "Very much. Thank you."

"It didn't cost me anything."

"That isn't what I meant. Today was a misery until now. Thank you for bringing me here. Your city is beautiful."

He turned his head, smiled. "You are welcome."

Lena tipped her head back as they passed beneath the aqueduct. "I wonder how far up it goes."

"Ninety-two feet." Cas reached out, fingers brushing the stone base.

"That's very exact." Lena craned her neck even more. "This is the first working aqueduct I've come across. The one near Elvira is a ruin."

"There's another one in the south. It's even older than this one. The upkeep is prohibitive for most cities."

"But not here?"

"We don't really have a choice. It's the lifeblood of our city, being so far in the mountains."

Lena looked thoughtful. "Lord Ventillas is a soldier *and* an engineer. Is that what you are?"

Not quite. It was how he had spent his days, before. Helping to maintain the city walls, the bridges, the aqueduct, the roads. Scouting the outlying areas for signs of threat. Ensuring the food and water stores were plentiful in case of siege. It was what he had been taught to do since he was very young: watch over Palmerin in his brother's absence, for he was the second son.

Cas said, "I'm not an engineer yet. I haven't finished my training." When he had left home, he still had several years of study to complete, overseen by Ventillas and Captain Lorenz.

Lena was frowning. "That's hardly fair. You built a bridge while you were a prisoner. Surely that counts for something."

It was the first time he could think back to his imprisonment and find something to smile about. "Good point. I'll ask."

Lena was looking past him. "That lake. Is that where . . . ?"

"Yes."

They crossed another square, riding past the church where the prince's naming ceremony had taken place, and made for the bridge. They stopped halfway across before dismounting. Cas shoved their empty bowls and spoons into his saddlebag. Two old women on horseback rode by, eyeing them curiously.

"Which one is it?" Holding the mare's reins, Lena scanned the homes and shops across the lake, looking for the archer's window.

Cas pointed. "That one there."

She studied the attic window belonging to Master Dimas, then turned back to the bridge. "It only took one arrow? That is extraordinary. Not for the nurse, of course. Or my sweet nephew."

"Can you shoot?"

"Badly" came her prompt reply, making him smile. "Can you?"

"Not as well as that." Another look from window to bridge. "Ventillas could do it. He's better with a bow and arrow."

"Jehan could too." At Cas' skeptical look, she said, "It's true. Rayan wrote about it in a letter. He's seen her practice in your arena. She was trained by Brisa's royal archer. Lady Mari was too."

It took Cas a moment to recall the queen's friend who had sailed with her to Oliveras. "Lady Mari who died?"

Lena nodded, saying absently, "She caught the pestilence outside Gregoria. They had to leave her at a hospital there. Cas, why are we here?"

"Because of the chickens."

She turned a blank look on him. He waved a hand. *Never mind.* "I was thinking about something Ventillas said last night. That Master Dimas, the owner of that house, gave his servants the day off for the naming ceremony."

Her brows drew together. "Yes?"

"You've met our stablemaster, Jon?"

Her expression cleared. "Of course. He's a very nice man."

"Jon used to work for Master Dimas. As a groom. He left his service because those who work for Dimas are not given time off, ever."

"What? Not even a half day?"

"No."

"Not even for a funeral?"

Cas shook his head. "Never."

"That's barbaric," Lena said, appalled.

Cas was in agreement. "It's why Dimas has never been able to keep staff. He hires those who are very young, like Jon and his brother were at the time. Or desperate, and they move on as soon as they're able. And yet on the day of the naming ceremony, the day a stranger breaks into his home, every servant is given a day off."

Lena was quiet. "Hm."

That was what Cas had thought. *Hm.*

Lena said, "Although, for argument's sake . . . you've met this Master Dimas?"

"Many times." He was one of the richest men in town. He did not let anyone forget it.

"But you haven't seen him in three years," she said. "People change, Cas. Perhaps he's grown wiser, decided to be kinder to his servants. The pestilence changed people."

True. It had changed him. He looked at the house across the lake and said, "Let's go find out."

## ᠊ 13 ᠊

THE RICE MERCHANT'S SHOP had a bright, prosperous look to it. A freshly painted sign hung above the door, the image that of a smiling girl holding a heaping bowl of rice. Hellin, Master Dimas' daughter. Inside the shop, open rice barrels lined the walls. Three clerks rushed about, filling orders for waiting customers. One female clerk was elderly, stooped and bony. The other two were girls no older than ten.

Cas and Lena stood in a corner out of everyone's way. Cas had declined the old clerk's offer to wait upstairs in the family's living quarters. Master Dimas was expected back shortly. A groom had been sent to fetch him. A few of the customers recognized Cas, though none approached. He thought nothing of it until Lena commented, "Do you know, you can look very scary when you wish it."

Cas had been deep in thought. He had not realized he was scowling. Now he saw the customers giving him a wide berth as they exited the shop, clutching burlap sacks of rice. He rearranged his face into something more neutral, much to Lena's amusement.

"You're not scared of me," he said, contemplating her down length of his nose.

"Why should I be?" Lena took a scoop off a wall hook and poked about a rice barrel. "We're friends. You saved my life. We share a horse."

"We do not share a horse."

She gave him a crooked smile. "Did you know Lord Amador's great-great-grandfather died in a rice barrel?"

Cas only looked at her.

"It's true," she insisted. "His middle son hit him on the head during an argument and then buried him under the rice until he suffocated."

"I . . . How do you know this?"

"It was in a book I read." Lena gave the rice one last poke before returning the scoop to its hook. "I wonder how long it would have taken."

"Lord Cassia!"

Master Dimas was as Cas remembered. Curly black hair and a full bushy beard. Shaped roughly like one of his rice barrels. His black robe matched his velvet cap, which was topped with a goose feather. A heavy gold chain served as a belt. Behind him was his daughter, Hellin.

"I almost fell over when I heard you'd come back! Keeled right onto the floor! Is that not so, Hellin?" Master Dimas spoke in booms, one volume only, the first of which made Lena jump.

"Nearly so, Papa." Hellin's smile was indulgent. She was Cas' age, curly black hair spilling well past her shoulders. She wore a green cloak, as Lena did, though hers was lighter, like a crisp green apple. "We are so pleased to see you safe, my lord Cassia." She turned to Lena and curtsied. "Lady Analena, welcome. Here is the king's sister, Papa."

Beaming, Master Dimas greeted Lena, whipping off his cap with a flourish. Lena was polite. She was not friendly.

"But why do you wear your cloaks?" Master Dimas asked. "Why

have you not been shown upstairs?" He pinned the older clerk with a glare. She froze like a trapped rabbit.

Cas said, "It was offered, Master Dimas. We can't stay long. We're here about your archer."

Master Dimas glanced quickly around the shop to see if the customers had overheard. They had. "Not *my* archer," he said with a grimace. "I do not claim him."

Lena said, "No, I would not want to claim him either."

"Ventillas told us the archer broke into your attic. May we see it?" Cas asked.

"There's nothing *to* see," Master Dimas protested. "The king's men were all over here two days ago. In and out. Up and down. They found nothing."

"Nevertheless."

"Certainly you may." Hellin placed a soothing hand on her father's arm. "We, too, wish to learn who would do such a thing. Please, follow me."

They left the rice shop behind. Hellin led them out a back door and into a courtyard. A stone wall blocked the view of the lake. Plump, clucking chickens roamed freely. Lena paused at the sight of the birds, frowning.

"The house was built strangely," Master Dimas explained, the feather in his cap nearly flattened by the wind. "The attic can only be accessed through a separate stairwell, just here." He pulled a key from his robes and turned the lock. "Inconvenient. But one cannot fault the location. Buildings by the lake are rarely for sale."

Cas nudged aside a chicken pecking at his boot. "The lock was broken, I heard."

"Yes," Master Dimas said. "This one is new."

"Where is the old one? May I see it?" Cas could feel Lena watching him, wondering what he was up to.

Father and daughter exchanged a glance.

"I threw it away," Hellin said. "Into the lake. I was upset. Forgive me, Lord Cassia. I did not realize it was important."

Cas assured her it was not. They climbed the narrow stairwell to the very top. Four stories in total. By the time they reached the attic door, Master Dimas huffed and puffed. The attic was completely empty, the floor thick with dust and covered with hundreds of footprints.

"We are still moving our belongings from the old house," Hellin said. "The attic will be the last of it. I hate to think that someone used our home for such evil." She turned to Lena. "The little prince is well, I hope?"

"Very well. Thank you."

"And the nurse? The one who was hurt?"

"Her shoulder will heal," Lena said. "She's badly shaken, however, and no longer wishes to be a nurse. She'll go home to her parents."

Hellin made sympathetic noises. "How very sad."

Cas crossed the chamber to the window. A rusted latch took some doing but he managed to push it open. The wind rushed in, blowing dust off the floor and into swirls and motes. From this vantage point, the archer's skill was even more impressive. To be able to stand here and miss so small a target by inches. Incredible. Master Dimas and Hellin remained by the door, speaking among themselves.

Lena came to stand beside Cas. "Faustina was supposed to have carried the baby out of the church," she said. "Did you know?"

"Yes. Her leg was troubling her." The old nurse had said so in the carriage, afterward.

Lena placed both hands on the windowsill and leaned out. "She's grown frail since I last saw her. I'm glad she wasn't on the bridge. I'm not sure she would have recovered as well." She leaned out even farther and Cas, afraid she would tumble out in the wind, reached for her cloak and tugged her back in.

He turned. Father and daughter fell silent, looking at him expectantly. "You gave the servants the day off," Cas said.

"Yes." Master Dimas' chest puffed out, magnanimous. "I thought they would enjoy the celebrations. They are hard workers."

"Papa is very kind," Hellin added.

"Very," Cas echoed. "If there were no servants about, how would someone enter the back courtyard?"

Hellin said, "They could use the servants' gate. It leads around the side of the building. We use it for deliveries and such. Or one could come through the gate in the back wall. It leads directly to the lake and the alleyways."

"The servants' gate and the back gate," Cas repeated. "Were those locks also broken?"

Silence. Once again, father and daughter looked at each other.

"They were not," Master Dimas said at last. The boom had gone from his voice. Caution had taken its place.

"Strange," Cas said. "How would someone access the attic door if they could not even get into the courtyard?"

Lena offered, "He could have climbed over the back wall?"

"Yes!" Master Dimas seized on that explanation. "That is true. He climbed the back wall."

"When?" Cas asked. "A royal naming ceremony is rare, even in the capital. We've never had one in Palmerin. There would have been people gathering by the lake a day, two days, before then to claim their spot. There would have been crowds right outside your wall. Someone climbing the wall would have been seen."

More silence.

"We really could not say, Lord Cassia," Hellin said quietly.

Why had Cas come here today? Lena had wondered. He had come because Ventillas had spoken to Master Dimas, had taken him at his word. And therein lay the problem. "Master Dimas, do you know a toll keeper named Izaro?"

Neither the rice merchant nor his daughter could mask their shock. The question had come from nowhere. Cas had meant it to.

*A man came by. He took the toll. He took my chickens.*

*Were you . . . ?*

*Dead? Not yet. He came in long enough to hunt down the coin. Didn't say a word to me. Wouldn't give me water when I asked. Took my axe, too. Heard him tell his girl to gather up the birds.*

*Who was it?*

*That fat rice merchant. With the curly hair. Dimas.*

"You do know him." Cas leaned against the window ledge. For Lena's benefit he said, "Months ago, you both visited the home of Lord Ruben's toll keeper, who was ill from plague. You took the chickens from his yard. The same ones, I think, that are now in your courtyard. You took the coin he kept beneath his floorboards. You stole from a dying man, Master Dimas, and then you left his body for the dogs."

"How could you possibly—?" Hellin began before her father's look stopped her.

Lena stood very still, listening.

Master Dimas' face had turned an alarming red. "I'm afraid, Lord Cassia, that I am very insulted. Very insulted! Your brother will hear of this—"

"If that is your wish," Cas said mildly.

That stopped Master Dimas. Suspicious, he said, "What do you mean?"

"I'm not here about Izaro," Cas said. "There's something about this archer that you're not telling us. I want to know what it is."

Hellin wrapped her arms around herself. Master Dimas came farther into the attic. The open window had let in the cold as well as the wind. It did nothing to stop the sweat beading his forehead. "I did not know what she intended. I swear it."

"*She?*" Lena turned shocked eyes on Cas.

Cas had not been certain. But he had wondered. It could have been a woman that day, standing by this window.

Master Dimas took off his velvet cap and used it to mop his face. "A woman stopped me on the street three days ago. She was a visitor from Elvira, she said, who wished to see the procession. But she did not like to stand by the lake with the rabble. Might she have use of my attic chamber? She could see it would have an excellent view. It would only be for a few hours and she would pay handsomely. I said yes."

Cas said, "You left a stranger alone in your home?"

"Not the whole house!" Master Dimas snapped. "Just the attic. I left the servants' gate unlocked. And the attic door. There was nothing for her to steal except the chickens . . ." Color flooded his face as he heard his own words. Sullenly, he finished, "She did not look like an assassin."

Lena said, "What *did* she look like?"

"Rich" was his blunt response. "She was a widow. Or at least she looked like one. She wore black. Her dress. Her veil."

Cas and Lena shared a grimace. A veil. Frustrated, Cas said, "You did not see her face."

"No."

Cas turned to Hellin. "Did you speak with her?"

"I did not," Hellin said to the floor. "This will ruin us, Lord Cassia. If people learn we took payment from a prince killer —"

"The prince is alive, no thanks to you," Lena said with little sympathy. She turned to Master Dimas. "You didn't see her face, but you heard her. Did she sound young? Old?"

"Young. Like you."

"And she was from Elvira?" Lena pressed.

"She said so."

"What does that mean, sir? You didn't believe her?"

Master Dimas hesitated. "Her Oliveran was perfect. Without the patois. It was . . ."

"Too perfect?" Lena guessed. "A second language, perhaps?"

A shrug. "Maybe, Lady Analena. I don't know."

They did not know what the archer looked like. They did not know where she came from. Cas said, "What name did she give you?"

"Madame Faustina. What?" Master Dimas took in Cas' expression, then turned to Lena, who looked as stunned as Cas felt. "Who is Faustina?"

No one answered. Cas' mind raced. Faustina. The little prince's trusted nurse. The archer might not have known that the nurses had been switched at the last moment. Had her aim been true after all? But why would anyone want to kill an old woman?

"Here, take this." Master Dimas fumbled with the purse at his belt. He came forward, holding up a coin. "She left it on the window ledge."

Cas took the coin, Lena leaning in for a closer look. On one side was the royal emblem, the bull and the pomegranate flower. The other side depicted the Oliveran god Zacarias. An ancient god, worshiped long ago when Oliveras was still a pagan kingdom. He was pictured with two heads attached at the back of the skull, one facing forward to the future, the other looking back to the past. Zacarias, Cas remembered, was the god of doorways and transitions, of new beginnings. He said to Lena, "Do you recognize it?" Because he did not.

She shook her head. "It's not from the mint. I've never seen it before."

"You're certain?"

"Yes. Grandfather and I made a record of all official coins. I had to draw them, front and back, beside his descriptions. This was not one of them."

Strange. Turning to Master Dimas, Cas said, "This coin was your payment?"

"No. She paid regular gold in advance. I will give you those, too, if you wish it," Master Dimas said grudgingly.

Cas did not bother to answer. He said to Lena, "We should go."

They drew abreast of Hellin, standing frozen by the door. "Lord Cassia, must you speak of this to anyone?"

Cas held up the coin. "I can't keep this from the king. You know I can't."

Master Dimas had trailed after them. "And . . . the other? The toll keeper? Must he be mentioned? It was a moment of weakness. We were passing over the bridge and . . . I've regretted it ever since. I pray for forgiveness every day."

Though Cas held back a snort, Lena could not manage it. Hellin glared at her.

Cas said, "I don't have an answer for you. It will have to wait."

Cas tucked the coin away. They left father and daughter behind and did not speak until Lena stopped halfway down the stairwell.

"Cas," she began. "When I saw you by the river, that first day, you were holding a shovel." Her words were careful, as though she were trying to work through a puzzle.

Cas tensed. "Yes."

Her eyes searched his. "You buried the toll keeper. Izaro."

"Yes."

"Was he alive when you found him?"

His answer came slowly. "He was long dead."

"Then how . . . ?" Lena stopped. How had he known about the stolen chickens, the missing toll? Cas had not told anyone about the spirits. Ventillas had enough to worry about. As for everyone else, it had never felt safe enough to share his secrets. But he would not lie to her.

Quietly, he said, "Ask me. And I'll tell you."

Lena did not answer right away. She lifted a hand and held it between them, waiting, he thought, to see if he would back away.

When he did not, she placed her hand on his chest and felt the frantic beating of his heart.

Cas did not know how long they stood there, or what she thought. The vein at his neck thrummed. Eventually, her hand fell away. She said, "I won't ask. Not just yet. Come on, let's go back to the keep. You can ride the mare."

## 14

"I HAVE NEVER seen it before," Queen Jehan said. "Faustina?"

"No, Your Grace," the old nurse answered. "Nor I."

They had gathered in the king and queen's outer chambers. Cas stood by the fireplace, dressed in clothing that fit perfectly and felt extraordinary. He had clasped his hands behind his back so that he would not be tempted to stroke the fine wool of his coat, a deep Palmerin red, or fiddle with the onyx buttons, each stamped with the face of a lynx. Ventillas had already caught him at it, covering his laugh with a cough.

King Rayan held the gold coin up to the firelight, turned it this way and that. "It's a curious piece. You're absolutely certain it isn't ours, Amador?"

"Lady Analena was correct, Your Grace. It did not come from our treasury." Lord Amador had welcomed Cas back with a faint frown, which he took no offense at. Cas had never once seen him smile or laugh, not in all the years of their acquaintance. He wore the formal black robes and stiff lace collar of a high councilor. The lace was also black. For Cas, the entire effect had always brought to mind a reaper, a short one.

"Ventillas, what do you make of this?" King Rayan asked.

Ventillas stood beside Cas, drink in hand. Their clothing was identical. "The archer knows who Faustina is. Knows she's dear to the queen. It's no secret. Not everyone desires peace between Brisa and Oliveras. She's likely some obsessive still upset by your marriage. This was her way of showing it."

Queen Jehan occupied the chair closest to Cas. She said, almost to herself, "Faustina. She wished to harm *Faustina*." The nurse sat beside her and patted her hand, appearing more concerned for her former charge than she did for herself.

"Yes, Faustina," King Rayan said, his expression darkening, "with our son the extra cream in the custard." Standing opposite his queen, he tossed the coin onto the table, where it landed face-up on the god Zacarias. "A war obsessive. What lice they are."

Cas had shown them the coin and shared the rice merchant's tale. He had made no mention of Izaro. Several eyebrows had risen when Lena, carrying the prince in her arms and circling the chamber, had confirmed Cas' story.

"You went into town?" King Rayan had asked her, the displeasure in his voice apparent. "We had an agreement, Analena."

Lena had also changed for supper. She wore a dress of pale blue velvet and was attempting to untangle the prince's little fist from her braid. "I did as you asked. I broke no rules. You knighted him yourself."

King Rayan had looked at Cas. The frown, faint between his eyes, had softened into reluctant amusement. "A man-at-arms. So I did, little sister."

Now Lord Amador studied Cas with his beetle-black eyes. "How is it the rice merchant confesses all to you, after telling an entirely different story two days ago?"

Camphor. That was something Cas had forgotten. For some reason, the high councilor always smelled of camphor. "I can't speak for Master Dimas. Maybe his conscience weighed on him."

The beetle eyes narrowed. "An interesting theory. What business brought you to his home in the first place?"

Across the chamber, Lena lost the struggle over the braid. She looked at Cas. Her eyes met his over the prince's head. She had been true to her word, handing him the reins to his own horse, as though the mare were a beloved childhood toy and Cas in desperate need of its comfort. On the ride back to the keep, she had spoken of everything and anything, except Izaro and the shovel that had been used to bury him.

It was Ventillas who answered Lord Amador's question. "Why does that matter?"

"I am merely curious." Lord Amador brushed an imaginary piece of nothing from his sleeve.

"My brother does not answer to you, High Councilor." Ventillas' words were cool. "Not in this city, where he is my second and *you* are my guest."

"Always so hospitable, Commander. Well, whatever the rice merchant has done, he has lied to the king's men and must be dealt with. I will see to it."

"I think you won't," Ventillas said softly. Cas was not the only one who heard the underlying threat.

"Let it be, Amador," King Rayan said.

"Of course, Your Grace." Lord Amador bowed, but not before sending Ventillas a dark look. They had come of age together, Ventillas, King Rayan, and Lord Amador. There had been no love lost between Ventillas and the high councilor. Until now, Cas had never been curious enough to wonder why.

King Rayan offered a hand to his queen, who had reached across the table for the gold coin. "Come, my dear. Don't worry. Ventillas is right. She's a fanatic, no more, and long gone. We have seen the last of her."

***

At supper, Cas found himself seated beside Palmerin's newest priest, Father Emil, a slight, curly-haired man whose mustache and beard struggled to take root. Cas managed to hold his tongue over three courses. The partridge was quietly consumed, along with the cabbage dumplings and the roasted aubergine. But he was human, after all, and curiosity drove him to say, "Forgive the question, Father, but how old are you?"

"Cassia," Ventillas said.

His brother had always had the ears of a lammergeier. Four others dined between them. Not only that, the entire keep had gathered for supper. A hundred different conversations took place, ebbing and flowing around the sound of bandurrias plucked by musicians with lightning fingers. It was loud in here.

"I am eighteen, Lord Cassia. I understand we are the same age." Father Emil smiled. "You are wondering why the church has sent someone like me to your great city in the mountains."

Cas could guess why. "Because there was no one else to send."

"*Cassia.*" Ventillas leaned around Queen Jehan to fix Cas with a warning look. Cas ignored him.

"It is the truth," Father Emil admitted, his smile gone. "I come from a parish in Ollala. Most of my fellow priests died while helping in the hospitals and churches. I did not die, and so I find myself here."

Ventillas said, "We're pleased to have you here, Father. Do forgive my brother, who has returned to us a little rough around the seams." The look he gave Cas said, clearly, *Mind yourself or else.*

Cas said dismissively, "I'm sure you're a fine priest, Father, but I can't imagine there's any sort of queue outside your confessional." Who would admit their sins to an eighteen-year-old priest? He would not, that was certain.

"Lord Cassiapeus," Queen Jehan said. A softer voice than his brother's, but somehow more threatening. She did not glance up from her supper, which she had barely touched. Even Lena and King Rayan were looking over with identical expressions of disapproval. Cas raised a hand. Peace. He had not meant to harass the priest. He just did not see the point of priests.

Or prayer. Neither had ever done any good for him. He pushed aside the memory of Izaro asking for a final prayer Cas could not give.

Father Emil wore a rueful expression. "No one comes to the confessional. Except the children. I imagine it would be like confessing to a son, or a grandson." He sipped his wine. "I know I will have to earn trust here, Lord Cassia. Until then, I believe I may still do some good."

Disinterested, Cas reached for some bread. "Really? How so?"

Father Emil brightened. "Well, Lord Ventillas has kindly donated the old market building to the church. The one in the eastern quarter. I hope to turn it into an orphanage someday. The current one is vastly overcrowded and . . ."

As Father Emil shared his plans, his vision, the others joined in, asking questions. Cas remained silent. But he listened. The priest wore no rings, he noticed. No jeweled medallions. His brown cassock was simple, even for supper with the king and queen. Unusual among holy men who, in Cas' experience, usually favored robes made of gold and purple silk. As for Father Emil, even Cas could not deny his earnestness. By the time dessert came around — figs cooked in anise and a custard — an idea had taken hold.

Cas said, "How much do you require, Father?"

The priest was taken aback. Such things were not discussed over supper. "How . . . ah . . . a specific number? Now?"

"That would be best."

The priest named an amount. Cas asked a passing servant to bring parchment, ink, and wax. Ignoring the bemused looks from those nearest, he shoved aside platters and plates and wrote a letter to Master Dimas. He mentioned the priest, the orphanage, and the very specific number the rice merchant might consider donating before the week was out. Once the ink was dry, he borrowed his brother's signet ring to press into the wax seal. His own had been taken from him after his capture. Cas offered the letter to Father Emil along with directions to the rice merchant's home. Master Dimas was looking for a new charity to patronize, Cas had heard. The orphanage would be just the thing.

Lena started to laugh.

Ventillas had only watched until now. After the stunned and delighted priest thanked Cas, Ventillas said, "Do I need to speak with Master Dimas about his attic?"

Cas said, "I think this settles the matter."

Ventillas was quiet. "I will not ask," he decided.

"Best not to." Head down, Cas dug into his custard. A warm, heavy weight on his boots announced the presence of a lynx beneath the table.

Queen Jehan said, "I believe you may be a lamb in wolf's clothing, my lord Cassiapeus. However much you try to hide it."

Cas turned his head, frowned at her.

King Rayan remarked, "Yes. Sweet and furry, that is our Cassia."

Father Emil wore a puzzled look during the exchange. Queen Jehan only smiled faintly and poked at her figs. Cas went back to his dessert. The amount in the letter was far more than Master Dimas had stolen from Izaro. It was extortion. Cas did not let that bother him. Heavy was the price for his silence.

***

Cas found Lena in the kitchen, by the hearth, fanning sheets of parchment above a simmering cauldron. The only other occupant was an undercook, kneading dough at the far end of the chamber. And Cook's little boy. The spirit had curled up with a lynx in a corner. Both appeared fast asleep. Cas wondered if the boy felt any warmth from the living animal, or if it was merely the memory of a pet that offered comfort.

Cas went to stand beside Lena, still dressed for supper in sky-blue velvet. Six wrinkled sheets of parchment had been left on the floor to dry.

"It worked," he said.

"So far. These last two are being stubborn." Lena turned the pages over every few seconds to evenly distribute the steam. Her other hand was planted on a hip. "How does it feel to pay for a new orphanage with someone else's gold?" A sideways glance caught his smile. She laughed. "That man is going to despise you, if he doesn't already."

"I will live."

"You don't think he'll take it out on Father Emil, do you?"

"No. Once he gets over the rage, he'll make it look like it was his idea. Everyone in Palmerin will know that he is the orphanage's biggest, most generous benefactor."

Lena made a face. "That part is not as satisfying."

Someone had stacked empty crates along the wall, floor to ceiling. They had not been there this morning.

Lena saw him looking. "It's going to be a mass exodus. We're going home."

"When?" He felt an odd pang in his heart at the thought of her leaving.

"Three days? Four? Poor Master Jacomel will have the keep to himself again."

Cas did not answer. He hunkered down and picked up the closest page. "'Ten bolts of red wool for a traveling suit,'" he read, squinting to see past the heavier tomato stains. "'Ten bolts of green velvet for a hunting dress. Twenty-four buttons, silver gilt and enamel . . .'" He glanced over the other pages. "This is all clothing."

"Jehan's. Faustina said it took up the hold of an entire ship." Lena turned the pages over. "Everything was lost."

"How is that possible?" Cas asked in amazement.

"Everything was stored on the carriages. The carriages were abandoned." Lena removed the stuck-together parchment from the steam and tried to tease the pages apart. It did not work. "Oh, Grandpapa," she said. She returned them to the steam.

Cas studied a different sheet. "Rakematiz." He glanced up. "That's some sort of fabric, isn't it?"

"Yes. It's a very thick silk. Costly."

He read aloud, "'Four hundred and sixty-eight feet of cream rakematiz, woven with gold, the pattern one of stars, crescents, and diamonds, for a wedding gown.'" Cas whistled.

"It is depressing," Lena said, shaking her head. "Jehan borrowed one of my dresses for the wedding. There was no time to make one.

It was my best gown, but . . ." She lifted a shoulder. "It was not the sort of wedding one dreams of."

The lynx yawned and stretched, turning on its side and rolling the sleeping ghost with it. Lena watched the cat with wary eyes.

"She won't hurt you," Cas assured her.

"I don't believe you. The last cat I came across tried to eat me." Lena lowered her voice. "Why are they so *large*? The one in the copse was nowhere near this size."

"She's not so big for a city cat. I've seen bigger."

"Lovely."

Cas sat crossed-legged on the hearthstones. The fire offered a pleasant warmth. "The way the story goes, the lynx lived on these lands long before man. They were here when the giants ruled the mountains."

Lena turned a skeptical glance on him. "What giants?"

Cas waved a hand in the air. "You know, the giants," he said. "Palmerin is said to have been built on the ruins of a great city of giants. These giants kept little cats as pets. The cats slept on the giants' shoulders. They were fed off the giants' plates. When the lady giants went to call on their friends in town, they carried their cats inside little baskets. Their race eventually died out, but their pets remain in Palmerin."

Lena was smiling. "Who told you this story?"

"My mother."

Lena turned the pages over, her expression thoughtful. "There are stories I've never heard of, and food I've never tasted. It feels like a foreign kingdom sometimes, your Palmerin."

A piece of ash clung to her hem. He brushed it away. "Abril wasn't at supper." He had not realized it until much later, after the guests had retired to their chambers and the servants had spread their sleeping pallets along the great hall. The painter had missed her meeting with Lena in the archives, and she had not come to the keep to dine.

"No," Lena said, frowning. "She was supposed to meet with the weavers this afternoon. She did not appear for that, either." A long, frustrated sigh followed. "I'll go to her inn tomorrow and tell her she doesn't need to hide from me."

"What about your grandfather's history?"

"I will finish it," Lena promised. "The best I can. But when it comes to Abril, or Jehan, or Lord Ventillas for that matter, I'm not sure history is entitled to a person's . . ."

Cas waited for her to finish. When she did not, he offered, "Suffering."

"Yes." A look passed between them. "To their grief. Some things are private. I am not certain my grandfather would have agreed with me."

The undercook took no interest in them. Kneading dough, yawning over her task. At this distance, she could not hear their conversation. He said, "I used to like people. Before."

Lena turned her head and waited for him to make sense.

Cas tried to explain. "Ventillas was the quiet one in our family. I was the opposite. I liked the hunting parties and the balls. The noise. I would have liked having all these guests." He gestured toward the upper floors. "It doesn't suit me anymore. I'm not sure how to be around other people."

Lena sat beside him on the stone, the parchment on her lap. Her dress billowed about and covered his knee. "By giving it one day," she said. "And then one day after that, and another after that. And if, after all those days, you still don't like people" — they smiled at each other — "what of it? It's no great crime to prefer the quiet." A glance at the parchment brought a small sound of triumph. "It worked!" She eased the pages apart and studied the one that had previously been obscured. "Look! These were to be wedding gifts for Rayan. 'A sword made by Brisa's finest bladesmith. A miniature of the princess Jehan. A jeweled dagger. One hundred —'" She stopped.

"What?" Cas leaned closer. "One hundred what?"

Wordlessly, she handed him the sheet. He angled it toward the firelight. Sword, miniature, dagger. And then, *One hundred gold coins to commemorate the wedding between King Rayan of Oliveras and Princess Jehan of Brisa and to celebrate the newfound peace between the two kingdoms. One side of the coin is stamped with the royal emblem of Oliveras, the bull and the pomegranate flower. The other side is an image of the Oliveran god Zacarias, god of new beginnings. These coins were commissioned by the princess Jehan, with the guidance of her father the king's master goldsmith.*

Cas raised his head. He pictured Queen Jehan, only hours ago, examining the coin.

*I have never seen it before.*

Lena's words were quiet, barely heard over the crackle of fire.

"I don't understand. Why did she lie to us?"

# ❧ 15 ❧

IN THE SMALL HOURS of the morning, Cas sat in his chamber by the fire, boots propped on the table, waiting up for Ventillas like a nursemaid.

He needed his brother's counsel. There was no reason Ventillas would have seen the coin before. But Queen Jehan had recognized it, had *commissioned* it, and said otherwise.

"Why would she say such a thing," Cas had asked Lena, "when she knows you can disprove it so easily? You have your grandfather's inventory." Almost immediately, he remembered. "They don't know you have it."

"No." Lena had paled considerably. "I meant to tell them after I'd finished here. Once I knew what it said."

They spoke in lowered voices, though the undercook had finished her task and slipped away, the lynx padding after her. Only the boy remained. He had scooted closer, sitting on the floor by the parchment. He gave Cas a hopeful smile, like a pet that just wanted to play. Up close, Cas could see it clearly. The boy looked like Cook. He had her eyes.

Cas turned away, rattled. "Will you tell her now?" he asked Lena.

She gathered the parchment from the floor, her hair falling forward. The boy tried to touch it, but she tucked the strands behind her ear, out of his reach. "Yes," she said finally. "Tomorrow. There's a perfectly good explanation for this, Cas. We just don't know what it is yet."

Lena and Jehan were family. Bound by marriage and, with the birth of Prince Ventillas, bound by blood. She had to reserve judgment. He understood this.

Cas was not family.

The archer had left the coin behind. It was meant to be found. Not by the rice merchant but by the king's soldiers. And the use of Faustina's name? It felt like a taunt. Someone was sending a message to the queen, one filled with malice. But who? And what, Cas wanted to know, was the message?

After a troubled Lena went off to bed, Cas stayed crouched by the fire. It was only after her footsteps had faded away that Cas spoke aloud in the empty room.

"How are you still here, little one?"

The boy's face lit up. He had given up on Cas acknowledging his presence. He pointed to a peg on the wall where Cook's apron hung, white and crisp, ready for a new day.

Cas understood. "You're waiting for your mother?"

The boy nodded. He did not speak, not like Izaro. Was it because his death was not as recent? Would Izaro, too, lose his voice?

Cas said, "Is there anything I can do for you?"

The boy pointed to the corner where he had been asleep. He bared his little teeth and made pawing motions with his hands.

Cas smiled. "The lynx? You want her back?"

The boy nodded, pleased to have been understood.

"Must it be the same one?" The lynx had likely followed the undercook to the servants' quarters. Cas preferred not to go poking around up there at so late an hour.

The boy shook his head. Any lynx would do.

Cas got to his feet. "I'll come back."

He left the kitchen and went roaming the halls with only the occasional firefly globe in a niche to light his way. In the great hall, he tread carefully. Hundreds had bedded down for the night, soldiers and servants who had come with the keep's guests. The chambers above could hold no more. There were no torches or globes here, but moonlight poured in through the rosetta window, making it possible to navigate the space without stepping on anyone. The sounds of snoring were tremendous. It was like trying to sleep beside Ventillas, only far worse. He stopped when a hand reached out and wrapped itself around his boot-encased ankle. A voice, gruff with sleep, murmured, "Esti, my sweet." It was the soldier Bittor, looking blearily up at Cas from a pallet. Recognition broke through the fog. "Oh, it's you." The hand fell away. "What's wrong?"

Cas kept his voice low. "Nothing. I'm looking for one of the cats." Then, "Who's Esti?"

"Only a goddess," Bittor informed him. "There's one there. By the doors." He turned over and covered his face with an arm.

Cas murmured thanks. A lynx guarded the main doors. It was awake, watching Cas in the gloom with amber eyes. Cas crooked a finger. Slowly, the lynx rose, stretched, and followed Cas across the hall. The grunts and curses suggested the animal was not as careful as he, wending its way among the slumberers.

In the kitchen, a second undercook had arrived to watch over the fires and prepare for the day. He greeted Cas quietly while plucking feathers from a goose. Cook's little boy was delighted to see the giant cat. Cas waited until they had settled in a corner by the fire before leaving them to their rest.

Cas must have nodded off waiting for his brother's return. When he woke, it was to the sound of stone against stone. A replica of Palmerin's amphitheater had been placed on a table across the chamber, a model he had completed three years ago. The stones beneath the table shifted, revealing an opening in the floor. The sight jolted him awake. His slingshot lay on the rug. By the time a dark head popped up, Cas had loaded a spiked ball and aimed.

"Whoa," the intruder said mildly, holding a blazing torch. His broad shoulders appeared through the opening, followed by the rest of him. "No need for that. It's only me."

Only? Cas lowered his weapon, shaken to realize how close he had come to sending spikes into his king's eye. Tossing the slingshot aside, he rose. "Your Grace."

"Cassia." King Rayan handed the torch off to Cas, then went to stand by the fire. He wore a cloak but no gloves, and stuck his hands close to the flames. "I'll never get used to the cold here. It's barely autumn!"

Cas set the torch in a niche on the wall. "My mother used to say the same." She had grown up far away, in the warmer climates of Elvira.

"I was very fond of your mother. Ventillas and I used to ride the lynx down the corridors when we were boys. Like ponies. She never scolded."

"Master Jac would have." There was a pitcher and glasses on the table. Cas poured wine for the king.

He accepted with a laugh. "He was not steward then. We would not have dared if he was." King Rayan drank deeply. "This keep needs a lady, Cassia. It's been without one for too long."

The likelihood of his brother marrying, having children, was not good. Cas had known this for many years. "Yes. Well, I'll be sure to remind Ventillas —"

"Your brother doesn't need a reminder. He's been a hunted man in his own household, with so many unmarried women about."

There was something in King Rayan's voice. For Cas, confusion turned to caution. Why was he here? Where was Ventillas? Cas poured wine for himself.

King Rayan, still looking into the fire, said, "I fell off my horse some weeks back. Hurt my shoulder. It is nothing," he dismissed, seeing Cas' expression. "But it's best not to carry heavy loads just yet. Will you help me?"

Cas' glass came down hard on the table. "Is my brother hurt?"

"He'll be fine." King Rayan drained his glass and left it on the mantel. "Come on, then. Bring your cloak. And the torch."

Cas did as he was told. He also found two pairs of gloves. He offered one pair to the king, who accepted it with a smile and tugged them on.

The opening in the floor led to a steep staircase. King Rayan went first, then Cas. Running a hand along the wall, Cas searched for the anomaly, a smooth patch on an otherwise rough surface. He found it at knee level and pushed. The stone floor above their heads swung shut and settled in place.

They traveled down stairwells and passageways festooned with cobwebs. The torchlight picked up the occasional snakeskin left on the ground, dry and papery, its owner long vanished. "I hate snakes," King Rayan muttered. He navigated the corridors like a man who had spent his boyhood at Palmerin Keep, serving as page to Cas' father. Cas was not surprised the king knew every way in and out of a keep that sheltered his family.

Cas knew the passageways too, was well aware he and King Rayan were headed outside the city walls, beyond the eastern gates. He could hear the sound of rushing water. After a time, they came to a door. Cas knelt and lifted a particular stone paver. A key rested in the dirt; one needed the key to get out. The door opened into a chamber housing the aqueduct's distribution basin. From here, water would be piped throughout the city. To the fountains, the public baths, the keep itself. The door they exited was positioned directly behind the basin so that anyone entering from the aqueduct's main entrance would see *only* the basin, two stories tall, the door carefully hidden behind it.

They left the aqueduct and stepped into the night. It was a good thing they had brought a torch. Heavy clouds had rolled in, and the moon was no longer visible. At their backs lay Palmerin's outer walls. Before them was a graveyard that had not been there three years ago.

"They were buried as one," King Rayan said quietly. "It had to be done quickly. There were hundreds. But later, Ventillas made sure they had their own gravestones. He would not have them forgotten."

Cas could not forget them if he wanted. He could *see* them. Not hundreds, but fifty or so spirits drifting among the stones. A woman laughed, on and on, there was no end to it. The sound had Cas taking a step back.

"Cassia?"

King Rayan had gone ahead and was looking back at him now, clearly wondering why Cas had not followed. "What's wrong?"

"Nothing." Cas hustled to keep pace. They pulled up their hoods, protection against the bitter wind. "Where did the trees come from?"

Flame trees, fully grown, surrounded much of the graveyard. Even in the dark, he could see their leaves were a brilliant orange. As bright as sunset. The trees had not been planted three years ago. They should not have grown so tall, so fast.

"It's the strangest thing," King Rayan said. "We planted them six months ago. From *seed*. The next day, they looked like this. No saplings. No one knows how."

When they entered the graveyard, Cas was careful to keep his expression blank, though it was hard to pretend. This was not like Izaro or Cook's little boy. A solitary spirit here and there. There were too many present and not one was a stranger. He knew their names, their faces.

"Ventillas is just there." King Rayan pointed.

Cas saw a headstone, five feet tall, and then he saw his brother. His heart turned cold.

Ventillas lay face-down in the dirt in a posture of deep mourning. His legs were straight and his arms stretched over his head, bare fingertips brushing the gravestone.

Cas rushed to his brother's side and dropped to his knees. "Ventillas." Cas shook him, gently at first, then harder. Ventillas did not stir. Cas leaned down and sniffed, dismayed at the smell of smoke and mandrake. Cas rolled him over. He brushed the dirt and grass from his brother's face. He wiped the tears from his cheeks. Then he held the torch close to the grave marker, to better see the name inscribed.

*This is the grave of Kemen*
*Son, Brother, Soldier*
*Honored friend to Palmerin*

Cas sucked in a breath. Ventillas and Kemen. They had been

friends for years, rarely apart. Neither had married. Neither had ever shown an inclination to. And now King Rayan stood here, watching his commander drugged and weeping over the grave of another man. Cas had always known. But the king? His expression told Cas nothing.

A very real fear settled in his heart. "Your Grace —"

"Give me the torch," King Rayan said. "You carry him. I've knocked him about already. He won't wake up." For emphasis, he reached down and gave Ventillas several brisk pats on the cheek. Ventillas grunted but did not open his eyes. "You see?"

"Yes." Cas handed off the torch, flickering wildly in the wind. "How did you know he was here?"

King Rayan shrugged. "I like to go on walks sometimes. It helps me think. I saw him leave through the gates."

That brought Cas' head around. "You go walking . . . alone?"

"Yes." A pause. "Don't tell my sister."

One of the spirits, a woman, reached out to touch Cas' hand. She used to sell beads in the market, he remembered. Bracelets, necklaces, charms. Coral beads for luck. He forced himself not to flinch as her hand brushed his. It did not feel like the touch of another person; it only left him nauseated. He hoisted his brother over his shoulder. Ventillas' head and arms hung limp behind him. Cas staggered. It was like carrying a dead ox.

"Will you make it?" King Rayan asked.

"Yes."

Silently, Cas and the king retraced their steps past the spirits and out of the graveyard.

"Cassia."

Unthinking, Cas turned.

Kemen stood just beyond the graveyard beneath a flame tree, leaves rustling in the wind. Dressed in red, in the uniform of a Palmerin captain. He smiled at Cas' dismay. "You hide it well, but I saw when she touched you. Your eye started to twitch."

"What is it?" King Rayan scanned the graveyard. One hand rested on the hilt of his sword.

"I thought I saw something." Cas shifted his brother, held him a little tighter. "A mistake."

Kemen said, "Don't let Ventillas come again. Please, Cassia. He's here almost every night. It is not good for him." He took a step back. "You don't have to answer. Go."

Cas went. But when King Rayan was busy unlocking the door to the aqueduct chamber, Cas turned around. Kemen was a silhouette, barely visible in the distance. Cas raised a hand. In farewell. And to show he understood.

*** 

It was a long slog carrying his brother through passageways and up staircases. At last they reached Cas' chamber. Gasping, he dumped Ventillas onto the bed. A single firefly globe lit the room. King Rayan was making sure the secret entrance was well concealed. Satisfied, he came into the bedchamber. "I'll leave you to the rest of it, then. Good night."

Cas said nothing. He did not know what to say.

King Rayan tugged off his borrowed gloves and dropped them on the bed. "What do you think of me? That I would turn on your brother because . . ." He made a vague gesture that could mean anything. "I am not Lord Amador. I would lose half my army if I were so particular. And I would lose my good friend."

Cas sat on the bed by his brother's boots. "Forgive me. I didn't mean . . ."

"I know it." King Rayan spotted a carafe and two cups on the bedside table. This time it was he who poured the wine and handed a glass to Cas. Settling in a chair, he said, "You're not a boy any longer, Cassia. I won't treat you like one." A pause. "Analena calls you Cas. Is that your preference?"

"Yes."

King Rayan nodded. "Ventillas has offered his resignation as high commander of Oliveras."

Cas would have fallen over if he had not already been sitting. "What?"

"I've refused it, of course." King Rayan's expression was grim. "But, and I tell you this in confidence, I worry. He is flailing. He has gone off, for days at a time, sometimes a week. Without telling anyone where or why."

This was not the brother he knew. "Not even Captain Lorenz?"

"Not even him. Your brother's men try to cover for him. But it's getting harder and harder for everyone to pretend." King Rayan set his glass aside. "I do not begrudge the man time to himself. We have invaded his home after all. But it is not only that. His judgment in some matters has been . . . unsound. And when I yell at him about it, his only answer is to offer me his resignation."

"How many times has he offered?"

"Four." A single word, heavy with frustration. King Rayan rose. "He is my brother too. I love him as one. And he has offered my family sanctuary. This is a debt that can never be repaid. But Ventillas and Amador and I are responsible for the safety and governance of this kingdom. I must consider this, too."

Cas was quiet. "What would you have me do?"

"Nothing, Cas. Not just yet. I only wanted you to know." King Rayan looked down at Ventillas, adding very quietly, "We grieve in different ways. We do the best we can."

After King Rayan had gone, Cas removed his brother's cloak and set it aside. He tugged off a boot. Ventillas finally woke as Cas struggled to pull the other free. He propped himself on his elbows and looked blearily down the length of the bed.

"What are you doing?"

Cas held up the boot. "What does it look like?"

Ventillas glanced around the chamber. Awareness flickered. Abruptly, he sat up, then clutched his head with a groan. Cas poured water into a cup and handed it to Ventillas, who finished it in one great gulp.

"How am I here?"

"I carried you."

Ventillas' expression was one of utter mortification. "Through the *keep?*"

"I took the passageways, don't worry. No one saw."

Ventillas closed his eyes in relief. When he opened them again, he asked, "How did you know where I was?"

Cas made the king's story his own. "I went for a walk. I saw you leave through the gates."

"Oh."

Cas sat in the chair by the bed. "I'm sorry about Kemen. So sorry, Brother. I didn't even realize . . ."

Ventillas brushed aside the apology. "You haven't been home long enough to realize." He handed Cas the cup. "Sometimes even I forget. For an hour, or two, I forget everything. And other times . . ."

"It is like yesterday," Cas finished.

"Yes." Ventillas fell back on the bed and stared at the ceiling. Some time passed before he said, "Sorne is gone."

From Kemen to Sorne. It took Cas a moment. "What?"

"She left a note with Cook. Some merchants were leaving the city, headed south. She went with them."

"Did . . . What else did she say?"

Ventillas turned his head toward Cas. "That she was sorry about Faro. She thought leaving was best for everyone. She hoped you would not think too badly of her, forever."

Guilt was a burden, heavier than carrying his brother across half the city. "Ventillas. This is her home."

"And it was her decision to leave it. She has been well provided for, Cassia. Sometimes starting over is best." Ventillas closed his eyes and within moments, his breathing evened out. He'd fallen asleep.

The gold coin, the queen. Those questions would have to wait. Cas set about undressing his brother and putting him to bed, as though Ventillas were the child and he the adult, their roles reversed, another odd thing in this strange new world.

# 16

ABRIL HAD NOT been seen in days. This Lena and Cas learned when they arrived at her inn the following morning.

"The painter?" the innkeeper said after greeting Cas with surprised delight. A spare man with a welcoming smile and a large mole on his cheek, he had known Cas since he was a boy. His was a comfortable establishment, a crackling fire in the hearth, sprigs of rosemary strewn about the rushes. The tables were empty. Most guests would be in their chambers still, preparing for the day. "Why, I have not seen her since yesterday . . . no, the night before that. That's right."

"Two days ago?" Lena pushed back the hood of her green cloak. Her nose and cheeks were red with cold. Beside her, Cas blew warm air into his hands and eyed the fire with longing. They had ridden here through a morning fog, the frost seeping into their bones.

"Yes, Lady. She has these terrible headaches," the innkeeper explained. "The kind that knocks you flat. Her sister has been fetching her meals."

"I didn't know she had a sister." Lena's expression wavered between concern and resignation. She said to Cas, "Well, that is the end of it. I can hardly bother someone who's ill. I'll check on them at least. Abril might need a doctor."

Cas did not envy her this day. After meeting with Abril, Lena would show her grandfather's inventory to the king and queen. It had been too early to speak to them before Cas and Lena had left for the inn. The innkeeper waylaid a passing servant, a girl of about fourteen who turned out to be his daughter. Lena followed her up the stairs. Cas hung his cloak on a hook by the fire and sat at the counter across from the innkeeper, prepared for a wait. To his relief, there were no prying questions. Nothing about his imprisonment or Faro in the dungeon. The innkeeper poured Cas a black tea, the leaves of which he had just acquired from the southern islands. The first sip cleared the cobwebs right out of Cas' head, like a brisk sweep of a broom.

"Well? What is your opinion?" The innkeeper leaned across the counter, expectant.

Cas held up both hands, palms down, to show him. The second sip had left them trembling.

The innkeeper sighed his disappointment. "The brew is too strong. I thought it might be different, seeing as you're bigger than most, but no."

"You could weaken it," Cas suggested.

"That *is* weaker" was the innkeeper's rueful response. He poured cider into a fresh cup and slid it before Cas. "And my foolish son bought eight crates' worth. Such a waste." He set a platter of fried bunubunus beside the cup. "Have one, or three! It's apple. My dear wife made them fresh this morning . . ." As Cas reached for a pastry, the innkeeper looked past him, words trailing off in consternation.

A man Cas knew came stomping in from the back kitchen. The city inspector, Gaspar, who had returned his mare to the stables. No small daughter on his shoulders this time. He wore a blue cloak and held a burlap sack that bulged. There must have been a hole in the bottom, because what looked to be a rat's tail hung straight down from it, unmoving. Scurrying about his boots were two cats. Not lynx. These were regular black cats of regular size. Rat catchers.

The city inspector stopped beside Cas but did not spare him a glance. He lifted the burlap sack and glared at the man across the counter. "Ten rats, innkeeper. In the kitchen alone. This is unacceptable."

Cas, about to take his first bite of bunubunus, returned the pastry to its plate.

The innkeeper's pleasant countenance had turned mulish. "We live in a city, Inspector. Rats are a part of life."

"They do not have to be. They should not be. It is as simple as disposing of your garbage and keeping your premises clean." The city inspector shook the burlap for emphasis, the lone rat tail whipping about. "Filth attracts rats. Rats bring on the plague—"

"So says you." The innkeeper's tone, weariness and skepticism combined, only riled the inspector further.

"So says the physicians, sir! Scientific minds—" The inspector threw his hand up and finally looked Cas' way. He blinked. "My lord Cassia."

"City Inspector Gaspar." Cas dipped his head in greeting. "Thank you for returning my horse."

"It was my pleasure." The inspector bowed. As graceful as one could be while holding a bag full of rats. "You have become my daughter's new hero. She has spoken of nothing else since that day."

Cas smiled before bringing the topic back around. "Who are these scientific minds? We've always been told that plague is spread through the air."

"Don't get him started," the innkeeper advised.

But City Inspector Gaspar ignored him. "That is part of it, I think. But there's a study written by a physician in Caffa. It's a kingdom in the far, far west," he added, seeing their blank looks. "And she believes that plague may also be spread through fleas. Fleas that are carried on the backs of rats."

The innkeeper sniffed. *"She?"*

"Yes, she," City Inspector Gaspar said, weary. "The physician is a woman, famous in Caffa. Her name is Blaise. And it makes a terrible sort of sense, does it not? What creature travels as far and as wide as man?"

Cas said thoughtfully, "In the hold of a ship. In a caravan across the desert . . ."

"Roams the common rat." City Inspector Gaspar wore the smile of a man who was finally being listened to. "I would be pleased to show you the report, Lord Cassia, if you wish it."

"I do," Cas said. At the innkeeper's wounded look, he added, "I was told Palmerin did not suffer as greatly as we might have, and that is largely because of our city inspector." This at least the innkeeper did not dispute. City Inspector Gaspar appeared baffled by Cas' words, as though recognition was something he rarely heard. "I have known plague, sirs. Rather too well. If there's a way to keep it far from our gates, then I would like to know about it."

A shriek came from the second floor, freezing everyone down below. They turned as one toward the stairs. The innkeeper exclaimed, "Why, that is my girl —!" Cas was already halfway across the room when he heard Lena, somewhere above, shouting his name.

"Cas! Cas, come quick!"

***

There would be no stories shared by Abril. Not today. Not ever. She lay on a narrow bed in a tiny room, as perfectly arranged as if she were in a coffin. Her hands were folded across her chest. She wore an elaborate gown the color of fresh cream. It flowed off the bed to form a heavy puddle on the floor. As for Lena, she stood frozen by an easel and paint box near the window.

Cas gripped both sides of the door frame, breath ragged from the panicked sprint up the stairs. A crowd had gathered behind him in the corridor. Guests and servants lured by the screams. The innkeeper's daughter wept in her father's arms.

Cas said, "Lena."

His voice jolted her from her trance. "We knocked and knocked but no one answered. We had to go find a key. But when we opened the door . . ."

Cas approached the bed. Even he, who had seen so much death, was unsettled. A gold coin covered each eye. A startled glance at Lena said she recognized them too. The two-faced god Zacarias, turning up in the strangest places.

"I don't even know how she died," Lena said. "There's no blood, Cas. She looks like she's sleeping, except for those horrible coins." She stepped forward suddenly, hopeful. "What if she's not—?"

Cas placed two fingers on Abril's neck and felt the cold clamminess of her skin. "She's gone." There was no sign of a pulse beneath his fingertips, which brushed the ribbon tied around her neck. A black ribbon, two inches wide. It was loosely secured. Cas' touch had it drooping even farther to reveal a pinprick marked by a spot of dried blood. Lena came to stand beside him. Their backs prevented the others from seeing much. She kept her voice low. "That looks like a needle mark."

"Yes."

"Poison?"

It could be. "I'm no expert on poisons."

"Cas . . ." Lena lowered her voice even further. "The dress. Do you recognize it?"

He was no expert on dresses, either. It looked costly, with gold threading and all those stars — Cas felt the hairs rise along his arms. "Is this . . . ?"

"Yes." Lena recited from memory: "Four hundred and sixty-eight feet of cream rakematiz, woven with gold, the pattern one of stars, crescents, and diamonds. This is the queen's wedding dress." She studied the folds gathered on the floor. "Part of it, at least. What is happening here?"

"Lord Cassia?" The city inspector's voice broke through their whispers. He stood beside the innkeeper and his daughter, the bag of rats nowhere in sight. "Should I send for the death wagon?"

"Yes. And Lord Ventillas. Wait." Cas had nearly forgotten. A small chest sat by the easel, the lid open, only half-full of clothing. The room was neat and spare and lonely. Nothing suggested a second person had ever slept here, helping Abril through her terrible headaches. "Where is her sister?"

\*\*\*

The coroner's wagon attracted more onlookers outside the inn. Ventillas was there as Abril was carried out, his rage quiet in the face of so many watchful eyes. He had known her. Cas thought they might have been friends in better times. And from Ventillas, they had learned another truth. Abril had never had a sister. She had been an orphan, raised by aunts.

"Cassia," Ventillas said. "Lady Analena. What do you know?"

Cas and Lena exchanged a glance. They knew Queen Jehan had lied about recognizing the coin, but Cas did not think Lena would want to mention it here, not before she had spoken to her family. He was right.

"Abril stayed at the inn for months," Lena told Ventillas. "Everyone knows she's been working on the tapestry. But the servants only remember seeing the sister, whoever she is, these last few days."

"No one saw her face," Cas added. "The innkeeper says she always wore a veil, a black one. They thought she was a widow." Dimas, the rice merchant, had said the same.

"What name did she give?" Ventillas asked. "This false sister?"

"Faustina again, Lord Ventillas," Lena said. His brother's only reaction was a slight flaring of the nostrils.

Cas said, "First Faustina, now Abril. Someone isn't happy with the queen, *or* her traveling companions."

"So it would seem."

Was that all his brother would say? Did he truly not see it? Cas spoke bluntly. "Ventillas. That includes you. You could be in danger."

Ventillas smiled thinly. "When am I not, little brother?" And when Cas opened his mouth, Ventillas added, "This has nothing to do with me."

"You can't know that. Why are you —?"

"Later, Cassia. Now is not the time." He turned to Lena. "Lady, I'll see you back to the keep."

It was like trying to talk to a tree. Frustrated, Cas turned away. The innkeeper hovered by his front door, deeply unhappy. A guest, mysteriously dead. Not the sort of thing a man of hospitality would wish to be known for. Ventillas' men surrounded the coroner's wagon, keeping the shrouded Abril away from prying eyes. Merchants gossiped from their doorsteps, their backs turned on the city inspector, who kept somber companionship with the priest, Father

Emil. There were people on horseback and people in carts. Across the square, diagonal to where Cas stood, was a woman on a horse. Cas looked past her.

And then he looked back.

She wore a riding dress the color of rust. Her posture was straight as a trained soldier's. Her hat reminded him of the sweeping head covers worn by rice farmers in the fields. Only this hat, the same autumn shade as her dress, was far larger. It swooped two feet on each side of her head and was low enough to shield her eyes. All Cas could see was her smile. A woman alone, smiling as a corpse rolled away in a death wagon.

Cas stepped forward, silencing whatever it was Ventillas said to Lena. They turned to see what Cas looked at. The lady on the horse tipped her head back, too quick for Cas to catch more than the briefest glimpse of her face. She saw Cas staring and her smile vanished. Even as she turned her horse around, Cas was running.

***

Cas had not forgotten his city. The streets and back alleys, the market squares. He knew exactly where he was as he chased after the woman. He rode a horse that was not his own, for he had stolen the closest one. Its owner had been too shocked to protest when Cas had flung himself into the saddle and ridden off. A quick glance over his shoulder showed a man standing by Ventillas, shaking his fist and shouting.

The woman veered right and disappeared from view. He could not ride as fast as he wished. There were children playing and women with market baskets, all clogging the streets. Cas' warning cries only slowed the people further. They looked around in confusion before the sight of him sent them leaping out of the way in a panic. He turned the corner just in time to see a horse tail whip into an alley behind a butcher's shop.

The alley was dangerously slick with blood and discarded body parts. Flies swarmed. Cursing, he slowed the horse. The butcher poked his head out a window. First in curiosity and then in pained resignation when Cas, glaring, pointed to the rabbit heads and tails strewn everywhere. If he did not break his neck, he would be giving City Inspector Gaspar this address. The horse picked its way to the end of the alley. The woman was nowhere to be seen, but a boy standing in a doorway called out, "Lord Cassia!" and pointed left.

Offering a salute, he went left. The horse gained speed; Cas could see her now, up ahead. This street led to the western gates. Beyond them, the road ran straight across the valley into the forest. If she reached the shelter of the trees, he would lose her. But the gap between them had narrowed. She glanced back at him with greater and greater frequency. The gates loomed ahead. Wide open. Guarded by men in Palmerin red.

This was Abril's false sister. This was Faustina's archer. Riding on that horse was the answer to a great many questions.

"Help!" the woman cried suddenly. "Please help me!" She waved at the guards, then pointed behind her. At Cas. "He's trying to hurt me!"

In disbelief, Cas watched her race right through the gates while a line of guards closed behind her, blocking his path.

"Stop!" a guard shouted.          `

Cas slowed the horse. They did not give him a chance to explain. One man grabbed the reins; another yanked Cas right out of the saddle and thumped him into the dirt. A kick to his side followed. Stunned, Cas could think only that it had been a long time since he had been beaten like this. How easily one forgot the pain. "Who do you think you are, chasing decent women in the street —?"

"Stop! Ho!" Another guard came running over, horrified. "Let him go, man! That's Lord Cassia!"

"What!"

Snarling, Cas shoved aside hands that were suddenly helpful and solicitous. Clutching his ribs, he half stumbled, half ran to the gates.

Too late.

She raced down the road. Away from the city, and a reckoning. She grew smaller in the distance until, just shy of the forest, she stopped. She turned the horse around and faced the gates. Cas knew she saw him. A second later, she raised her hat high and waved.

Cas braced a palm against the wall, breath coming in sharp, angry pants. He could not see her face. She was too far away. But he knew, without a shred of doubt, that she was laughing.

H OW COULD THEY not recognize you? Look, just look at you! You were gone for three years, not twenty!"

Lena wrung out the cloth with a violent twist, but her hands on his face were gentle. They were back at the keep in Master Jacomel's work chambers. Cas perched on a table while Lena cleaned the blood and dirt from his cuts. Over by the window, Master Jacomel stirred something foul-smelling in a cup.

Cas inhaled deeply, past the pain. "They thought I would hurt her. You would have believed her too if you had been there." A terrified woman in need of rescuing. She had played the part brilliantly.

The soldiers had been shamefaced and full of mumbled apologies. And when they learned they had allowed the prince's near assassin to ride right past them, their mortification had been complete. Cas had almost felt sorry for them when Ventillas had ridden up to the western gates.

"I don't blame them for stopping you. But *this*" — outraged, Lena took in his battered face and leather tunic, worn once, now beyond repair — "without giving you a chance to speak. What will happen to them, Master Jacomel?"

The steward tapped a spoon against the cup and set it on a plate. He headed their way, cup in hand. "Oh, I think they are already punishing themselves quite thoroughly. The other men will not let them forget, and seeing as there's nothing broken —" He stopped, having caught the grimace Cas could not quite hide in time. "What is it?"

The pain along his ribs felt like fire. "Nothing."

Now two sets of eyes looked at him with suspicion. Lena set the cloth aside. His tunic, ripped and torn, was subject to such close scrutiny he thought she could see right through it. "Cas, are you hurt somewhere else?"

"No."

Master Jacomel appeared by Lena's side. Black robes, keys jangling. He set the foul-smelling cup on the table. "You are lying. I can always tell."

"They're just bruises." Cas touched his ribs lightly, very lightly. "Nothing's broken. I know the difference."

"Take it off," Master Jacomel ordered. "Let me see."

Cas had removed his tunic during his fitting. Nearly all of the keep had seen his scars. But Lena had not. He would keep it that way. "No."

Master Jacomel, who was not without mercy, said, "My dear lady, perhaps —"

"I'm not going anywhere, Master Jacomel. You will have to pick me up and make me." Lena's expression was set.

Cas bowed his head. This was what shame felt like, a hollowness in his gut. "Lena. It's awful."

"I know, Cas," she said quietly. "Stop this. Did you hurt your ribs?"

She knew. Someone must have told her of his scars. Cas would not win this argument. He could tell just by looking at her. He pulled off the tunic with painful slowness and heard Master Jacomel's sharply drawn breath.

"You idiot child. Were you truly going to say nothing?"

Cas did not look at either of them. As Master Jacomel railed on about his new wounds — a vicious scrape across the entire right half of his torso and the deep bruising beneath it — Cas kept his head bent and followed the pattern on Lena's blue dress, tiny silver falcons perched on branches. Master Jacomel marched back to the table by the window, which held an assortment of bottles and jars, each carefully labeled.

Lena had not spoken a word or moved an inch. When he could bear it no longer, Cas turned his head.

She was trying very hard not to cry. Even as he watched, a single tear fell. His heart sank. The sight of him made her weep.

Cas crumpled the discarded tunic in a fist. "I tried to warn you."

"I hate them all." Her voice was low and fierce. Another tear fell.

"Don't." Cas looked down at his new injuries, winced. "This was a mistake. It will heal. And this . . ." The whiplash, the crescents, the old scars. "These men are all dead. There's no point hating them."

Master Jacomel returned with an open jar. The salve within, a thick, green substance, smelled of mint. He scooped it out with his fingers, then rubbed it briskly between both hands to warm it. "Lift your arm." When Cas obeyed, Master Jacomel spread the ointment onto the scrape from top to bottom. Instantly, Cas felt better. The steward did not comment on Lena's tears, which fell freely now, but he said, in a far gentler voice than he had used with Cas, "If it will make you feel better, Lady, I can make sure those men are given some sort of terrible latrine duty for the next month or so. Will that do?"

Lena's smile wobbled. "It would make me feel better, Master Jacomel."

"Good. Consider it done." The steward wiped the salve from his hands with a cloth. "Come now, help me with these bindings."

The task distracted her. Cas knew this was Master Jacomel's intent. Lena brushed aside her tears, and together, she and Master Jacomel unwound a bolt of linen and wrapped it tight around Cas' chest. A servant poked his head in to say Master Jacomel was needed in the great hall. There was some sort of catastrophe surrounding the packing of musical instruments.

"Catastrophes everywhere," Master Jacomel said with a sigh. He pointed to the foul-smelling cup, ordered Cas to "Drink it all, every last drop," and then he was gone.

Neither Cas nor Lena spoke as she helped him back into his tunic. She picked up his cup and sniffed. The mysterious concoction, a gray sludge, resembled the sort that clogged gutters in the streets. Not Palmerin's streets, not with the city inspector. Other streets.

Lena made a face. "What did he put in it? It smells like feet."

Cas grimaced. Now that she mentioned it, it did bring to mind a room full of soldiers removing their boots. "Best not to know."

She offered him the cup, then hopped onto the table beside him, her shoulder brushing his. Neither was in a hurry to speak. Lena studied the painting on the wall opposite them. A life-size portrait of a woman in a blue cloak, standing on the peak of a mountain and looking off into the distance. She held a long wooden staff in her right hand. Below her, cloud cover shielded the landscape.

"Who is she?" Lena asked.

"I don't know," Cas told her. "I used to ask when I was a boy. He would only say she was an old friend."

"She's beautiful." Lena's eyes shifted to his, curious. "Did Master Jacomel ever marry?"

Cas shook his head. Glancing down, he said, "Your hands. Are they . . . ?"

She turned them over. The scrapes and cuts were nearly healed.

"You'll be back climbing trees before you know it."

Her smile was quick, fading as she said, "I have to tell Jehan about the coins. And my brother. I can't put it off any longer."

"No." Cas shook the cup slightly. The sludge did not move. "Ventillas thinks this woman is a stranger. Someone upset by the king's marriage."

"You don't?"

"It's possible," Cas admitted. "But I've been wondering . . . Imagine you're part of Princess Jehan's cortege. You've left your country behind to serve her faithfully, and now you're racing across Oliveras trying to outrun the plague."

Lena folded her hands on her lap and nodded once. "I am imagining."

Cas glanced at her, smiling briefly. "Now imagine you catch the pestilence and are left behind. How would you feel?"

A frown. "I would not have time to feel much of anything. I would be dead."

"But what if you *didn't* die?" Cas countered. "What if you were left in a hospital or village or the side of the road, and you survived? What would you think about the people who left you there?"

Lena was quiet. "Jehan's safety was their mission. If it were me, I would understand that they had no choice, that their decision was made for the greater good."

Cas looked at her. He said nothing.

"I might be a little resentful," Lena admitted.

"Anger doesn't always make sense." Cas knew this very well. "Master Dimas said the woman spoke too-perfect Oliveran. It's possible she came from another kingdom. Brisa maybe. Do you have a list of people who were part of that cortege?"

"Yes. My grandfather kept one. What are you looking for?"

Cas set the cup down. He was not drinking this. Master Jacomel could not force him if he was not here. "The women. The names of the servants, the ladies in waiting, anyone from Brisa."

"I don't need to look at a list," Lena said. "Nearly everyone was Oliveran. The soldiers, the servants. Rayan sent them. Jehan knew it would be a hardship for her ladies to join her here. They had lives in Brisa, families. She only brought two women with her. Faustina and . . ." Lena stopped.

"Lady Mari," Cas finished. "That's her name, isn't it? The queen's oldest friend?"

A nod. "They left her at a hospital in Gregoria. She died there."

"I know what hospitals are like during a plague, Lena. Did anyone see her body?"

## ❧ 18 ❧

C AS SPENT THE rest of the afternoon trying to be invisible. Few at the keep had known Abril. She was not from Palmerin. She had done her work and kept to herself. Which meant that, while the tapestry weavers wept, few others mourned her. That did not stop them from wanting to know the grisly details of her death, and Cas found himself peppered with question after question from everyone he came across.

The guests would be leaving in two days' time, every last one of them, and preparation had begun in earnest. Master Jacomel was in his element as he directed the packing of trunks and the loading of carts. Staggering amounts of bedding were made ready, from bundled pallets to wool blankets. Silver candlesticks were carefully packed alongside porcelain dishes. Essentials for the road. The musicians would also be returning to Elvira, which meant space had to be found for the bandurrias, tambours, pipes, and accordions. In the kitchen, Cook and her undercooks were run ragged filling crates of fruit, vegetables, cured meats, and salted fish. Cas slunk in long enough to pilfer bread and sausage, then took himself down to the amphitheater.

Captain Lorenz found Cas sitting alone in the stands, watching the soldiers at practice. The men were on horseback, charging one another with drawn swords.

"Interesting day for you," Captain Lorenz commented, his craggy face red with cold. The chill transformed his words into puffs of air. He remained standing in the aisle.

Cas snorted. That was one way of putting it. A woman dead. A failed chase. A beating. "Yes."

Captain Lorenz gestured toward the amphitheater floor. "You could join them."

Cas wanted nothing more. He had missed training, the concentration and discipline it demanded. He had missed being a part of the king's army. "Maybe tomorrow."

Captain Lorenz took in his battered face and the hand pressed gingerly against his ribs. "Maybe next month."

Cas laughed, then winced at the pain it caused.

Captain Lorenz shook his head. "Come with me, lad."

The captain walked off before Cas could ask *where to*. Curious, he followed him down the steps into the amphitheater's labyrinthine underground. There were enough people down here to populate a small city, a shadowy one lit by torches and candles. The tunnels and corridors smelled as he remembered, of metal and of sweat. Cas spent some time greeting men and women he had not seen in years. Armorers, soldiers, animal trainers, the tavern keeper and her grandson who ran the underground alehouse. And for a short time, he managed to forget all about Abril and that awful woman on the horse.

In the captain's work chambers, parchment was spread across a large table, the pages covered with sketches and handwriting Cas recognized as his brother's.

Captain Lorenz said, "Lord Ventillas has plans to expand the amphitheater. We're running out of room here."

Cas moved a brass compass aside to better see the drawing beneath it. "I remember him talking about it, years ago."

"Yes, well, we're still talking. And we're behind on some repairs, mainly to the façade and the upper tiers. These are his notes, his sketches." Captain Lorenz riffled the parchment. "But the man is busy. You used to enjoy this. Will you take it over? Draw up the final sketches? Prepare a plan I can work with?"

"I . . . Yes, absolutely I will." Cas smiled across the table at the older man. "Thank you, Captain."

"You are the one doing me the favor." Captain Lorenz came around the table, placed a heavy hand on his shoulder. Cas managed to control a flinch. "As far as homecomings go, yours has been a shoddy one. We will make it up to you, Cassia."

When the captain had gone, Cas studied the plans in detail. He read over his brother's notes, several times, then found ink, parchment, and a ruler and began making his own. When Bittor found him to say the queen wished to speak with him, Cas realized that hours had passed and night had fallen.

* * *

The chapel was tucked away in a corner of the keep, rarely used since his mother's passing. It was small, meant only for family, with stained-glass windows and elm wood pews. The first thing Cas saw was Abril laid out on the altar. She was bound simply in strips of burial linen. Without the grand wedding dress, she looked very small and alone.

*I am cast into the mire. I am become like dust and ashes.*

The memory came to him. His mother had lain on that very altar. A priest had spoken those words on her last day above the earth.

Queen Jehan knelt before Abril in prayer. Three others were present. Lena in a front pew. Ventillas and King Rayan stood at opposite walls, the king by an alcove window, looking out into the darkness. The two friends were as far apart as they could be in the small chapel. That was Cas' first warning.

At his entrance, everyone turned.

"You sent for me, Your Grace?"

"Come in, Lord Cassiapeus," Queen Jehan said, rising. All around her, candlelight threw shadows onto the stone. "I was very sorry to hear you were hurt."

"It was just a scratch." Cas walked up the aisle. Ventillas gave him a brief, grim nod, the greeting echoed by the king. Cas stopped beside Lena, sitting at the end of the pew. Her lips barely moving, she said, "I wish I were anywhere but here."

That was the second warning.

Queen Jehan came up to him. "Lena has shown me her grandfather's list. I hoped to tell you in person about the coins." She held out a hand, and when Cas did the same, she dropped three gold coins onto his open palm. "Will you stay?"

Cas studied the god Zacarias with his two heads, one looking back, the other forward. Ill at ease, he said, "You don't owe me an explanation."

Queen Jehan's expression said she agreed with him. She glanced at her stonefaced husband. "Nevertheless," she said.

All was not well between the king and his queen. Cas could see it. Even more, he could *feel* it, a heaviness in the air that made him want to flee the chapel right alongside Lena. Queen Jehan had lied to Cas about the coins. But he was not the only person she had lied to.

Having little choice, Cas said, "Of course I'll stay."

Queen Jehan wrapped her arms around herself as she spoke, the shrouded Abril directly behind her. "Mari and I grew up together. Her mother died when we were very young. Her father was an ambassador of Brisa. He traveled often, and when he did, she lived in the palace with me. We did everything together. When the time came to sail to Oliveras, I brought her with me. Her and Faustina.

"Mari fell ill outside Gregoria. Ventillas knew of a hospital, a good one, in that city. We brought her there. The last time I saw those coins, Lord Cassiapeus, they were with Mari. Sewn into the lining of her dress."

Cas closed his fist around the coins. "But why . . . ?"

"Why did I lie to you?" Another glance at her husband. "To everyone? It was foolish. I'm aware. I knew . . . I knew that if I told you about the coins, you would blame Mari. And you would be wrong."

Cas did not understand. Who else could it be besides Lady Mari? He turned to Ventillas. "You've seen these before?"

"Yes."

In the alcove, King Rayan turned his head and looked at his friend. Ventillas stared straight at the floor.

"Do not blame Ventillas," Queen Jehan said. "His only crime was in not wanting to call me a liar in front of others. I put him in a wretched position, and I regret it."

Cas said, "Your Grace, how can you be sure Lady Mari died in Gregoria?"

"We went back for her," Queen Jehan said. "When it was safer to travel, we sent men to look for her. There was no death record, no grave marker. Nothing. But you did not see her when we left her there. She could not have survived."

King Rayan spoke at last. "And yet Cas did. He is standing right here, against every odd."

Silence. Lena slipped a little farther down in her seat.

Cas tried to work through his thoughts. "Your Grace, you left Lady Mari with the coins, and there is no absolute certainty she died. Not only that, she is an expert with bow and arrow, as you are. Shooting the nurse on the bridge would not have been difficult for her. We know from Master Dimas that the archer spoke Oliveran as though it was not the language of her birth. She spoke a formal, perfect version." A dull ache rolled over him. Cas pressed a hand against his side and felt Lena's eyes on him. Master Jacomel's salve was wearing off. He finished, "That is how you speak our language, Your Grace. You speak it better than we do."

Queen Jehan turned away, toward Abril.

Something else bothered Cas. "Where would she have found the dress? Was it left with her?"

When no one else spoke, Lena said, "It wasn't. But I found my grandfather's list by chance. She could have found another carriage the same way." Lena held out a hand to Cas, who gave her the coins. "The inventory didn't list a dress. Just the bolts of cloth. Jehan, did Lady Mari know how to sew?"

"No," Queen Jehan said without turning. "She was terrible at it."

Lena turned a coin over, studying both sides. "Then someone else made the dress. I wonder who."

Her voice muted, Queen Jehan said, "Lord Cassiapeus, the woman on the horse . . . why did you chase her in the first place?"

Cas looked at Abril, all alone atop the altar. He crossed himself. "Because she was smiling," he explained. "Abril was being taken away, and she was the only person in the crowd who looked happy about it."

Queen Jehan's entire frame had stiffened. Across the chapel, the king's eyes remained fixed on her.

Cas said, "I don't want to upset you, but my brother was part of your cortege —"

Ventillas stirred. "Cassia . . ."

"Don't 'Cassia' me, Ventillas. You are not invincible, however much you think it." Cas counted to five, long enough to rein in his annoyance, and spoke to the queen's back. "Your Grace, I want Lady Mari found, *before* my brother ends up with an arrow in his heart or poison in his throat."

Queen Jehan spun around to face him. "This is why I said nothing! You see Mari, only Mari, and your minds are closed to all else. Mari does not murder people and *smile* about it afterward, Lord Cassiapeus. The notion is absurd. Mari *would not hurt me.* She would not hurt Faustina. I will never believe it. However wretched this looks, there is another explanation."

"People change," Cas said. "The pestilence changed people. It changed me." Lena had said something similar, just the other day.

"Did it truly?" Queen Jehan countered, her color high and rising. "By all accounts, you left Palmerin a good person. You returned a good person. The essence of you has not changed. I believe the same of Mari."

*Going to hell, am I? I'll take you with me.*

Cas spoke quietly. "With respect, Queen Jehan, you don't know the things I've done."

The ensuing silence was deafening.

King Rayan came forward. Gently, he took his queen's arm. "Sit, Jehan." When she did so, beside Lena, he said, "Everyone is upset. Whoever she may be, Mari, not Mari, there's nothing we can do about it tonight. Cas, Ventillas has offered additional escort back to Elvira. He will ride with us. I understand you were hurt today, but I hope you will come as well."

King Rayan's request seemed to surprise everyone. Not just Cas. When he had returned home, mere days ago, he had not intended to leave for a very long time. Instead, after a glance at Lena, he found himself bowing, however painfully, and saying yes, of course, he would be pleased to come.

"Good," King Rayan said. Just then, the chapel doors opened. Father Emil came in, followed by Master Jacomel and several dozen women. The weavers Abril had spent her days with. King Rayan added, "Now. We are here to say farewell to Abril, a daughter of Oliveras, who honored us with her gifts. Everything else can wait."

***

"I feel terrible," Lena said.

"Why?" Cas asked. "What did you do?"

They had left the chapel together, headed to the main part of the keep. The path took them outdoors and past covered archways. No one else was about in the dark, quiet night.

Lena said, "Rayan was nearly betrothed to someone else before. Did you know?"

Cas looked at her quickly. "To whom?"

"Lady Rondilla. Yes, I know," Lena said at Cas' strangled cough. "It looked like an excellent match on parchment. Her brother is high councilor, and they are richer than the moon and the stars. The exchequer would have had enough gold for the next ten generations."

"What happened?"

"Jehan's father proposed a truce, with marriage to his daughter as a condition. He had never been open to a truce before. Rayan leapt at the offer."

Cas whistled softly. "Bad luck for Lady Rondilla."

"Good luck for me," Lena said. "I used to visit him sometimes at the palace. They weren't even betrothed yet, but Lady Rondilla was already there, ordering the servants about and redecorating the queen's chambers. She can be unpleasant."

He halted. "To you?"

Lena tugged his arm long enough to keep him walking. "My mother was a king's mistress. One of many. Lady Rondilla was only horrid when Rayan was not around to hear, and she did not say anything I had not heard before."

Cas stopped again, outraged on her behalf. "Did you tell the king?"

Another tug. "Of course not. It is the last thing he needs. The only reason I mention it is because Jehan is nothing like her. From the very beginning, she has treated me like a sister. I hate that I've caused trouble for them."

"All you did was show them your grandfather's list."

Lena was quiet. "I don't think Rayan believes her. I don't think he believes Lord Ventillas, either."

Cas had seen the way the king looked at his queen and his closest friend. There had been anger there, and hurt. "Do you?"

She glanced up at him, troubled. "Something does not feel right. I don't know what, or —" This time, it was Lena who stopped.

They had entered the passageway by the back gardens. In the space where Cas' ugly statue had once stood, someone had built a roaring fire. Not anyone — Bittor. He walked toward the flames, carrying what Cas first thought was a sleeping woman in his arms, until he realized it was Queen Jehan's wedding dress.

Seeing them, Bittor paused. "What?" he called out. "Why are you looking at me like that?"

Lena's hand had flown to her throat. "I thought he . . . a body . . ."

"So did I," Cas admitted, rattled.

"What are you doing?" Lena demanded when they reached him.

"Getting rid of this dress," Bittor informed them. "The king wants it burned."

"Why?" Cas asked.

"He did not confide in me," Bittor said, "but if I were to guess, I would say it is because a woman was murdered in it. And therefore it is a very creepy thing to have around."

Lena reached out and touched a sleeve, wistful. "It's so beautiful. Such a waste."

"Would you wear it?" Bittor asked.

Lena dropped her hand. "No."

"Well, then. Step back." Bittor made to heave the dress into the flames.

"Bittor, wait." Lena turned to Cas. "May I borrow your dagger?"

Cas reached for his belt, handed her the dagger hilt first.

"Not everyone can make a dress from silk rakematiz," Lena explained. "Certainly not one like this. It requires great skill. I wonder . . ." Using his dagger, she sliced off the right sleeve.

Cas understood. "If we can find out who made it . . ."

"We can find out who wanted it made," Lena finished with a small smile. "Hopefully."

"You are finishing each other's sentences," Bittor pointed out with a pained expression. "Already."

They ignored him. "Where would we start?" Cas asked.

Her face fell. "Oh, who knows. Let me think on it."

Bittor broke in, sounding annoyed. "Is someone going to tell me what this is about?"

"No," Cas and Lena said at the same time.

"*Fine.* Step back."

When they did, Bittor gathered up the dress, folds and all, and tossed it into the flames.

BEFORE HE LEFT Palmerin Keep, Cas made one last stop. He knew he should not do it. No good could come from seeing Faro again. He told himself this even as he descended the tower steps into the deepest, darkest part of the keep. The air chilled him. His nose twitched at the first sour waft coming from below.

There had been no chance to confront Faro privately, to speak aloud the names of the three men who had lost their lives because of him.

Jorge.

Sans.

Arias.

But then, why would Faro care? In one fell swoop, he had lost his hand, his beloved, his good name. Soon he would lose his country, once Ventillas sent him off to the border to be tossed from a cart onto the roadside. Like the core of an apple just eaten. Like a pet no longer wanted. Pity came to Cas. Unbidden, unwanted. He hunched his shoulders and hardened his heart. It was as Lena had said that night in the stables. Faro still had his life. It was more than he allowed the others.

Jorge.

Sans.

Arias.

The farther down he went, the worse it smelled. Unwashed bodies and moldy cells. The sharp, acrid sting of misery. He had known a similar place once, not so long ago.

Cas reached the bottom of the stairwell and ducked through a doorway. The dungeon was round, in keeping with the shape of the tower. Cells took up the entire perimeter with the exception of the doorway. A guard occupied a table in the center of the room. Cas had found him taking a bite from his breakfast. Two pieces of bread with a slab of meat between them. When he recognized Cas, he jumped to his feet, and a violent fit of coughing seized him.

Cas thumped him on the back. Three times, hard. A piece of chewed-up, greasy-looking sausage flew from the guard's mouth and landed on the stones.

"Better?" Cas asked, concerned.

"*Yes, yes,*" the guard gasped, one hand around his throat. "Welcome home . . . Lord Cassia."

"Thank you." Cas picked up a tankard from the table and handed it to the guard, who took it gratefully. Cas glanced around in puzzlement.

"Who are you guarding?" From where he stood, the cells looked empty. Aside from the guard gulping down his wine, all was quiet. Where had they put Faro?

"What? Oh, Lord Tuli is back there." The guard pointed. "Sleeping, not dead. I just checked."

"Lord Tuli?" Cas lowered his voice. "What's he in for?"

The guard wiped his mouth with his sleeve. "Burned down the village near his manor. Thought the fire would keep the pestilence away from his family."

Aghast, Cas said, "Did anyone escape?"

"Only two out of a hundred. The fire started at night." The guard picked the sausage off the floor. "No gallows for him, though."

"Why not?"

"He saved Captain Lorenz's life in the war. The captain asked for mercy." The guard dusted off the sausage and popped it in his mouth.

Cas said, "Where is his family?"

"Plague took them." The guard spoke around the sausage. "His wife, sons, grandsons. The fire did not help them in the end."

Disturbed, Cas went to have a look. Through the bars, he saw a figure lying on a pallet on the floor. A blanket, formerly white, now gray, covered him from head to toe. He looked dead.

"Lord Tuli," Cas said, to check.

"It is not my fault." The figure spoke, puffing out the blanket around his mouth. His voice was hoarse, thready, but recognizable. "I thought the fire would save them. Not my fault."

A sound followed, muffled but unmistakable. Cas moved past Lord Tuli's cell to the one beside it. A pallet on the floor. A bucket in the corner. Rusty chains and fetters left in a heap. Cas was quiet a long time. He spoke without turning. "Where is he?"

The guard came to stand beside him. "Ah, this was the scribe's cell." He looked from the pallet to Cas, clearly wondering how Cas had figured that out.

"Where. Is. He?" Cas repeated.

"Ah . . ." The guard scratched his neck, ill at ease. "Well . . ."

He broke off as footsteps sounded on the stairs. Ventillas appeared, dressed for travel, as Cas was. A heavy cloak and a sword at his back.

"Master Jac saw you come down here," Ventillas said, frowning.

Cas wrapped a hand around a bar. "I wanted to speak to him."

"To what end?" Ventillas said with some impatience. When Cas did not answer, he said, "I had him taken away last night. I wanted him gone. He'll be put on a ship in the south. Are you ready? We should go."

The guard was carefully studying the paving stones.

"It is not my fault," Lord Tuli said.

"Save your breath, old man." Ventillas turned to Cas, waiting.

"I'm ready." Cas followed his brother out of the dungeon and up the stairs. Knowing that Ventillas lied to him.

Faro was not on his way to some ship. Cas did not know what had been done to his body. But Cas had seen him in his cell, a figure not whole or solid. He sat on his pallet with his arms wrapped around his knees and his hand a bloody stump. Rocking himself back and forth. Whispering one word over and over again.

A name.

*Sorne. Sorne. Sorne.*

## ❧ 20 ❧

A MASS EXODUS TOOK place throughout the morning. Wagons, packhorses, and carriages streamed past the keep's doors as guests departed one by one. Ventillas had gone ahead to lead the train, leaving Cas with unanswered questions. He found Master Jacomel directing all from the bottom steps. Not grinning, exactly. A good steward was the soul of discretion. But as each visitor rode away, it seemed to Cas that Master Jacomel's eyes gleamed brighter and his spirit grew freer.

Dark as his mood was, Cas had to laugh. "You have the keep to yourself. At long last."

But Master Jacomel surprised him. "I imagine I'll enjoy it for a day or so before it starts to feel *too* quiet. It was nice to have women in the keep. And children," he added with a meaningful look in Cas' direction.

"Not you, too." Master Jacomel sounded like the king. Cas took in their surroundings, made sure no one could hear their conversation amid the noise and bustle. "Master Jac?"

"Mm?" The steward had turned his attention upward, where the sun held court in a cloudless sky. A smile appeared beneath his heavy mustache. "Ha. I could not have asked for better weather."

"What happened to Faro?"

Master Jacomel's head came down quickly. The smile vanished. "What do you mean?"

"He's dead. I know he is. What happened to him?"

Thankfully, Master Jacomel did not ask Cas how he knew this. "Have you spoken to your brother?"

Cas waited until a group of nursemaids hurried by, each carrying a bundled infant. "He says Faro was taken away last night. To be put on a ship in the south."

Master Jacomel was quiet. "Then that is what happened."

"Master Jac—"

"If that is what he said, then I cannot tell you otherwise."

Cas would find no answers here. The master steward served the lord of Palmerin, and that was Ventillas. A page sprinted by carrying a birdcage, the owl within hooting frantically. The boy slowed his steps, throwing back a sheepish grin when Master Jacomel called his name, ordering him to *walk, do not run.*

Cas turned at the sound of footsteps. Lena came down dressed for riding in forest green, hair gathered in a braid. Two lynx reclined halfway up the steps, eyeing her. One licked its paw. She gave them both a wide berth.

Cas said, "I thought you'd gone."

"I've been hiding." Lena stopped a few steps above him so that they stood eye to eye, and smiled. "Otherwise, I would have to share a carriage with Lady Rondilla, and that would not be good for anyone." She turned to the steward. "Might I beg a horse from you, Master Jacomel?"

"Of course, Lady. Will he do?"

As the last of the carriages rolled away, Jon from the stables approached leading two horses: Cas' white mare and a brown stallion. He was a beautiful horse, tall and proud, with a flowing black mane. But Lena did not want him. She descended the steps, murmured, "My, aren't you a pretty one?" to the stallion, and walked right past him to the mare. Horse and girl greeted each other like old friends.

Master Jacomel regarded the mace on Cas' back with disfavor. "That should have been returned to storage. We have swords to spare. I'll have one fetched for you."

"I like this mace."

The look on Master Jacomel's face said he would choose his battles. This was not one of them. "Your sword will be ready when you return. One month, is it?"

"Maybe more, maybe less. Don't worry."

Leading an entire court back to Elvira would take time. Longer if the weather did not hold, or if there were other unforeseen delays, which there always were. They would make camp on some nights. Others would be spent at inns and estates along the way. Cas did not know how long Ventillas planned to remain in Elvira, but with luck, they would return long before the cold dug its claws into the mountains.

Master Jacomel did not answer. Seeing the look in his eyes, Cas remembered the last time he had told him not to worry. It was the day he had set off to inspect the aqueducts. Three years ago. Deliberately, Cas placed a hand on his shoulder. "I'll send word if we're delayed."

Master Jacomel's hand came up to cover his in a firm grip. "See that you do."

Lena loitered by his horse. She threw a look of mute appeal at Cas, who said, with amused resignation, "Just for today."

His words were met with a wide smile. Declining Jon's help, she placed her boot in the stirrup and swung onto Cas' mare.

Master Jacomel took all of this in. "Women and children," he murmured.

"Stop."

***

Traveling as part of a train was vastly different from traveling on one's own. Stops were frequent. To eat, to stretch, to walk pets, mostly tiny dogs and bad-tempered ferrets that did not actually walk — they were carried. The court's first night would be spent in the open, as they were too far away from any manor or town.

Cas had been summoned to the front of the train, where he found Captain Lorenz chuckling and Ventillas shaking his head.

Captain Lorenz explained. "I was reminding your brother of the time you climbed to the top of the aqueduct and could not get down again." He tipped his chin at the arches rising high on their right. The sound of water could be heard rushing through the pipes. "How old were you then? Four? Five?"

Cas had no recollection of it. "I don't remember."

"He was four," Ventillas said, riding in the center.

"Makes my heart stop just thinking about it." Captain Lorenz kneaded his chest with a gloved fist. "Ventillas would have been fourteen. He had to climb up and get you."

"And my reward was a walloping from Father," Ventillas added. "That was fair."

"You were supposed to be watching him," Captain Lorenz said dryly. "And somehow he ends up outside the city gates on top of the aqueduct, of all things. A walloping was a mercy."

They rode past arches with footholds cut into the stone. Cas would have gone up that way. It was strange to think of his brother rescuing him, or neglecting him, in a time before his earliest memory.

Ventillas glanced over. "You're very quiet. Something wrong?"

And Cas found he could not pretend. "You know what's wrong."

The captain's eyebrows rose. Cas saw no reason not to speak in front of him. If Faro had been killed, his body removed, the captain likely knew about it.

Ventillas' grip tightened on the reins. "I already —"

"I'm not a boy anymore, Ventillas. Easily tricked. I know Faro is dead."

Captain Lorenz turned in his saddle. His hand came up to shield his eyes from the sun. "Ah. Something's off with the supply wagon. I'll just go see —"

"Stay, Captain," Ventillas ordered softly.

Captain Lorenz sighed, straightening in the saddle.

Ventillas said, "Who told you?"

Cas turned his head, glared. "You just did."

"Cassia."

"What does it matter, who?" Cas demanded. "I did not want him dead. You swore you would not kill him."

Ventillas looked away. A good distance separated them from the next line of soldiers. Close enough to hear their laughter. Far enough away not to make out their words. After a long while, his brother said, "I meant it at the time."

"I've been home less than a week," Cas said, incredulous. "Six days. Does your word last no longer than that anymore?"

"Cassia!" Captain Lorenz snapped. "You will remember who you're speaking to."

"I'm not the one in the wrong here, Captain." Cas' blood was up, and he didn't care. Everywhere he went, he saw the dead. He had not wanted to add to their ranks. Not any more than he had already.

"Faro tried to kill my brother," Ventillas said very quietly. "My only brother, who he knew I loved above all else. And then for three years afterward, he slept under my roof and ate my food and spent my silver." His knuckles on the reins had whitened. "Yesterday I went to his cell and put a dagger in him." Turning his head, Ventillas looked Cas in the eye. "And even now, seeing how you look at me, I don't regret it. I would do it again."

Cas could not find the words to speak. It turned out he did not have to, because Captain Lorenz leaned around Ventillas to snap, "That's enough out of you. Get to the back of the train."

***

Banished from the front, Cas sped off toward the rear of the train until he heard his name called. Lena beckoned him over; she was in a group of happy, laughing travelers. Cas hesitated, torn between a desire to ride with her and the knowledge that it might be better to go off alone and steep in his own sour company. Better for her at least.

"Cas!" Lena waved again.

He rode up beside her. And he made sure to pin on a pleasant expression, which cracked slightly when Bittor appeared, wedging his horse, a piebald, between theirs.

"That is a nice cloak," Bittor observed, bringing his horse even closer and peering at Cas' outer garment, a gray so dark it appeared black. "Trastamarian wool, is it? Good choice. And the stitching is fine. What sort of lining do you have?"

"Black," Cas said.

"Black what? Silk? Fur?"

"Silk."

"The queen had it made for him," Lena added.

"Really? Impressive." Bittor reached over to touch his sleeve, then drew back at Cas' expression.

Lena said with a laugh, "Bittor's family are wool merchants in the north."

"Then why aren't you there?" Cas asked before he could help himself. "In the north?"

Bittor shrugged. "Because I am the cuckoo in the nest, or so my mother tells me. I prefer fighting to clothing fairs." He gave Cas another look over. "Are those trousers padded by any chance?"

Heads swiveled at the question, ladies and men both. Cas felt his face turn hot. "No," he snapped.

"Really? Impressive."

Lena's head was down, but her shoulders were shaking. "I want my horse back," Cas said, which only made her laugh harder.

As the day wore on, they veered east, leaving Palmerin and the aqueduct behind. They passed craggy mountains and tiny hamlets. Farmhouses appeared after long intervals. Cas had drifted off to one side, lost in his thoughts. Lady Mari. Queen Jehan. Ventillas most of all. At first, he thought the music came from one of the travelers. A piper playing a lament, something sad and mournful. He looked around to see who it was, but no one else appeared to be listening. And then he realized the music drifted not from the train, but from the side of the road, just beyond a giant boulder. Curious, he broke away from the others and went to have a look. The smell served as a warning. He rounded the boulder and stopped. It was not his choice alone. The horse would go no farther.

Unlike Izaro, these bodies were newly dead. A day or two, that was all. The man and woman lay face-up on the grass, clothing and skin torn to shreds, bags and walking sticks strewn about. A boil oozed just above the woman's collarbone. She had not lived long enough for it to grow larger than a thumbnail.

A spirit sat cross-legged by the bodies. A man not much older than Ventillas. The bones on his face stood out in a way that suggested hunger had once been a close companion. It was too late for Cas to pretend not to see him, and the spirit, lowering his pipe, did not seem to care either way.

Cas asked, "What happened?"

The spirit set his pipe on the grass. "We stopped to rest, my wife and I. We'd been traveling for days. The lynx . . . came from nowhere."

Cas took in the wounds on the bodies, the shredded skin. "More than one?"

"Three. Their eyes were bloody, and I knew . . ."

Cas waited, but the spirit stopped speaking. Cas scanned the area. Ventillas and his hunting party had found one such lynx, days ago. They had burned it in the fields. "When was this?"

"Two days ago. My wife . . . she did not die right away." The spirit looked at the boil on his wife's collarbone. His lips trembled. "You could smell it on them, the pestilence. You could smell the rot." He focused on Cas for the first time. "They are not far. In the Desfilad." Bitterness twisted his smile. "I can sense them. Now."

Dread had overtaken Cas. The train headed toward a cleft in the mountains, one known as the Desfilad. A narrow road wide enough to fit a cart, no more. By his reckoning, the very first of the travelers would reach the entrance to the cleft within the hour.

Cas turned the horse around, only to see Lena and Bittor not twenty paces away, watching him with identical expressions of unease.

Bittor looked at the bodies. He looked at Cas. "Who are you talking to?"

Lena remained silent.

"I was praying." Cas brought his horse beside them. "There are lynx in the Desfilad. Rabid. We have to warn the others."

Bittor did not move. "How do you know this?"

Cas was careful not to glance at the spirit, who had taken up his pipe. No one heard the lament but Cas. "I know what a lynx attack looks like, and I know what plague looks like —"

Both flinched at the word *plague*.

"But why do you think they're in the Desfilad?" Bittor asked. A reasonable question, considering. One Cas could not answer. "They could be anywhere —"

"Bittor!" Lena said. "You can play grand inquisitor later. You have to warn Lord Ventillas."

"Do I? Because —"

Cas gave Lena a grateful look. He said to her, "They need to be burned."

"I'll see it's done." Lena studied the bodies on the ground, her brown eyes filled with pity. "Be careful, Cas."

She did not understand how or why, but she believed him. She did not think he was mad. At least not completely. Unsure how to feel about that, Cas rode off. He heard, "But how —?" followed by cursing and the sound of Bittor in pursuit.

It took a good hour to reach the front of the train, which had just begun to form a single line. Ventillas and Captain Lorenz were there. Cas' whistle brought their heads around.

"What is it?" Ventillas demanded the second Cas stopped in front of him.

Their argument loomed between them, but it would have to wait. Cas said, "We found a man and woman back that way. Killed."

Captain Lorenz turned his horse in the direction from which Cas had come. "Killed how?"

"Lynx," Cas answered. "Maybe more than one."

Bittor stayed mercifully silent. Guards had gathered close to listen.

Ventillas said, "Recent?"

"I think so. Ventillas, the woman had a boil here." Cas tapped his neck with one finger.

The royal carriage was nearby. Queen Jehan watched them through the window, the prince resting against her shoulder. King Rayan came over on horseback.

"Bad cats," Ventillas said at the king's look of inquiry. "I'll take some men and ride through the cleft, make sure they're not hiding on the ledges."

King Rayan said, "Do you have something to add, Bittor?"

All eyes turned to Bittor, who looked as though he badly wanted to say something. Cas tensed, until Bittor shot him a look and said, "No, Your Grace."

"Then let's go." Ventillas chose Cas and Bittor to accompany him, along with two archers.

They rode with their eyes peeled. In the Desfilad, the mountains rose steeply on both sides before vanishing into the clouds. The rockface was broken occasionally by ledges that jutted out, wide enough for something — an animal, a man — to crouch and watch.

When the first ledge came into view, Ventillas stopped. He said to Cas, "Do you have your sling?"

Cas reached for it. "Yes."

"Good. Shoot the rocks by that ledge. Make it noisy."

One of the archers said doubtfully, "If they're asleep, should we wake them?"

"Better they wake now than later," Ventillas said, "when the queen and the prince pass through."

Cas took aim. The resulting shot sent rocks raining down onto the road in front of them. Ventillas held up a hand for silence. There was no sound from the ledge. After some minutes, Ventillas motioned them forward.

Cas did the same with the second ledge and the third. By the time they rode past the eighth ledge, he could feel the looks from the other men, especially Bittor, who rode beside him.

"I'm not mad," Cas said to himself, not realizing until it was too late that he had spoken aloud, and Bittor had heard.

"Are you sure?" Bittor asked. "Because I'm beginning to think—"

A lynx sprang from the ninth ledge, so suddenly the horses reared in fright. Bittor flew off his piebald and landed in the dirt.

Ventillas shouted, "Archers!"

The lynx was no easy target. It sprang from the ledge to one directly opposite, claws scraping for purchase before it leapt straight at the first archer, whose arrow missed by inches. The second archer came to the rescue. His arrow struck the lynx in the neck. A thud followed. By then, two more cats had appeared on a ledge. Hissing, they skidded down the mountain in a shower of pebbles and rocks.

Cas aimed his sling, but a clear shot was impossible. He vaulted from his horse, grabbed the mace at his back, and waited for them to come to him. The blood beat in his ears.

And then Ventillas was there.

He rode in front of Cas. From his bow, two arrows flew as one. Both lynx fell over dead. Ventillas whipped his horse around to glare at Cas, furious. "Get on your horse!" he yelled.

Three lynx dead. The piper had said there were three. Breathing hard, Cas raised a hand to say *yes, yes, he understood,* then reached down and pulled Bittor to his feet. "Anything broken?"

"No," Bittor said, blood on his lip. "Did you see that? Two arrows at the same time! How —?"

Behind him came the sound of brush rustling. With a yelp, Cas swung the mace upward, catching the lynx in the chest as it sprang from a hidden cave at ground level. Cas and Bittor stared at the dead cat, then at each other, mouths agape.

Ventillas yanked Cas around. "Are you hurt?"

"No," Cas said, heart pounding. Where had that fourth cat come from?

His brother muttered something rude. Cas was given such a thorough inspection that he felt his face turning red. "Ventillas," he grumbled, aware the others watched.

Ventillas saw them too. He stepped back. "Not a boy anymore," he murmured. "I forget." Turning away, he said, "Not too close," when Bittor would have ventured over to the animals for a better look. "There are other ledges. We clear them all."

They continued on, inspecting the ledges and checking behind shrubs. Bittor rode beside Cas, who could feel his stare boring into his left ear. Finally, Cas said, *"What?"*

"You've ripped the sleeve on that cloak," Bittor informed him. "Already. Leave it with me tonight. I'll fix it for you."

Startled, Cas turned his head, but Bittor, who came from a family of wool merchants in the north, stared straight in front of him. Cas inspected his torn sleeve. The offer was a thank-you of sorts. Cas would not turn it down. He liked this cloak.

Ventillas rode ahead of them. Alone. His brother, whose first duty had always been to keep him safe. Climbing the aqueduct, shooting the lynx. Those were just a few. Suddenly, Cas understood why Faro would never have boarded a ship in the south.

*And even now, seeing how you look at me, I don't regret it. I would do it again.*

Remorse filled him, sharp and pinching.

When they reached the end of the Desfilad, they retraced their steps and set fire to the corpses. They did not return to the others until every lynx had burned to ash.

# 21

THE FOLLOWING DAY the rains came. It poured and it poured, turning the roads to muddy rivers and trapping two food wagons in the muck.

Every other word uttered by Ventillas was a curse as he joined the men trying to pull the wagons free. He shouted orders at Cas, who rode to the front of the train and rapped on a carriage window.

King Rayan pulled aside the covering, his clothes enviously dry. He took one look at Cas, every inch of him drenched, and winced in sympathy. "You're a miserable sight! Analena, a towel!"

Cas grinned, shaking his head and spraying rainwater everywhere. "It's no use! Ventillas says we can't stay out here much longer. There's a castle, not far that way." He pointed. "It's abandoned. We'll make camp there until this blows over."

"Abandoned?" Queen Jehan sat across from Faustina, who held the sleeping prince. "Is it safe?"

"I'll ride there now and clear it. If there's a problem, I'll come back."

Lightning flashed, turning the afternoon sky a brilliant white and striking a tree across the field. It burst into flames. Cas thought he could hear his brother's curses all the way from the back of the train.

Lena reached past the king, covered Cas' head with a warm towel, and rubbed vigorously. When she pulled the towel away, everyone in the carriage smiled. He could only imagine what he looked like, hair stuck out in every direction. "It will be dark soon." Lena swiped at his face with a gentler hand. "Be careful."

"Lady." Cas returned her smile and rode off.

He took Bittor and two others with him. They rode as fast as the storm allowed, dodging holes and keeping a sharp eye out for wolves and lynx. Neither were spotted, but Cas heard them occasionally. Howling from the mountains. Hissing in the rain.

A stone arch signaled the entrance to the castle. They rode beneath it, their pace slowing considerably as they navigated the overgrown path. Trees and ivy closed in on both sides. The carriages would only just be able to travel through. Cas and his companions came to a halt at the end of the road and stared in dismay.

Bittor was the first to speak, rainwater dripping off his nose. "I say we risk the storm."

"Hear, hear," another soldier muttered.

Cas was tempted. A less welcoming home he had yet to see. This was not the place he remembered visiting during his boyhood. The castle stood three stories tall, built of pewter stone that mimicked the color of the sky. Black slate tiles covered the roof. Half the windows were broken. The wind and rain whipped the draperies out into the open between the shards and the cracks. Steps led up to a set of doors, each bearing a red cross. Faded, but still unsettling. This had once been a house of plague.

Lightning struck again, followed by the long, ominous roll of thunder.

From Ventillas, Cas had learned that the pestilence had struck Lord Pastor and his entire family. A wife and two young children. None had survived. The closest sheriff lived in a town days away. He had come, eventually, to see to their burials and to wrap chains around the front doors. By then, the servants had died or fled, and the house had been looted down to the floorboards. All that had been left were the corpses, moldering in their beds. A tragic place.

Still, they needed whatever shelter it could provide. "We're too near the river," Cas said. "We can't risk the carriages being caught in a flood."

"What about . . . ?" One of the soldiers gestured at the painted crosses on the doors.

"It's been a year. It doesn't linger in a home for so long."

Cas directed one man to check the stables, another to locate a brush to scrub away the crosses. For that, rainwater would be useful. Cas made quick work of the chains on the doors with his mace, prompting Bittor to say he would be getting one of his own at the first opportunity. Cas shoved open the doors.

Even with Ventillas' warning, he was unprepared for the sight of the great hall. He remembered gracious furniture and tapestries on the walls. There had been blazing torchlight and a fireplace so large ten men could stand shoulder to shoulder within its vastness. The fireplace was still here, cold and dark. Everything else was gone.

Bittor whistled. "This is brazen work. Did you know the family?"

"A little." Cas turned full circle, heart heavy with the sorrow of their passing. "We came for the children's naming ceremonies. Pastor would have been . . . ten? Clara five by now. They were a nice family."

Bittor went to stand in front of the fireplace. His sopping cloak left great puddles in his wake. With his back to Cas, he said, "My sister's name was Clara."

"Was?"

When Bittor turned, his expression was unreadable. "A year ago. She was twelve."

Cas remembered standing by the lake in Palmerin, believing his own brother had been taken by the plague. It had felt like the end of the world. He placed a hand over his heart. "I am sorry."

Bittor looked away. He cleared his throat. "I say we skip the clearing. No one's been here in ages."

Bittor had a point. The dust was thick beneath their boots. No prints but their own were visible. "I told Ventillas we'd clear it. You start back there. I'll go upstairs."

Sighing, Bittor walked off. While one soldier scrubbed industriously at the red paint, the second came in from the rain. The stable was empty, he said. Every saddle gone. Every iron bucket. Someone had even removed the wooden boards separating the stalls and carried them away. Cas sent him to help Bittor.

Cas went upstairs, bringing a torch with him. It was colder here, wetter. All these broken windows. The wind whistled through the fractured panes, causing his torchlight to sputter and dance. Cas shivered. This floor was not as empty as the one below. Furniture had been left behind. Giant trunks and carved chests, heavy mahogany bed frames. Pieces too cumbersome for thieves to transport. The mattress ticking was nowhere to be seen, and he could only hope someone had taken the time to burn it.

Two chambers looked as if they had once been meant for a boy and a girl. He did not linger in those rooms.

"Oy!" Bittor hollered from below. "There's no one here. What now?"

Cas retraced his steps. The men were gathered near the front door, where the crosses were no longer visible. He sent Bittor and one other to meet the train. They would need help avoiding the ruts and pits in the gathering darkness. The third soldier would stand guard by the main entry, beneath the arch.

As soon as they departed, Cas started on the fire. He collected pieces of broken furniture, a chair leg here, a shattered table there, and tossed them into the fireplace. There was no way of knowing beforehand if birds had built nests high in the chute. Once the flames caught hold, he watched with bated breath to see if a sparrow or robin would tumble down. To his relief, no birds appeared. The fire burned clean.

When that was done, Cas went upstairs to search the rest of the castle. The torchlight threw shadows into every corner. On the second floor, he found a smaller stairwell, steep and narrow, that led to the third floor. It was only because he was looking down, making certain he did not miss a step, that he saw them.

Footprints in the dust.

They went up and they went down. The prints overlapped one another. He lifted the torch high and considered. It was too late to climb the steps quietly. They creaked and groaned beneath his weight. If there was someone hiding above, they knew he was coming. He left his mace at his back. Maybe he would have cause to regret it, but he did not want to risk frightening whoever was up there. The footsteps he followed belonged to a child. One who wore no shoes on this wet, miserable autumn day.

The attic took up the entire length of the house. Centuries' worth of discarded furniture had been relegated here. Scavengers had made their mark, leaving behind the heaviest pieces, absconding with the rest. Perhaps in a fit of goodwill, they had decided against breaking the windows. Every one of them remained intact, which meant the space was dry and relatively warm.

Cas stood by the door. The little footsteps disappeared into the maze of overturned trunks and broken armoires. "Hello?" he called. There was no answer. "Hello there?"

How had the child entered the house in the first place? Not through front doors wrapped in chains. Cas thought of Palmerin Keep with its hidden passageways and secret doors. There were any number of ways in and out of a home. If one knew where to look.

He said, "Is anyone here? My name is Cas. I mean you no harm." He stayed where he was. It occurred to him that the sound of heavy, measured footsteps walking up and down the chamber might be terrifying to a small someone trying to hide. "I live at Palmerin Keep. Do you know it? It's not far from here. My elder brother is Lord Ventillas. Do you have a brother?"

There. Halfway down the chamber, to the right, a shadow moved.

Cas focused on that spot. "Most days I like my brother. He taught me how to fish." Also how to fight with a sword, shoot with a bow and arrow, scale a castle wall, throw a dagger directly into a man's throat. But these were not things you mentioned to someone you were trying to put at ease. "Some days I don't like him as much. Elder brothers like to tell you what to do, which can be tedious. I would have liked to have had a sister. Do you have a sister?"

Another shift, a small sound.

Cas raised the torch. "Do you live up here? I used to visit sometimes when I was a boy."

A minute passed. Cas began to feel like a lump. There was no one here. He was talking to air. Good thing Bittor was not around to see. Whoever had left those footprints had come and gone. There were mice in this attic. That was all. He had heard nothing more than the scuttling and scraping of claws.

Even so, he tried one last thing. He took an apple from his pocket, one that had been meant for his horse. He had forgotten it was there. He placed it on the floor, shiny and red amid the dust. "Are you hungry? I have an apple. I'll leave it here for you and then I'll go. You can eat in peace." He took a step back, feeling more and more foolish as the seconds passed. "There's food downstairs. A warm fire. You have my word no harm will come to you . . ." Nothing. He sighed and turned around. Under his breath, he said, "Wasting food on a mouse."

***

Downstairs, Cas opened the front doors and peered down the path. It was impossible to see anything through the sheets of rain. His saddlebag had been brought in and left by the fireplace. Crouching, he rifled through the contents. He had pillaged the food wagon before riding here. Wrapped in various cloths were bread, cheese, grapes, and olives. Sticks of meat, dried and salted. He could have sworn . . . *ah*. And a large slice of olive oil cake wrapped in more cloth.

Cas heard nothing over the crackling fire and the pouring rain, but something had him turning his head toward the stairs.

A small figure stood on the bottom step. A little girl, hair a wild tangle, feet bare. She wore what appeared to be a collection of tattered blankets around her shoulders, and Cas was reminded of the old crones from his childhood tales. Except this crone was three feet tall, if that. She looked scared. Cas knew what had drawn her from her hiding place, for she could not take her eyes from the food he had spread out by the fire.

Cas remained kneeling. "Hello there. I was just about to have supper. Will you join me?"

She took a few steps toward him, then stopped. Cas had never seen such a quiet, watchful child. "I have bread and cheese. The grapes are very sweet." He laid two squares of cloth on the floor and divided the food in half.

Hunger won out over fear. Several blankets were discarded as she hurried over and knelt before her share of the food. Her reek nearly knocked him over. It reminded him of his time in prison. The smell was the same. Cas watched her fall on the meal, inhaling more than eating. Like a wild animal, feral. He should tell her to slow down — she might be sick otherwise — but he did not have the heart to.

Not a crumb was left on her napkin. Immediately, she eyed his untouched meal.

Cas said, "Drink first." Slowly, so as not to scare her, he reached for his water flask, pulled off the cap, and offered it to her.

She snatched it away and drank, watching him the entire time with wide, unblinking eyes. When he gauged she had consumed half the flask, he held out his hand. Only a slight hesitation before she returned it. She turned back to his napkin, waiting.

Cas asked her a question, though he knew the answer already. He had seen the birthmark on her cheek and recognized it. As big as his thumbnail, it reminded him of the rosetta window at Palmerin Keep. He had first seen it at her naming ceremony five years ago. "What is your name?"

She reached for more bread. Cas held up a palm, stopping her. "Do you remember your name?"

"Clara." It was a strange voice, with the high-pitched tone of a child, but full of rust, like a hermit unused to speech. "I am Clara."

# ❦ 22 ❦

WHEN THE ROYAL household arrived, full dark had fallen. The doors were thrown open and they poured in, tired and damp, happy to be out of the storm. They stopped at the sight that greeted them. Directly ahead was a massive stone staircase. Cas sat on the bottom step, elbows on bent knees. Beside him was a small girl, five or so, wearing a heap of ancient, holey blankets.

Queen Jehan was the first to approach. Her cloak was a rich purple, the hood lined with black fur. She pushed it back, revealing dark hair gathered in cauls above her ears. Clara shrank against Cas.

Queen Jehan paused. She said something to one of the soldiers, who immediately began steering everyone toward the fire and away from the staircase.

"Who do we have here?" Queen Jehan smiled. She was close enough to see the girl's condition, to smell her. Nothing showed on her face except a mild curiosity.

Cas tried to stand; he needed to greet the queen properly, but Clara hung on to him with both arms. "It's all right. No one will hurt you here. This is Queen Jehan." Clara only buried herself deeper into his armpit. Queen Jehan shook her head slightly at Cas' apologetic look. By then, a small crowd had gathered beside her. King Rayan, Ventillas, Lena, Bittor, and High Councilor Amador, who covered his nose with a handkerchief until the queen turned and looked at him. The handkerchief disappeared but the pinched expression remained.

Bittor swiped rainwater from his face, baffled. "Where did she come from?"

"I found her in the attic," Cas said. "I think she's been alone since . . . for some time. I don't know what she's been eating." The girl peeked out from under Cas' arm, the birthmark clearly visible.

There was a strangled sound from Ventillas. "Cassia. That's —"

"Yes." Cas explained to the others, "This is Clara, Lord Pastor's daughter."

"How is this possible?" King Rayan asked, appalled.

"There must be some mistake," Lord Amador said. "One does not simply *misplace* a nobleman's daughter —"

"We will untangle this mystery, of course," Queen Jehan said. "But not tonight. We are all tired and hungry." She smiled at Clara, then turned as her old nurse approached, carrying the prince. "Faustina?"

Faustina handed the prince over to Lena. "I will see to her bath, Your Grace." She held out her hand to Clara, her manner one of brisk kindness. "Come with me, child. There's a good girl."

But Clara would not go without Cas. She clung and whimpered. And that was how he found himself on a stool by the fire as Faustina transformed a tiny old crone back into a little girl. At least on the surface.

Ventillas had decided that everyone would sleep in the great hall. It would make leaving the following day simpler if they didn't have to waste time searching the estate for stray travelers. Some had chosen to put up tents indoors for privacy. Most spread about on blankets and within bedrolls, as close to the fire as possible.

A tub had been filled with hot water. Faustina removed Clara's blankets, layer by filthy layer. The blankets would have to be burned. They weren't fit for the horses. Beneath the blankets was an ill-fitting nightgown that had once been white. Legs and arms poked out. Cas guessed it had fit perfectly a year ago. Silence fell as the nightgown was removed, a quiet filled with horror and pity. Clara was thin, covered with bites and scratches. Cas knew it should not have been a surprise given the state of her clothing, but it was. He was deeply and profoundly shocked. Even worse was seeing her stand there, shoulders hunched, shivering despite standing so near the fire. Faustina, unflappable, efficient, stood frozen, so Cas lifted Clara up by her armpits and said, "Come on, Clara, in you go."

He held her over the tub. Instantly, she yanked her feet high as though he were about to drop her into a pit full of snakes. He smiled reassuringly. "You'll like a bath. I promise." He lowered her into the tub. The expression on her face — filled with wonder and bliss — had him swallowing. He remembered his first real bath after the prison and plague. He had earned some money digging graves and had gone to the public baths. Hot water, soap, a little extra paid for the owner's daughter to cut his hair. It had felt like a small step toward his old life. Toward dignity.

Several women watched Clara with tears in their eyes. Recovering, Faustina reached for a cloth. The queen stopped her, saying quietly, "No, I will do it."

Queen Jehan had exchanged her traveling costume for a simpler, blue dress. She knelt beside the tub, opposite Cas, picked up a cloth, and began to wash the child.

Lady Rondilla hovered over her, arms folded. She was not one of the women with tears in her eyes. Her expression showed revulsion, and at that moment, she looked very much like her brother and twin, High Councilor Amador. Sharp-featured, dressed in black, a single heavy line between her brows. "Your Grace," she protested. "The child is filthy. Surely a servant—"

"I'm perfectly capable of giving a child a bath, my lady Rondilla." Queen Jehan's voice was mild. How did she feel, Cas wondered, knowing Lady Rondilla had nearly married the king? Would have married him, if not for Brisa's offer of peace.

"It is a commoner's task, not fit for a king's wife," Lady Rondilla said. "Not in this kingdom, at least."

Lena stood off to one side, pretending to eat the prince's small fist and making him giggle. At Lady Rondilla's remark, she looked over at Cas and crossed her eyes. Beside Cas, Ventillas tried to mask a laugh with a cough.

Cas barely heard him, his attention on the woman by Lena. She was not much older than Ventillas, small and pretty. Her dark hair looked as if it had been freshly brushed. It hung loose past her shoulders, so long it nearly touched the stones. She wore a white nightgown, similar to the one that had just been peeled from her daughter. Years had passed since Cas had last seen Lady Danna. She had been alive then. Not like she was here, pale and transparent among the living.

"Do you see me, Lord Cassia?" Lady Danna asked.

Cas looked away. He shook his head quickly, earning strange looks from Lena and his brother.

"A king's wife?" Queen Jehan repeated. Her tone was less mild. "Do you mean the queen, Lady Rondilla? Your queen?"

Lady Rondilla's lips thinned. "I only meant—"

"Am I only to be queen to a few? To the privileged and perfumed? Do I shun all others?"

Lady Rondilla turned crimson. "No, certainly not, Your Grace." A quick, barely respectful curtsy before she hurried away.

With Clara, Queen Jehan was gentle but efficient. Every inch was scrubbed. The water quickly turned a grayish brown. The queen had pushed up her sleeves, which made no difference because the entire front of her dress was soaked from Clara splashing about. Clara kept reaching for Cas' hand, then letting go when diverted. Her mother, Lady Danna, knelt beside the queen, unable to take her eyes off her daughter.

Lena appeared with an armful of clothing. "These are from Lady Sol's granddaughter. They might be a little large, but they should stay on."

Queen Jehan scrubbed Clara's neck, saying absently, "Lady Rondilla's ward is also five, dear heart. She will have something more suitable."

"I did ask." Lena's voice was neutral. "Regretfully, her clothing could not be spared."

The queen looked up at that, eyes narrowing. She made no comment other than to thank Lena.

The queen kept her words light as she bathed the girl, humming occasionally, and soon after, three musicians gathered and began to play. At the first sound of the lute, Clara, distracted by her ear being scrubbed out, bolted upright and stared, making those nearby laugh. She had not spoken a word beyond telling Cas her name.

Queen Jehan said, "Do you sing, Lord Cassiapeus?"

Cas opened his mouth, but before he could lie to his queen, Ventillas, playing a game of chess with King Rayan, answered. "Like an angel, Your Grace. If I had a brother to spare, I would have sent this one to the monks for their choir."

Cas glared at his brother, who grinned while the others laughed. Queen Jehan, smiling, said, "An angel? Then you must sing for us."

"Oh no. I'm not sure I remember —" His protests mattered to no one. Not even Lena, who put in a request. "Sing something cheery." Clara watched expectantly.

"Come, Lord Cassia," the head minstrel urged, "what will you sing? We will play along."

Cas had not sung in a long time. Not since he had set off with his friends on a journey that had ended terribly. He was not sure he *could* still sing. Or if his voice would fail him.

Lady Danna spoke softly. "Do you know 'My Horse Thinks He's a Prince'?"

Cas snuck a glance at her.

"It was Clara's favorite," Lady Danna explained.

Cas scratched the back of his neck. He said to the head minstrel, "Do you know 'My Horse Thinks He's a Prince'?"

"Ah!" the head minstrel cried. "I have seven children. Of course we know that one!" He snapped his fingers three times and the trio struck up the familiar tune.

Cas listened for the correct note and then began to sing. He repeated the song twice and the refrain three times. His voice carried no rust, as he had feared, and he found, strangely, that he was enjoying himself. Before the last note ended, the hall had erupted in applause and demands for more. So Cas sang "There's a Candle in My Ear," about a boy with too much earwax. Another suggestion by Lady Danna. The last was a request from Lena, "My Beard Is Longer Than Your Beard." Clara, sitting on a stool and wrapped in a giant towel, clapped her hands. Lena twirled Prince Ventillas in her arms, both of them laughing. She smiled at Cas, and he found he could not look away.

King Rayan applauded. "I would have given him up to the monks, Ventillas. Even without the spare." And Queen Jehan said, "That was very well done."

"Thank you, Your Grace."

Lady Danna had vanished from Clara's side. Cas searched the great hall but could not find her. She had gone as quietly as she had come.

One thing soon became clear. Clara's hair could not be saved. Most of it would have to go, Queen Jehan said. The knots were too many. Tangled, twisted, they could not be undone with a comb. It would take an age, and it would be painful. When Clara heard this, the tears began to fall. It was the first time she had cried. Cas' heart clenched when she looked at him, eyes wide and pleading. "Hair," she said.

The second time she had spoken tonight.

Cas took in the women around him, every one of them with long hair. Braided, twisted, rolled, pinned. Black, brown, white, and gray. Whatever the color, however groomed, it was their crowning glory. And it was *long.* Cas said to the queen, "Surely, Your Grace . . ."

"These knots cannot be undone," Queen Jehan said, regretful. "It would hurt her tremendously to try."

Lena returned the baby to Faustina. She knelt before Clara and said, with a bright smile, "What luck! Do you know, I've thought about cutting my hair too." She held up her braid. "It gets in the way of everything. *Such* a bother. But it is a big decision, I wasn't sure I was brave enough. Why don't we *both* cut our hair? I'll go first."

There was a shocked silence. Lena's hair reached past her waist, a rich, glorious tumble when she wore it loose. Even Queen Jehan murmured, "Analena."

Lena's voice was matter-of-fact. "It's only hair, Jehan. It will grow back if we change our minds." She brushed a gnarled strand off Clara's cheek. "What do you say? Yes? We'll look like sisters!"

Clara had stopped crying. She nodded uncertainly. A pretty nursemaid with hair-trimming skills was summoned to the task. Her name was Esti, and Cas, after a moment, remembered where he had heard the name before. Bittor on a pallet in Palmerin's great hall, talking in his sleep. Esti. This was Bittor's goddess. Sure enough, when Cas searched the crowd, he found the soldier leaning against a wall, watching the nursemaid with a foolish expression on his face. Cas shook his head and turned away.

Lena, as promised, went first. When the initial snip was made, several women flinched. Queen Jehan had to look away. Lena's hair was trimmed so that the waves fell just below her ears, exposing the nape of her neck. When she was done, Lena smiled at Clara and said, "See?"

Clara's cut mirrored Lena's. The little girl fell asleep on a pallet by the fire under Faustina's watchful eye. Lady Danna did not reappear. Once Cas was certain the girl was asleep, he grabbed a torch and picked his way past the bedrolls. Bittor had told him the library was at the back of the house on the first floor. Someone was already there, as he knew she would be. He could see the light of a candle flickering. As he drew closer, the light went out. Undeterred, he walked into a chamber where manuscripts and scrolls lay scattered on the floor, trampled and torn. He located the wisps of smoke coming from behind a table. Lena huddled on the floor, back against a wall, weeping quietly into her hands. Her shoulders shook. She didn't look up as he placed the torch in a bracket and sat beside her in the dust.

After a moment, he said, "You never once thought about cutting your hair, did you?"

"*Never.*" Lena spoke into her hands, her words muffled. "*Ever.* I loved my hair." A fresh round of sobbing commenced.

"Lena." And Cas, who did not like to be touched, wrapped an arm around her shoulders and pulled her close, tucking her head beneath his chin. "Why did you do it?"

A sniffle. "She looked so sad. And she's so small. Her family died when she was *four,* Cas. I don't understand how she could have been here alone all this time."

"So you cut your hair?"

"Yes." Lena wiped her nose with the back of her hand and brooded. "You think I'm vapid and shallow."

"I think you're beautiful," Cas said quietly. "I think you're kind."

Lena looked up, startled. Her face was splotchy, her eyes red. Her nose dripped, dripped, dripped.

"Well," Cas amended, patting around his tunic until he found a handkerchief. "You are usually beautiful."

Lena laughed. She took the handkerchief and dried her tears and blew her nose. It was made of white linen, with the letters *CP* embroidered on one corner. Cas of Palmerin. One of the many items that had appeared in his trunk, courtesy of the queen and her tailors.

They sat for a time in silence as the sounds from the great hall grew quieter. Lena spoke first. "Does it still hurt?" She was studying his wrists, where the sleeves inched back, exposing the scars.

Cas did not yank his sleeves down as he wished to. "No."

"They look like they're from chains."

"They are." From iron cuffs. From trying, whenever the guards turned their backs, to pull himself free.

More silence. "Have you always seen them?" She no longer spoke of chains.

"No," Cas told her. "When I woke at the hospital, they were there. Everywhere. I don't know why I can see them. I don't know why I can only see some of them."

Izaro had seen a spirit that Cas had not. Hundreds had been buried in Palmerin's plague graveyard, but Cas had not seen hundreds when he had gone to fetch his brother. Fifty only, no more.

"Do they frighten you?"

"At first," Cas admitted. "Most of them are confused. Or sad. They've never hurt me." He hesitated, wondering if he should tell her. "Clara's mother was kneeling by the bathtub."

Lena stilled. "Lady Danna?"

Cas nodded. "She was dressed in a white nightgown. She told me what Clara's favorite songs were."

"Is she still there? Or . . . here?" Lena searched the shadows beyond the torchlight. Her voice had dropped to a whisper.

"I think she's gone." He reached up, twirling a strand of her hair with a finger. "Why do you believe me? Why don't you think I'm mad?"

"Oh, I do think it," she assured him, and Cas smiled. "But this past year . . . I wonder if we've all gone mad, just a little bit."

"Lady Analena?" A serving girl had appeared in the doorway. "The queen is asking for you."

Cas slipped his arm away and stood.

"I'll be right there," Lena called back. The girl retreated but remained in sight.

Cas held out a hand and pulled Lena to her feet. "Good night," he said.

"Good night." Lena's hand fell away from his. She offered him his handkerchief back, laughing a little when he said, "No thank you." He watched her go, navigating around ruined books and forgotten scrolls, until she was out of sight.

***

In the morning, Clara led them to the food stores. Accessed through an opening in the kitchen floor, they had been overlooked by pillagers, mercifully preserved so that a little girl would be able to feed herself for a year. There was very little left. Upstairs, Cas found the space she had made for herself in the attic. More blankets, a doll, a small painting of a woman in a yellow dress. Lady Danna.

When the train departed, Clara rode with them, an official ward of the court. She brought her doll and her painting and left everything else behind.

# 23

C AS TOSSED ANOTHER branch onto the fire as dusk settled over their camp in the woods. Colorful tents filled the clearing, along with the chatter of many. The smell of roast pig wafted pleasantly from cookfires. When a lady came by holding a small boy's hand, Cas rose from his crouch and offered a polite greeting.

The boy was about five, Clara's age, his attention focused on the stick of sugar cane in his hand. At first glance, sugar cane might be mistaken for a piper's pipe; the size and shape were similar. But this pipe had been chewed nearly flat, sucked dry of every last bit of sweetness.

The woman said with an indulgent look at the child, "I promised him a treat if he was good today. He does not forget a promise."

She wore a hooded cloak. Beneath it, her face was narrow; deep grooves bracketed her mouth and creased her forehead. She might have been twenty or forty. Time and again, he had seen how the pestilence had left its mark on the living, so that the young appeared old and the old appeared desiccated. Try as he might, he could not recall her name.

"I don't blame him," Cas said with a smile. Smiling came easier with each passing day, he had found. The way things do with practice. Like singing in front of others. Or tolerating Bittor. "My father used to bring them home whenever he visited the southern isles.

Enough for every child in the keep. We nearly mauled him at the doors when he walked in."

She reached into her cloak, pulled out a stick of sugar cane, and offered it to Cas. "It's from my family home in the south. The purest cane in Oliveras."

"I can't take your son's treat, Lady."

A laugh. "Oh, there's more where this came from. Please take it." When Cas held up a hand, refusing, she returned the cane to her cloak with good grace.

What *was* her name? "My apologies, I don't remember . . ."

"Lady Noa," she said, her smile showing no insult was taken. "We met at the keep, though I cannot blame you for not remembering. What a time you've had of it, Lord Cassiapeus."

Cas sighed inwardly. He truly hated that name. He gestured toward the fire and the stool beside it. "Please."

"Just for a moment." Lady Noa seated herself while her son flopped down on the grass by her feet. The boy had curly brown hair and round cheeks, red from the cold. Cas wished the same for Clara. Good health and few cares besides a treat freely offered. He could see Clara now, walking hand in hand with Lena toward the cooking tent. Lady Noa brought his attention back to his own fire. "I've never been to the mountains before."

"Do you like it here?"

"It is cold," Lady Noa confessed, and Cas smiled again. "But beautiful. There are colors here one does not see on the islands."

A chill wind sent leaves scattering through the clearing. Cas tossed another stick onto the fire. "You'll only see the flame trees in the mountains." Here in the woods, they were surrounded by them. "It's my favorite season, autumn."

"We don't have seasons as you do here. We have rain, or we do not have rain. Have you been to the southern islands?"

"Not yet, Lady."

"Well, when you do, you will stay with us. Our home is open to you, Lord Cassiapeus. Agreed?"

*Our home.* Cas tried to conjure up an image of Lord Noa and failed. He had been away from court too long. "Agreed."

"Good."

Her hood covered much of her hair. Cas had thought it blond at first, rare in a kingdom where black hair was dominant. But it was white. Cas had seen such a thing before: a person's hair changed in a day, color and life gone from it. He did not have to ask Lady Noa if she had suffered some great loss. The answer was there. On her face, her hair, for all to see. It was only when she reached up to touch her hood self-consciously that he realized he was staring.

Cas bowed. "Apologies. I didn't mean to be rude."

"There's no need. My hair was as dark as his, not too long ago." Lady Noa reached down, smoothed her son's curls absently. The boy licked his fingers clean. "Loss is a part of life, my lord Cassiapeus, and grief is constant. It is unbearable at first. Then you find you can indeed bear it. Over and over again. As many times as necessary."

His parents, his friends, his freedom. Looking into the fire, Cas said quietly, "Yes."

The boy threw the mangled sugar cane into the fire, setting off sparks, and demanded, "More!"

"Of course, darling. Here, have two." Lady Noa retrieved two canes from her cloak. He snatched them from her without a word of thanks, and Cas felt his eye twitch. "I really shouldn't indulge him. It's nearly supper."

Around them travelers settled in for the evening. Laughter amid crackling fires. A whistling wind. Cas was glad for the warmth of his cloak, the sleeve of which Bittor had mended beautifully. Just then, someone called out in the distance. One voice joined by others. Gradually, their shouts formed a single recognizable word: *Luis!*

Lady Noa's head turned at the sound. Her expression changed. All traces of sadness vanished. She rose, her words brisk. "Time to go now, darling."

The little boy had also turned toward the cries. He stood, sugar cane clutched in each fist. "Mama," he called, his back to Lady Noa.

*Mama?* But wasn't Lady Noa . . . ? Cas looked at the boy. He looked at Lady Noa, who smiled.

She said softly, "I wanted to meet you, my lord of Palmerin. I was curious. And upset, I will admit it. I did not like having to flee your city in such a way. It was undignified."

Cas held himself very still as she spoke. Lady Noa no longer sounded as though she were from the southern islands. The lilt to her voice had gone. Her accent was of the north, the far north, in the kingdom of Brisa.

"Lady Mari."

Her smile grew. "Did your queen like the dress I made for her? We chose the silk together. What I would have given to have seen her face." Her smile vanished. "Do it now."

She had not spoken to Cas. He started to turn, sensing someone behind him, but before he could, pain exploded between his eyes and he felt himself falling, falling, as the fire went out.

\*\*\*

When Cas came to, he found himself flat on his back by the fire. Ventillas and Lena looked down at him with dual expressions of panic. Ventillas was yelling, something about sugar cane.

Cas tried to sit up, which made his brother's face split from one into two. "Stop. Shouting."

"Here, let me help you." Lena's arms came around his shoulders. She hauled him upright and did not let him go.

"The sugar cane, Cassia." Ventillas crouched before him, his tone urgent. "Did you eat any of it?"

"No."

Relief flooded his brother's face. Before Cas could ask him what had happened, Ventillas jumped up, swung onto a horse, and was gone.

Mere feet away, the doctor knelt on the ground beside the boy, Luis, who vomited in the dirt. The sounds Luis made turned Cas' stomach. His sugar canes were on the ground. One uneaten, the other half-chewed. A man and woman hovered, the woman crying, "Luis, Luis, oh, my baby." The man looked the way Cas felt, as though he had just been hit on the back of the head.

The doctor stuck his finger down the boy's throat. Luis vomited some more. The sight of it cut through the haze in Cas' mind. He turned to Lena.

"Poison?"

"We think so, yes," Lena said, pale but for two angry streaks along her cheekbones. "The doctor thought the sugar cane smelled strange, and poor Luis was turning purple." Lena glanced at the discarded canes. "He was playing with the other children. The nursemaid said she turned her back for a moment and he was gone."

Cas remembered the sugar cane he had refused. Had that been poisoned too? Lena helped him to his feet. He staggered over to the doctor and said, "He's had more than that." Cas gestured at the half-eaten sugar cane. "At least one. He threw it in the fire."

The doctor nodded grimly. The woman wailed even louder. "Will he die, Doctor?"

"I don't know anything just yet, Lady. I don't know what's been put on the sugar cane. There's nothing left in his stomach now. Let's hope it is enough."

A hand on Cas' arm. Queen Jehan stood there, white-faced, holding a sleeping prince against her shoulder. "I heard some of what happened." She inspected the back of Cas' head, hissed in sympathy. She eyed Luis with trepidation. "Poison, they said? And by a woman? What woman?"

Three guards fanned out behind her. Close enough to hear everything. Now was not the time to mention Lady Mari. "She said her name was Lady Noa."

A glance exchanged between Lena and the queen, who said, "*That* is Lady Noa." The wailing woman had gathered Luis into her arms.

"I must go to her," Queen Jehan said. "Lena, take Ventillas . . ." She trailed off, eyes riveted on the discarded sugar canes in the dirt. "What are those?"

"Sugar cane." Cas winced at the pounding between his eyes. "The doctor thinks they were poisoned."

The queen looked horrified. She thrust the prince at Lena. "Take him!" Lena barely had time to juggle the baby in her arms before the queen whirled around, picked up her skirts, and ran. After a shocked moment, one guard followed. Two stayed behind, for the prince.

Cas said to a wide-eyed Lena, "Stay here!"

Cas went after the guard who ran after the queen. He stumbled more than he ran. What had frightened her? She headed for the royal tent at the very center of the camp. He saw her fling aside the opening and disappear within, the guard following. A cry rang out. In the seconds before he saw her again, his imagination ran rampant. She had been stabbed, bludgeoned, set afire. Lady Mari had lain in wait and killed her friend.

Cas charged into the tent. The sudden stop made his head swim. The guard grabbed his arm — Cas would have fallen otherwise — and they stared in horror at the scene before them.

Queen Jehan knelt on the rugs with Faustina in her arms. The nurse shivered uncontrollably, her face drenched with sweat and her queen's tears. Her white wimple lay on its side nearby.

Cas kept his voice quiet. "Get the doctor." The guard bolted.

"It's just the two of us now, Faustina. Please, please do not leave me here." Queen Jehan kissed the nurse's hair.

Faustina's words were faint. "Jehan. Forgive her."

"I won't. Not ever."

"Jehan." The nurse's eyes closed and the only sound left was that of the queen weeping.

Clutching his head, Cas crossed the tent and knelt by the queen. A stick of sugar cane lay beside the wimple. No sharp-eyed physician had found Faustina in time to force the poison from her body. She was gone. Beside her was a small mountain of coins, as though someone had upended the entire contents of her purse. Cas picked one up. It bore the royal emblem, the bull and the flower. The opposite side showed a god with two faces, one looking forward to the future, the other looking back to the past.

Zacarias, god of beginnings and endings, in all their forms.

## ❧ 24 ❧

FOR CAS, it was the longest night in recent memory. Lena burst into the tent, holding the prince. Cas watched each horror register in her eyes — the nurse, the sugar cane, the gold coins — before she took over.

He found himself pushed into a chair directly outside the tent. Lena placed the sleeping prince in his arms. She spoke urgently. "Cas, I can't have the baby in there. I'm not sure it's safe for him."

His head throbbed. "Why not?"

"There's a strange smell . . . that sugar cane . . ." Distress cracked her voice. "Will you stay here with him? I need to help Jehan."

"Yes."

Lena kissed the baby's cheek and tugged the blanket up around his ears. "The doctor will come look you over soon. Your poor head! The guards will stay here." She looked behind her, received grim affirmation from Captain Lorenz, Bittor, and a dozen others before turning back to Cas. "Don't let anyone take Ventillas, do you understand? He's safe only with you."

"I understand, Lena. Go."

She placed a hand against his cheek, and then she went. Beyond the guards, a crowd watched and whispered in the light of a blood-red moon. Horses thundered past, soldiers called out to one another, as the hunt for Lady Mari raged on.

The doctor hurried over with his physician's box. He entered the tent first, and then, when it became clear his services were not needed, he returned to tend to Cas. He poured something bitter-smelling onto a cloth and pressed it against Cas' wound. The sting of it had him growling, but quietly, because he didn't want to wake the prince.

The doctor, too, minded his volume. "This will need sutures."

Cas had suspected. He nodded.

"Best to hand the prince off. You don't want to drop him."

"He stays with me."

Captain Lorenz was close enough to hear. He came over with a torch, giving the doctor the light he needed to do his work. While the doctor readied needle and thread, a nursemaid braved the wall of guards and came up to Cas. Her eyes were red from weeping. Faustina had been a mother figure, not just to the queen. Her name was Esti, he remembered. She had cut Lena's hair. Clara's, too.

Esti said, "I will take him for you, Lord Cassia."

"No." Cas held the prince closer. Esti hesitated and then melted back into the crowd.

Cas felt the scrape of a blade as a patch of hair was removed behind his right ear. The needle stung and was followed by the unpleasant tug and slide of threaded catgut. He gritted his teeth through the pain. Captain Lorenz shifted, still helpful to the doctor with his torch, but Cas knew he was ready to catch the prince should he drop him.

Prince Ventillas was a welcome distraction. Cas studied every inch of his little face. His black hair, as straight as Cas', though finer. The sweep of his lashes, the tiny, pointed chin. *So much danger around him,* Cas thought, before gasping at a particularly sharp tug of catgut. Captain Lorenz glared at the doctor, who murmured apologies.

The doctor worked quickly. It was not long before he said, "It's done," and began to pack up his box.

"You're all right, lad?" Captain Lorenz asked. When Cas answered yes, he moved away to speak with some guards, taking the torch with him.

"How is the boy?" Cas asked the doctor. "Luis?"

"Better. We will see." The doctor closed the box and hurried off in the direction from which he had come. The weeping had stopped inside the tent, or at least quieted enough that Cas no longer heard it.

Bittor came over and offered a flask. "Water," he said.

Cas hesitated.

Bittor tipped the flask back and drank. He offered it again. "Only water."

"Sorry." Cas shifted the prince to one arm. He took the flask and drank. "Thank you."

"You're right to be careful. That is one crazy woman on the loose." Bittor took the flask and went back to his post.

The prince woke briefly. He looked blearily at Cas, who looked blearily back. Cas was reminded of their first meeting on the shores of a lake back home. "So here we are again," he said, before the baby closed his eyes.

That was how King Rayan found them. He had joined the search early and had not heard what had happened in the royal tent. The guards moved aside so that he could ride through. He dismounted before Cas, who saw the fear in his eyes.

"Where is she?" King Rayan asked.

"The queen is safe," Cas assured him quickly. "Lena is with her. But Faustina was killed, Your Grace."

King Rayan inhaled sharply. Cas did not hear him exhale. He passed a hand over his son's head and Cas' shoulder before he slipped inside the tent.

***

In the end, three men were captured and questioned. All of them strapping brothers from a nearby farm whose sole job was to lead the king's men on a merry chase. Who hired them? Why, a woman wearing a hooded cloak. She did not give her name. They knew nothing about poisoned sugar cane. They did not even know what sugar cane was. Why had they agreed to such idiotic, suspicious employment? Well, because of the gold. Each brother held up a familiar coin.

They swore on their mother's life that they had not hit Cas. They quaked when Ventillas loomed over them, glowering. Two of the brothers wept, blubbering into their hands.

"It sounds so stupid I think it must be true," Ventillas said later, when he and Cas were alone in his tent. Lena had finally returned to take the prince from Cas.

"What will you do to them?" Cas asked.

"I haven't decided."

They stood by a table looking over a map. Neither had removed his cloak. "She escaped through here." Ventillas pointed to a crevice in the mountains, one even narrower than the Desfilad. "She didn't bother to hide her trail. By the time we tracked her it was too late. She had gone through one of the caves. We lost her there."

Cas eased himself into a chair. "How does a Brisan find her way through our caves?"

"She must have a guide. Someone who knows our mountains." He glanced at Cas. "Likely the same person who nearly knocked your head from your shoulders."

Cas tried to ignore the throbbing in his skull. "She walked right into our camp with sticks full of poison."

"Faustina couldn't resist the sugar cane," Ventillas said. "Queen Jehan made sure there was a ready supply on the ship. Lady Mari knew this. Even I knew this."

"What about Luis? Why would she hurt the boy?"

"A diversion?" Ventillas pinched the bridge of his nose, a sure sign of headache. "I don't know. Maybe she is just cruel."

Lady Mari had been smiling, even as she offered poison to a child. "Was she cruel before? What was she like?"

"She was not," Ventillas said after a moment. "She didn't want to be in Oliveras. I do not blame her for it. She came because it was her duty to come. Our exchanges were civil, and I like to think that, in time, they would have been more than that. But she was devoted to Jehan. And she loved Faustina." He stopped, his expression one of sorrow. "What she did, it is as unthinkable as you raising a hand against Master Jac."

Something Cas would never do. Under any circumstance. "She's smarter than us, Ventillas. She's escaped three times now."

Ventillas threw himself into a chair and brooded. "It's an embarrassment. But she's made mistakes. She shot the wrong nurse. She did not anticipate you showing up and saving the prince's life. I'll wager she did not like being chased through the streets of Palmerin."

No. Lady Mari had said as much. "She still escaped."

"One day she won't. She'll make another mistake, Cassia, and it will be her last."

The tent flap lifted; Bittor poked his head in. "My lord Ventillas, the king wishes to see you both."

***

They gathered before the king and queen: Cas, Ventillas, Lena, and High Councilor Amador. Lena and King Rayan stood near the rug where Faustina had breathed her last. There was no sign she had ever been there. No sugar cane. No wimple. The gold coins had been cleared away. There were no strange smells in the tent either, if one did not count the heavy cloud of camphor hanging over the high councilor.

No one sat, for Queen Jehan was on her feet, pacing restlessly before her chair. Her tears had dried. A quiet anger had settled in their place. The moment Cas and Ventillas appeared, she stopped pacing. She did not waste words.

"She has slipped through our fingers once again, Lord Ventillas. It will be the last time. Lord Cassiapeus, what did she say to you? I want her words precisely."

After a quick glance at Lena, who offered a weary smile, Cas told the queen everything, from the moment Lady Mari walked up to his fire with Luis. "She said she wanted to meet me. She was curious, and displeased about being chased out of Palmerin. She said it was undignified." Cas hesitated before forging ahead. "She asked if you liked the dress she had made for you, and told me that you had chosen the silk together. She said she would have given much to have seen your face."

Queen Jehan's eyes were as cold as winter's river. "There's something else you wish to say. Say it."

Lord Amador stepped forward. "Your Grace, the boy—"

"Are you Lord Cassiapeus?" Queen Jehan did not look at him.

Lord Amador clamped his mouth shut and bowed his head.

Cas said, "She's toying with us, Your Grace. With all of us, but especially Ventillas, and you most of all. I wonder if we should look at this a different way."

"And what way is that?"

Cas glanced at Ventillas, whose face gave away nothing. "We know Lady Mari is behind this. She answered to the name. The question is no longer *is it Lady Mari?* But *why is she so upset with you?* You, and the people who traveled with you? I think we must look deeper."

No one spoke or objected, so Cas continued. "She was ill when you last saw her. Too ill to care for herself. Which means someone may have helped her, sheltered her. Someone knows what happened. If it were me, I would ride to the hospital in . . ." He could not for the life of him remember the name of the town.

"Gregoria," Lena provided.

Cas bowed his head in thanks. "In Gregoria, and start there."

Queen Jehan's gaze settled, for the briefest of instances, on Ventillas. A look that was not missed by the king, who said suddenly to Cas, "Then that is what you'll do. You'll leave at dawn."

Cas said, "I— Your Grace?"

"What do you mean, Rayan?" Queen Jehan said, taken aback.

King Rayan did not look at his wife. "It has long been a tradition," he said, "for the king of Oliveras to appoint a queen's man. A man he trusts without question, whose first duty is to protect his queen. Is that not so, Analena?"

Lena's answer came slowly. "Yes, Your Grace."

"Good. Then I would be pleased if you would accept this role, Cas of Palmerin, in service to me."

Cas saw it, the look of dismay on Queen Jehan's face, before it vanished just as quickly. Ventillas showed no visible reaction. He did not have to. Cas knew his brother. He was as unhappy as the queen. Forcing Cas to ask himself, *Why?*

Lord Amador made no effort to hide his displeasure. "Lord Cassia is still young. A boy untried. There are far more suitable —"

"Are there really?" King Rayan said, his expression sardonic. "*Far* more suitable? Where are they? Sitting on their hands, it seems to me, allowing this woman to run rings around them." A searing contempt encompassed both the high councilor and Ventillas, who kept his head high even as a vein throbbed at his temple.

"I choose a *boy* who survived a Brisan prison with his soul intact. I choose a *boy* who saved my son before anyone else could pull off a boot. It is the *king* who chooses, not the overly ambitious high councilor. Tell me, Lord Amador, who am I?"

Lord Amador quaked. The high councilor dropped to one knee, head bowed. "You are the king, Your Grace. Forgive me."

King Rayan said, "Do you have any objection, Jehan?"

Queen Jehan looked at Cas. The tear tracks were still visible on her face. Just outside the tent, her old nurse lay cold in a horse cart. "No," she said at last. "Lord Cassiapeus is a fine choice. Let him find her. Let him put an end to this, for good."

Cas bowed. He tried not to look as overwhelmed as he felt. "Then I accept, Your Grace. I am humbled by the faith you place in me, and in my family." His antipathy toward the queen had thawed.

He could not despise someone who treated Clara as kindly as she had. But she was hiding something. He did not trust her. And neither, he thought, did the king.

A small box sat on a table. Lena brought it to King Rayan, who removed a gold ring and offered it to Cas. It bore the royal insignia, the bull and the flower. Cas slid it onto the middle finger of his right hand. It was slightly loose, which seemed to cheer Lord Amador, who had shuffled off to the side.

"Take this." Ventillas removed one of his own bands, held it out. "It will anchor it."

Cas took their father's ring and put it on. A perfect fit.

"That settles it," King Rayan said. "Cas, you'll leave for Gregoria at sunlight. Take whomever you wish. People you trust."

Cas did not look at Lena. "Whomever?"

The king paused. His gaze flickered toward his sister. "Whomever."

Lord Amador was the first to depart. Queen Jehan held Cas back long enough to say, "If you find her, Lord Cassiapeus . . . I loved her once. If it is possible, please do not harm her."

***

"Take this." Ventillas handed Cas a dagger.

Cas took it without speaking and strapped it to his belt.

It was dawn. They were by the horses. Alone, but not for long. Lena and Bittor approached from the far side of the camp. Cas had asked them both to come. Lena, because where would they be if she had not discovered the ships' inventory in the first place? Nowhere. This was her history to write. And he suspected she would not allow herself to *be* left behind. As for Bittor . . . well, Cas didn't know why he had invited him — he just had. He would likely come to regret it.

Most of the travelers were still asleep in their tents or wrapped up in blankets by small fires. Sleepy-eyed servants went about their early morning tasks, carrying buckets of water and armfuls of wood.

"Take this, too." Ventillas produced a pouch heavy with coin. "Master Jac sent word to the countinghouses, so they know you're alive. If you need more, show the ring."

"I know how a countinghouse works." Cas took the pouch, tucked it safely within the saddlebag strapped to his horse. When he turned back, his brother was frowning at him.

"What is it now?" Ventillas demanded, looking as bad-tempered as Cas felt.

*Nothing* lay on the tip of Cas' tongue, but Lena and Bittor had stopped to exchange words with a soldier. They were still out of earshot. Cas said, "What aren't you telling me?"

A guarded expression came over his brother's face. "About what?"

Cas wanted to shake him. But that would have hurt Cas more than his brother. His head pounded. "I saw the look the queen gave you. When I mentioned the hospital. Is there something I should know about Gregoria?"

"No."

Cas pulled his gloves on. *"Really."*

"Cassia. *Enough.*" Their snarls were attracting an audience. Two boys carrying rabbits walked by, their steps slowing and their eyes wide with interest.

"Fine. Don't tell me." Lena and Bittor were nearly upon them. Cas swung onto his horse and looked down at Ventillas, feeling a terrible sense of dread. "But whatever you're not saying, the king suspects. Brother, be careful."

## 25

THEY RODE EAST, past abandoned fields and empty farmhouses. Past olive groves, neglected and overgrown, the trees dotting the landscape in a distinct crisscross pattern. There were signs of graves everywhere if one cared to look. Sunken earth unmarked by headstones, the grass above impossibly green, fertilized by copious amounts of flesh and blood and sorrow. In some towns, the spirits outnumbered the living.

The farther they traveled, the more it struck Cas what a marvel Palmerin was. The city had not escaped death. The plague graveyard would always serve as a reminder. But the number of dead in relation to the living had been astonishingly low. *This* was the landscape he was accustomed to. Not the miracle that was his ancestral home. *Miracle.* Cas shied away from the word. It had been a long time since he had believed in miracles.

Three nights passed. They stayed at inns for two of those nights and camped beneath the stars on the third. As they rode past another deserted village, Bittor very helpfully informed him of the dangers of being a queen's man. It was a unique court position in that, although Cas had been appointed by King Rayan, his loyalties were to the queen first and foremost. Even if her wishes did not align with the king's.

Cas tried to unravel that convoluted knot. "That isn't good."

"It can be very bad," Lena agreed. She wore a hooded blue cloak, protection against the cold. Somehow, she had ended up on Cas' mare. "If you're not careful."

"Why didn't you say so before?" Cas said to her, askance.

"When? Who could have known Rayan would ask you? There hasn't been a queen's man in Oliveras for a hundred years."

"That's because most of them were killed," Bittor remarked. "No one wants the work."

"I remember a book in my grandfather's library . . ." Lena's expression turned thoughtful. "There was Queen Isabella's man. He murdered the king's favorite mistress because the queen wished it. I think he was beheaded."

Bittor mused, "Wasn't his horse beheaded too?"

"Yes!" Lena snapped her fingers and pointed at Bittor. "I'd forgotten! His horse was also killed, and both heads were left on pikes outside the castle."

Bittor whistled. Cas reached up and touched the tender skin at his throat.

"Then there was Queen Sophia's man," Lena continued. "He made the mistake of falling in love with his queen. The king, understandably, was displeased."

"That will not happen here," Cas said decisively.

Bittor asked, "Did he get the pike too?"

"No. He was castrated."

Cas and Bittor exchanged a startled glance and sat up very straight in their saddles.

"There are others," Lena said. "I'll have to go back and see. I'm sure Rayan forgot it was a cursed position when he offered it to you. It was a horrible night, after all."

Bittor glanced sidelong at Cas. He said dubiously, "Maybe you'll have better luck."

Beheadings. Castrations. Pikes. Cas could only hope.

\*\*\*

On the fourth day, they arrived in Gregoria. Once a bustling university town, it was now quiet. More than half the population had perished, Lena told them as they rode beneath the city gates.

They found the hospital near the University of Oliveras; it had been built to serve the needs of the young scholars and their teachers. A carving above the doors promised to treat the sick, the poor, the old, and the infirm. Inside, it was a large, airy space, elegant archways and windows set high in the stone. Beds lined the walls, sheets crisp and white. Most were empty. A nurse admitted them, then left to search for her superior, Sister Roslyn.

The hospital in Brisa had looked and smelled nothing like this. Cas remembered waking on a filthy pallet in the corner. There had been no sheets on the beds for those fortunate enough to have beds. Blood and worse had covered the stones. And the keening. It had been unspeakable. Cas stared off into the past, not realizing Sister Roslyn had arrived until Lena nudged his arm.

Sister Roslyn was not as helpful as they had hoped. "I arrived ten months ago," she explained, a brisk, tidy woman not much older than Ventillas. Her robes were the vivid yellow of an egg yolk. Her wimple was the king's blue. It was short and pointed, secured beneath her chin with a ribbon. "I was not here when your Lady Mari was admitted. It would have been very different then. Every bed filled. Patients on the floor. An equal number of the dead outside, with no one left to bury them. We lost most of our staff. Nurses, doctors, orderlies, gone. That is why I was sent here."

No different, then, from the hospital in Brisa. Disappointed, Cas said, "The previous head nurse died?"

"Not a nurse. The hospital was run by a doctor. He did not die. He . . . left."

"Why did he leave?" Lena asked. "When?"

"He was gone when I arrived. As to why, I could not say." Would not, Sister Roslyn's expression very clearly indicated.

Cas tried a different path. "Do you keep records of your patients?"

"Yes, of course." Sister Roslyn looked relieved at the change of topic. "Please follow me."

She led them through the ward, past the beds and nurses. They dressed similarly. Yellow robes and pointy blue wimples. One nurse had bent to lift a chamber pot from the floor. She caught sight of them, watched their approach until a patient drew her attention away.

Bittor spoke out of the side of his mouth. "She looked like she recognized you. Do you know her?"

Cas shook his head. He'd never seen her before.

Sister Roslyn brought them to a small alcove that held a desk and shelves. She pulled a ledger off a shelf and set it on the desk. "These were meticulous once. See here?"

They crowded around. Sister Roslyn had opened to a page dated just before the pestilence had struck. The entries were tidy, full of useful information: the patients' names, where they lived, the nature of their ailments, the treatment advised by the doctor. A receipt of payment followed each entry, along with the date the patient left the hospital's care.

When Sister Roslyn turned a few pages, Cas saw the difference right away. The entries grew less detailed. Sometimes only a name. Before long, even the names disappeared. In their place were tally marks, hastily scratched in, the ink smeared and careless.

Cas said, "One mark, one patient."

"Yes," Sister Roslyn admitted quietly. "As I said, we were overrun."

Bittor had moved away to lean against the wall and fold his arms, watching the other yellow-clad sisters tending to their patients.

"Sister," Lena said. "Is there anyone left on your staff from before? Someone who might remember?"

Sister Roslyn turned a thoughtful eye to the other nurses. "Sister Ivette was here. One moment, please."

As soon as she was out of earshot, Cas said, "What is she not telling us about that doctor?"

"I don't know," Lena said. "But this hospital has a royal charter. It's wealthy. You would not leave voluntarily if you were in charge here."

"This place makes my flesh creep," Bittor said.

Sister Roslyn returned with the nurse who had taken an interest in them earlier. The one with the chamber pot. Her name was Sister Ivette. She could not have been more than a few years older than Cas. There was no sign of the briskness evident in her superior. She was shy, soft-spoken, the sort of kindly nurse one would wish to have if one had to be in a hospital.

Lena questioned her. She described Lady Mari as she would have looked a year ago, not as Cas had seen her. A pretty young woman, richly dressed, speaking with a Brisan accent. Did Sister Ivette recall anyone who fit her description?

"It was a terrible time." Sister Ivette's voice faltered. Her eyes were cast down; her lips trembled. "I'm very sorry. I don't remember her."

"She would have been brought in by Lord Ventillas," Lena said. "Commander of the king's army. A hard man to forget once you've seen him."

"I did not see him."

"Truly?" Lena said pleasantly. "Then how do you explain this?" A leather cord, barely visible, hung from Sister Ivette's neck. Lena reached out and tugged sharply. A pendant came into view. No, not a pendant. A gold coin with a hole punched through for the cord.

"Lady Analena!" Sister Roslyn objected. "You have no right to —"

Cas was at the end of his patience. "That coin was to be a wedding gift for the king. It was one of many. They were left with Lady Mari, sewn into the lining of her dress. How do you come to have one, Sister Ivette?"

Sister Roslyn, bewildered, fell silent. The younger nurse had slapped a hand over the coin and stumbled from Lena's reach.

Lena stepped toward her, her voice sharpening. "Queen Jehan left her friend here. What happened to her?"

Sister Ivette looked behind her, but Bittor had shifted to the alcove's opening, blocking her path. When she turned back, an ugly look twisted her face. "She's no queen of mine. Her lady can rot with all the rest of them for all I care. Brisan filth."

"Sister Ivette!" Sister Roslyn exclaimed, shocked.

Cas said, "We'll be sure King Rayan knows how you feel about his queen. The lady asked you a question. Answer it now."

At the mention of the king, Sister Roslyn paled. Royal disfavor would mean terrible things for the hospital. She gripped Sister Ivette's elbow hard enough to make her flinch.

Sister Ivette yanked her arm free and rubbed it. "They came during a rainstorm. A soldier brought her." A sullen glance in Cas' direction. "He looked like you."

"My brother," Cas said for Sister Roslyn's benefit.

"He asked that I send him word. If she died, if she didn't, and he left payment for her care. I didn't know about the coins in her dress," Sister Ivette added resentfully. Sister Roslyn listened, her expression furious.

So did Lena. "And did you? Care for her?"

"There was nothing to be done. She was like all the others." Sister Ivette looked away. Cas thought he saw the briefest glimpse of shame. "One night, the doctor came by. He took her."

Sister Roslyn's lips parted. No sound emerged.

Cas tried to make sense of it all. "The doctor who used to work here?"

Sister Roslyn answered reluctantly. "Before I came to Gregoria, a doctor named Saulo ran this hospital. Until it was discovered he . . . did things to his patients."

Uneasy, Bittor said, "What sorts of things?"

"Experiments. Tests. Surgery," Sister Roslyn said. "Tests that had nothing to do with their ailments. One of the sisters reported him, but he must have been warned" — she sent an accusing look toward Sister Ivette — "because he vanished before the guards could arrive. I was sent to replace him."

Cas turned to Sister Ivette. "What do you mean he took her? Did he pay you?" Her silence was her answer. Incredulous, he said, "You *sold* the queen's closest friend to a *lunatic doctor?*"

"She was nearly dead," Sister Ivette protested.

"Which means she was still alive," Lena said, outraged. "When did he give you that coin?"

Sister Ivette shoved the pendant out of sight. "He came sometimes, very late. He took others. The nurses who worked those hours . . . he was good to us." She did not look at Sister Roslyn, who regarded her with revulsion. "That night, he paid me with this."

*Others,* Cas thought. Then, "When did you last see him?"

"Several months ago. He's never stayed away so long."

"Where does he take them? Where does he live? Do you know?"

Finally, Sister Ivette met his eyes. The tears began to fall. "He has a house in the hills. Not far from here."

## ❧ 26 ❧

SISTER ROSLYN RODE an ancient nag that wheezed and shuffled, slowing their pace considerably. She had insisted on accompanying them. The disgraced Sister Ivette shared a horse with Bittor. She wept the entire way. For his part, Bittor endured the pointed wimple that batted unceasingly against his face, poking at his nose and obscuring his vision. Under any other circumstance, the sight would have provoked Lena to laughter. But there was no sign of her good nature here. She rode beside Cas, every inch of her radiating anger.

They left Gregoria behind and traveled into the hills. Eventually, Sister Ivette pointed to a crumbling stone wall covered in vines. When Cas brushed them aside, he discovered an opening where a gate must have once stood. Beyond the wall was a muddy path, and at the end of the path was a cottage. White stone, a thatched roof. One look and Cas knew they were too late. There was no smoke from the chimney, though the day was a cool one. The front door stood wide open. As they rode closer, a pair of genets raced out of the cottage and up a tree, pointed muzzles and spotted coats disappearing into the leaves.

Cas asked Sister Ivette, "Does anyone else live here?"

"No," she mumbled.

"Family? Servants?"

"No one."

They tied their horses to a fence post. Cas reached for his mace, Bittor his sword, and with their weapons drawn, they entered the cottage, Lena at their heels. Even with the door open, the smell was hard to bear. *"Ugh!"* Lena slapped a hand over her mouth and nose. It was too much for Bittor. The sisters had crept in last. He barreled by them before emptying the contents of his stomach all over the front stoop.

A man lay dead on the floor. Eyes filmed over. Staring up at the beams. A leather apron covered his tunic and trousers. Whoever had stabbed him through the leather had left the dagger behind, protruding from his chest. Beside him was a table. What would have looked to Cas like any other supper table, except for the chains dangling from the corners. Sister Roslyn crossed herself.

Cas said to Sister Ivette, "Is this him?"

"Yes," Sister Ivette answered, eyes riveted on the doctor. The sight of him had stopped her tears.

Lena spoke through her fingers. "How long has he been . . . ?"

"Months? I'm not sure." Cas surveyed the rest of the chamber. A single room with low beams and steps in a corner leading below. Dark cloth had been nailed to the windows. The only light came from the open door. Hundreds of jars sat on a wall of shelves, big jars, little ones. In them were terrible things floating in thick, murky liquid.

Cas drew closer, fascinated and repulsed. The archive at Palmerin carried all sorts of books and manuscripts. He had spent many hours poring over the keep's medical treatises, for what could be more intriguing to a young boy than drawings of severed body parts and human organs?

Hearts and kidneys filled these jars. Human heads with milky, unseeing eyes. A single hand. A pair of feet. The doctor had not limited himself to man, Cas realized, when he spotted the jar holding a lynx cub. There were mice, turtles, ducks, genets. And in one jar, near the end of a row, something he could not identify.

Lena came up beside him. She grabbed his sleeve and whispered, "What is it?"

Sister Roslyn also stepped closer, peering into the jar. She stumbled back with a cry.

Lena reached for her, alarmed. "Sister?"

Stunned, Sister Roslyn said, "It is a woman's . . . It is a womb."

\*\*\*

Bittor could not enter the cottage. He tried again, and Lena showed him the womb. He fled. Out of sight this time, but the retching sounds were unmistakable. A soldier who reacted poorly, delicately even, to gore. Privately, Cas wondered at his decision to join the army.

Sister Roslyn, after one frozen moment gaping at the shelves, rounded on Sister Ivette in a fury. She struck the younger nurse twice across the face — "You wretched girl! You spawn of snakes!" — before Cas caught her arm and pulled her out of the cottage. Lena dragged the wailing Sister Ivette out as well.

Bittor sat on the ground by the horses. Cas hustled Sister Roslyn his way. "Will you keep them apart? She might kill her."

"Fine." Bittor wiped his mouth with his sleeve. "Anything but going back in there."

Sister Ivette crumpled beside him, crying into her hands. Sister Roslyn stalked off some ways to stand beneath a tree, her back to them.

Cas turned to Lena. "Stay with them. I'm going to look around."

Lena did not bother to argue. She gave Sister Ivette the evil eye, then simply turned on her heel and entered the cottage again, leaving Cas no choice but to follow.

***

Cas stepped around the doctor and examined the restraints on the table. Rust coated the iron cuffs, along with blood turned black with time. His mind shied away from the horrors that had taken place in this chamber.

Lena's eyes had filled with tears. Not all of them, Cas knew, were due to the stench. "He kept her here," she said. "Hurt her. All this time."

"Yes."

Lena snuck a glance at the womb. She shuddered. "Maybe it isn't hers." Then, "What am I saying? If it isn't Lady Mari's, it is someone else's." She regarded the doctor with loathing and said very softly, "I want to burn this house down."

The cuffs made him think of his own imprisonment. The shackles, the beatings. He had gone mad for a time, and he suspected his suffering had been nowhere near as wretched as Lady Mari's. He said, "Then let's burn it down."

They regarded each other across the table, and Lena saw that he meant what he said. She nodded slowly. "Then let's burn it down."

Outside, the weeping continued, followed by Bittor's bad-tempered "Oh, pipe it, won't you? If there's anyone who should be crying, it's me."

Cas found a candle on its side on the floor. "But first" — he indicated the stairs — "let's see what's down there."

***

There were no bodies or jars in the lower chamber. There was a bed, a chair, and a table piled high with books and parchment. A trunk had been placed at the foot of the bed.

And there were chains.

Three sets attached to separate walls. Lady Mari had not been the only person imprisoned here. Sister Ivette had sent others.

Cas set the candle on the table beside a ring of keys. For the cuffs, he guessed. The candle was made of cheap tallow. It offered a stingy yellow light and plenty of smoke.

Lena kicked at some chains and sent them rattling. "Where do I start?"

"The trunk?" Cas suggested. "I'll look through these."

Cas sifted through medical books and anatomical sketches, but could find nothing that told him where Lady Mari might have gone from here. Disappointed, he looked beneath the table and, to be thorough, checked under the chair. Lena had discovered her grandfather's inventory tucked behind the wheel of a carriage, he remembered. But he found nothing.

"Look at this!" Lena knelt by the open trunk. Cas hunkered down beside her. She held up a dress that had once been very fine, blue silk trimmed with black lace.

"The buttons are missing," he said, noting the rips and tears.

"A dress like this would have had silver buttons, or enamel. Maybe even seed pearls. They would have been easy to carry and easy to sell."

"Lady Mari's?" He eyed the three sets of chains. The dress could have belonged to someone else.

"Let me see." There was a brief rustling as she turned the dress inside out. "Yes! Look, the lining's been ripped free. This was where they hid the coins."

"What's this?" An object glinted on the floor, in the narrow space between trunk and bed. Cas reached for it. The square box, made of solid gold, fit in the palm of his hand.

"It's a portrait box!" Lena exclaimed.

Cas' mother had owned such a box. Hers had opened to a miniature of his father painted on the inside of the lid. The box had also held a lock of hair from each of her sons, snipped when they were babies.

Cas undid the clasp. He angled the lid toward the sputtering candle. He barely heard Lena's gasp, so loud was the buzzing in his head.

A portrait had been painted inside the lid. It was of a young woman, unsmiling but lovely, dressed in full court regalia: a white dress and robes, a crown, a scepter. Beneath the painting was an engraving. *For Rayan, My Husband, My King. Honor, Faith, Fidelity.* And a name: *Jehan of Brisa.*

Only the woman who gazed out at them was not the person Cas knew as Queen Jehan. This was the archer who had shot an arrow across a lake. Cas had chased her through the streets of Palmerin. The woman in this portrait had shared a conversation with him by an open fire, even as she poisoned an innocent boy and the nurse who raised her.

# ❧ 27 ❧

KING RAYAN HAD married the wrong woman. Unknowingly. He had fathered a child, the heir to the throne, not with Princess Jehan of Brisa, but with her friend Lady Mari.

And Ventillas had known.

His brother had left the real princess at the hospital, and then he had kept his silence. Had stood quietly by as his king — his friend! — married an imposter. Not a word had passed through his lips when their son was born and named for him.

Prince Ventillas.

Cas lurched to his feet. He was trembling. *Brother, what have you done?*

Lena rose too, slowly. "That isn't Jehan." She regarded the box in his hand as though it were some sort of incendiary. One that would go off at any moment, destroying everything it touched. "Is it?"

He did not answer. Lena was studying his face. "You recognize her. Is she . . . *Cas*. Tell me what I'm seeing is wrong."

Before he could speak, the box was plucked from his grasp.

"What's this?" Bittor squinted at the miniature. His other hand was pressed up against his nostrils, trying to block bad smells. Seconds later, the hand fell away. He glanced up, frowning. "Who is this?"

"Give it to me." Cas snatched at the box.

Bittor was fast. He held it out of reach, turned toward the

candlelight, and read the inscription beneath the portrait. "This isn't Queen Jehan. Who . . ." Cas saw the moment the truth hit him. Bittor's mouth hung open. Nothing came out.

Lena turned in a slow circle, studying the chains on the walls. "This is why she hates them. They stole her name, her life."

Cas could think of nothing beyond Ventillas, both parent and brother. What would the king do once he saw the miniature? No friendship could survive a betrayal such as this. Ventillas would lose his head. It would end up on a pike for the lammergeiers and the crows. Lord Amador would make sure of it.

"Bittor, give me that box."

"Why?" Bittor backed away, toward the stairs. "What will you do with it?"

Lena collapsed onto the lid of the trunk. "How did she think she could get away with such a thing?"

Cas said, "Bittor —"

"Cas, you can't destroy it." Bittor shoved the box into his cloak. There was pity in his eyes. He knew what this meant for Ventillas.

"I won't —"

"I can see it in your face. You will." Bittor stopped as his boot hit the bottom step. His expression changed. "The treaty. What will happen to it?"

Lena lifted her head, eyes wide. That part had not occurred to her. There were too many layers to this disaster.

Cas cared about only one of them. "I don't want to hurt you. I need that box."

"No. You may be the queen's man, but I am not —" Shock flickered in Bittor's eyes. It was only then that Cas realized he held his mace with both hands. He did not remember reaching for it.

"Cas!" Lena cried. "What are you doing?"

The shock did not hamper Bittor's reflexes. When the mace swung toward him, his sword was there to stop it.

The next few minutes passed in a blur of steel and a flash of iron. Cas could have been back in prison. Fighting without thought. Intent only on survival. But this time he was not fighting for himself. The shock had gone from Bittor's face, replaced by a tightlipped anger. From somewhere far away, Lena screamed at them to stop. The box was knocked free of Bittor's cloak . . . and swept up by Lena.

Cas stopped.

Lena looked at him as though she had never seen him before. Angry color slashed her cheekbones. "You would have killed him." She stood next to Bittor, who was bent over, gasping for breath. Blood trickled from his ear and down his neck. The sight of it sickened Cas.

He dropped the mace. "No."

Bittor snarled, "Liar!"

"Was I next?" Lena demanded. "The sisters? All your witnesses gone?"

"No!" Cas protested, horrified that she would think it. That she had cause to believe he would harm her. "Lena, I need time to warn my brother. Please —"

"Then go!" She pointed to the stairs. "*Warn* him. But you won't take this with you."

Lena and Bittor watched Cas with suspicious eyes. They did not know what he would do. They did not trust him anymore. His sutures had opened. He could feel the blood oozing into his sweat. A sourness clung to his skin, not to be blamed on the foulness wafting from above. He recognized the smell. Fear had its own peculiar stink.

"They will kill him," Cas said.

Tears sprang to Lena's eyes. "This is beyond us, Cas. It's not for you and me to decide what is to be done." She held up the gold box. "This belongs to the king. He will decide." She tucked the box into her cloak and ran for the stairs.

"Lena!" Cas did not charge after her. He was not so far gone as that. But he turned to watch her go, heartsick, and in that moment of inattention, Bittor brought the hilt of his sword down onto his head.

*** 

When Cas came to, he found himself alone. He sat up, groaning at the pain in his skull. Chains rattled. Cas lifted his hands, staring openmouthed at the iron cuffs around his wrists.

Bittor had chained him to the wall.

The candle sputtered across the chamber. Burned down to a stub. It would go out soon. Beside the candle were the keys, freedom, only his chains did not extend so far. He could not reach them.

Cas listened. Now, when he would have welcomed it, there was no weeping coming from above. He called out, "Lena?"

Nothing.

Louder, he said, "Bittor! God rot you! Get down here!"

Nothing. The smell of death drifted down the stairs.

"Sisters?"

No one answered, though he continued to call out, yanking on his chains and fighting a terrible panic. *Bittor Lena Sisters!* became *Lena Lena Lena!* She did not come. The cuffs sent him back to prison. His arms turned bloody trying to break free, and his voice went hoarse from screaming. She had left him here knowing what she knew. Having seen the scars, the branding on his wrists.

The candle flickered. It went out. Cas was left with his chains in the darkness. And something deep within him died.

***

"Cas?"

He turned his head, blinking at the sudden blinding light. He was huddled in a corner, arms wrapped around his knees. He could not stop shivering. The light came closer. A face appeared.

Lena.

A shocked whisper. "You're hurt." She knelt before him, reaching for hands gone sticky with blood.

"Don't touch me." He recognized that voice. Hoarse, lifeless, it came from a time before. Lena froze. He said, "The keys."

"Yes, of course." Lena jumped to her feet. The flames swung wide as she searched the room.

"The table."

Lena snatched the keys, speaking in a rush. "I didn't know he had cuffed you. I came back as soon as I heard." She placed the torch in a wall bracket. That was when she saw the vomit by his feet. Cas lowered his head. After a moment, he heard her say softly, "Hold out your hands."

Later, he would remember that she was crying. It took several tries before she unlocked the cuffs. Her hands shook. "Your head. Your poor wrists. I have bandages. Let me —"

Cas staggered to his feet. He braced himself against the wall. "Where is he?"

"Riding for Elvira. He has the box." Lena rose, stepped away. "When he caught up with me, he said that he had left you here, that the sisters were to let you go after a few hours so that you would not stop us from reaching the king. I turned around right away. I went to the hospital first, but those wretched sisters! Sister Ivette is in jail, and Sister Roslyn forgot all about you —"

"I don't care about the sisters. Where is my horse?"

"Outside this whole time," Lena admitted. "Cas. I am so desperately sorry."

Cas did not care if she was sorry. He thought only of getting to his horse and riding to Elvira. Ventillas would need him.

Lena watched him make his way to the stairs. "It's not safe for you to travel alone. You're hurt. Please let me help you."

Cas turned. He wanted to make sure she heard him. "You've helped enough, Lady. Don't come near me again."

She looked stricken. He left her there. Upstairs, the doctor lay on the floor. Outside, the moon settled high in the night. There were two horses. He untethered his mare and rode away without a backwards glance.

## ⤜ 28 ⤛

I N THE CAPITAL city of Elvira, Cas learned what it was to be out of favor with the king.

They would not let him beyond the palace gates. He, a lord of the realm, who had always been granted a guest chamber when he had visited with his brother, could go no farther than the jagged teeth of the portcullis. He had given his name, his title. He had flashed the rings on his hand. It made no difference. Even worse, the Palmerin soldiers were also shunned. They had been relegated to the outer barracks by the wharves, where the soldiers for hire usually slept.

"What can you tell me?" Captain Lorenz said when Cas tracked him down. They stood on the quay, the air smelling of seawater and rot, and watched the fishing boats return with the day's catch.

"Very little," Cas admitted. Two nights had passed since he had left the doctor's house of horrors. He had been forced to stop at an inn along the way. His mare had needed the rest. So had he. The innkeeper — a cheerful, inebriated man — had tended to the wound on his head. Cas looked behind them at the tumbledown barracks and felt a simmering anger. That the men of his city, loyal men, fighting men, who had protected the king and his family in Palmerin, should be treated this way. And it was all his brother's doing. A soldier, no matter the rank, shared in his lord's glory and in his disgrace. "What happened when you arrived?"

"Nothing out of the ordinary," Captain Lorenz said as a rat scuttled by. He kicked it, sending it flying into the water, where it landed with a splash. "We rode up to the palace, settled in the barracks there. Lord Ventillas took up his usual rooms. There was a feast to welcome the king and his family home. Everyone went back to their beds full of wine and food. Then your friend Bittor —"

"He's not my friend." Cas' teeth set.

A sideways glance. "Then the soldier Bittor tears into the courtyard, looking as though he'd been beaten by some very large men." Another assessing look. "Same as you. Everything changed after that. A note came from Lord Ventillas instructing me to comply with whatever the guards demanded and to await further orders."

"He'll send further orders?" Cas could have sunk to his knees with relief. That was a good sign. An *excellent* sign. It meant Ventillas wasn't chained up in some dungeon somewhere, tortured and maimed.

Captain Lorenz was quiet. "The note said to wait on orders from you, lad."

*Me?* Cas' heart plummeted. Panic wrapped around his throat, a chokehold. And the captain, who had known him all his life, missed nothing.

"Does he need rescuing?" Captain Lorenz asked, all practicality. "I have a plan."

"No." Cas looked again at the dingy barracks and the palace, high atop the hill. "I can tell you this, Captain, and trust in your silence. We're the ones in the wrong here. Ventillas has broken his oath to the king."

Captain Lorenz was shaking his head. "I can't believe that."

"Do you think *I* want to?" Another rat appeared nearby, this one sniffing around some discarded fish guts. "I'm not certain it can be made right. I'm going to try."

Silence. "Are the men in danger?"

"From the king? No," Cas said with absolute certainty.

"Are you?"

Cas hesitated. It had not occurred to him to wonder. "I don't think so."

"That is not comforting, Cassia." Captain Lorenz cupped his hands around his mouth and blew warmth into them. "I'll have the men work on drills. It will keep them out of trouble. We have your trunks here. Where do I send them?"

"Nowhere. I'll stay here."

Captain Lorenz said, askance, "This is no place for a lord of Palmerin."

"For you either, Captain. I'm not sleeping at an inn. If the men are here, then this is where I'll be."

\*\*\*

*I grew up in my grandfather's house, a small one in the middle of Elvira where the booksellers keep their shops.*

It cost him a half civet, paid to a young apple seller, to learn where the king's sister lived. Dusk had fallen by the time Cas found the townhouse in Elvira's central parish. The building was made of stone, tall and narrow, with a green door.

Cas did not knock or even approach the house. Instead, he crossed the street to a shop that was shuttered for the day. He settled in to wait.

Lena could not have been too far behind him. If she had followed the same route. If nothing had gone amiss. It was the last part that frightened him.

Cas was not a good person. Maybe before his imprisonment. He had been different then. Now he was the sort who deliberately infected men with plague. The sort who left a lady behind to ride alone, knowing full well the dangers that travelers faced, women in particular. And what about Bittor? His almost friend? Cas did not like to think what would have happened if Lena had not stepped between them. He thought he knew the answer, and it shamed him.

Two men on horseback cantered by. Lena's green door opened, but it was only a servant come to light the outer lanterns. Cas rubbed his hands together for warmth as the rain began to fall. Thankfully, the shop's roof jutted out overhead, protecting him from the worst of it.

This parish suited her. The street was full of bookstores and parchment sellers. The shop behind him sold bottles of fine ink. Cas could imagine her growing up here, easily.

An hour passed, then two. The rain grew heavy before finally tapering off. A rider appeared.

Surely she could hear Cas' heart beating all the way from here. Lena did not see him. She rode past the green door, dismounted before the stable gate, and pulled on a rope. A bell rang out. "Why, Lady Analena!" a man exclaimed when the gate opened. "But . . . are you alone? Where are your guards?" The man stuck his head out and looked up and down the street. Cas drew deeper into the shadows.

"It's just me." Lena's voice was quiet, weary. She said something else, too soft for Cas to hear. They disappeared behind the gate, leaving Cas alone in the night.

It was all he had come for. To see for himself that she made it home. But as he walked away, he only felt worse. Thinking of his last, bitter words to her. Wishing he could take them back.

*You've helped enough, Lady. Don't come near me again.*

\*\*\*

For the next ten days, it was the same. Cas slept in the barracks with his men. In the morning, while the others trained in a field just outside the city, he opened his trunks and dressed in clothing fine enough to be received at court. Black from head to boot. Best not to provoke anyone by wearing Palmerin red. From the dingy waterfront, he rode his horse to the palace gates and presented a note to be delivered to the high steward.

*Lord Cassiapeus of Palmerin, who is honored to have been of some small service to the royal family on the prince's naming day, humbly begs an audience with his sovereign and lord, Rayan.*

Cas signed the note and sealed it with his father's ring.

He waited all day, outside, for ten days. Standing apart from the others who also desired an audience with the king. Merchants and diplomats, officials from all over Oliveras and beyond. They were admitted. Cas was not. At dusk he was ordered to leave by guards who knew who he was and could no longer meet his eyes.

Once, Cas saw Lord Amador. The king's high councilor rode up on his horse, grim and humorless. He stopped just inside the gates and stared across at Cas. It took everything in Cas to stand tall and wipe his expression clean of all but contempt. Lord Amador would not see his desperation. That was the one thing Cas could control.

Finally, looking vaguely disappointed and without speaking to anyone, the high councilor turned his horse around and went away.

Each morning before he presented his note, Cas scanned the assortment of heads that had been left, piked and rotting, high on the city walls. He did not see his brother. He did not see his queen.

And this was the one thing that kept him from utter despair. There was no denouncement of the queen. He listened as others came and went. They spoke of her often. She was there in the palace, going about a queen's normal business. Accepting homage, for herself and for the prince. Sitting by the king's side each night as the welcoming feasts went on.

Cas slept poorly, and not only because of a thin mattress crawling with ticks. He no longer dreamt of rocks and drowning. He dreamt of Lena. He dreamt of Ventillas kneeling before a cheering crowd, an axe at his neck.

On the eleventh day, Cas did not make it to the palace gates. He had left his horse behind to be exercised by one of the soldiers. No sense in both of them standing about in idle misery. As he strode down a busy city street, only one removed from the palace, a cloaked figure stepped from an alley. Just long enough to show Cas he was there. Cas followed him, wending his way around piles of trash and swarming flies. Bittor drew back his hood, and they proceeded to glare at each other in mutual antagonism.

Bittor said, "You're an idiot, do you know that?"

Instantly riled, Cas opened his mouth . . . and snapped it shut. It was the truth. Bittor, more than most, had the right to tell him so.

Bittor threw his hands up. "Nothing to say? What a surprise."

Cas forced the words past his lips. "I am sorry."

Bittor sputtered. "That's all? *Sorry?* You nearly decapitated me with that stupid mace!" He pointed an accusing finger at the weapon strapped to Cas' back. "A mace, Cas! A spiked one!"

Cas, after a moment, said, "I am very sorry."

Bittor looked disgusted. "The king isn't receiving your notes."

Cas was silenced. "Who is?"

"Who do you think?"

High Councilor Amador. Cas ground his teeth.

"Lord Amador doesn't like you," Bittor said. "Lord Ventillas is, was, too high up in the king's confidences. And you were not far behind."

"Where is my brother? Have you seen him?"

"I haven't, but he's well enough. I know one of his guards. They have him in one of the old tower rooms. He's not allowed to send or receive messages. The king is still deciding what to do with him."

Cas sagged against the wall in relief. He would admit it to himself and no one else: he was shocked his brother's head was not on the city wall. "And the queen?"

Bittor did not answer right away. He looked troubled. "In front of others, they are the same. I think he doesn't know what to do with her, either."

The weight of it all settled between them, for that was King Rayan's dilemma. To denounce his queen was also to denounce his son. The treaty would mean nothing. War would come once again to their kingdom.

"What about Lady . . . Princess Jehan?"

"There's no sign of her. As usual. She's like an eel, that one."

Cas' next words were difficult. Swallowing his pride felt like swallowing knives. "Can you get me past Lord Amador?"

"No," Bittor said, and Cas looked away. "He's under the impression that we are friends, and I am being watched." Bittor peered past him to the street. "Hence the secret alley meeting. But you know someone who can help you."

Cas, understanding, shook his head. He could not ask Lena to help him. Not after the way they had parted.

"Do what you like," Bittor said. "I don't know if she'd help you anyway. She went back for you. Was frightened for you. And you left her behind, all alone, to ride home in the dark."

There was something in Bittor's voice. Past the anger. Cas had seen Lena ride up to her house. But he had not *seen* her. A chill stole over him. "Was she hurt?"

Bittor flicked up his hood. "See for yourself. Or not." He stalked off, leaving Cas in the filthy alley. Cas stepped into the street and waited until Bittor was out of sight.

Her grandfather's house. The house with the green door. Cas ran the entire way.

*** 

Cas was gasping for breath by the time he arrived at Lena's. The serving girl who opened the door gave him a wary look as he gripped the door frame with both hands. He could barely state his business. But his name was enough for entry into the solar while she went to find her lady.

Cas paced in circles around the chairs and tables. He would never forgive himself. Bittor had said she had been hurt. A dozen possibilities sprang to mind. Filled with self-loathing, he clutched his head in his hands as he considered each one.

"Are you well, Lord Cassia?"

The serving girl stood in the doorway. He had no idea how long she had watched him pacing and grabbing at his hair. Her expression said she had not just arrived.

He dropped his hands. "Perfectly."

The skepticism remained, but she informed him that Lady Analena would see him in the library.

Cas found Lena standing by a round table. With her were six old men in blue robes, each, it seemed, determined to grow the longest beard and the bushiest eyebrows. Spread before them were several dozen illuminated manuscripts. Cas inspected Lena as closely as he could from the opposite side of the table. She, too, wore robes of midnight, the collar rising to her ears. Whatever injuries she had suffered, the ones Bittor had hinted at, must be covered up, hidden behind all that cloth. Anxiousness and sweat trickled down his back.

"My lord Cassiapeus." Lena's expression was sober, her voice distant. Her hair had been brushed into two cloudlike puffs above her ears. A slender silver circlet sat on her brow. There were shadows beneath her eyes. She looked a far different person from the cheerful courier who had once stolen his horse. "Welcome."

Cassiapeus, not Cas. Those days were over.

"Lady Analena." Cas bowed, greeting the men as they were presented to him. All royal historians, as he had guessed. Guild masters.

When Lena finished introductions, she asked, "How may I help you?" The six old men listened expectantly.

Cas said, "Ah . . . I thought we might speak privately."

Silence. Bushy eyebrows drew together in disapproval. One historian eventually answered. "That is highly irregular, my lord Cassiapeus," he chided. "For a lady to converse with a man without a guardian present. Surely you know this."

Cas looked at him. He looked at all six of them. Another historian chuckled. "He means a young, handsome man. We don't count, clearly."

"You may speak freely here," Lena said, unsmiling. She indicated the note in his hands. "Is that for me?"

Cas held it out across the table. "I hoped you might see it delivered. On my behalf."

Lena took the note. She studied the name written on it, turned it over, examined Cas' family seal in the wax. There was a twitching and shifting among the historians. A few suspicious looks were thrown Cas' way. They were unused to seeing Lena so reserved, Cas suspected, and were now wondering what he had done to deserve it.

Lena lifted her head. She met Cas' gaze directly and nodded once. "I understand its importance. I'll see it's delivered into the right hands."

"Thank you." Then, because there was no other way and he had to know, "Bittor said you were injured."

As one, the six historians turned to Lena, alarmed. After a startled moment, understanding and irritation settled over her features. "He said those words to you? I was injured?"

Cas was beginning to harbor a terrible suspicion about Bittor. He thought back, revisiting their exchange in the alley. His hands curled into fists. "He implied it." That Bittor was a dead man.

Lena tapped the note against an open palm. "He enjoys needling you. As you know. I am perfectly well, Lord Cassiapeus. Thank you for your concern, and your visit." Her words held a dismissal.

Stung, Cas bowed. "I'll see myself out. Lady Analena, sirs." He made it to the doorway before he turned back to her. Their eyes met across the library. And he thought that, for the briefest span of time, she did not look at him as though he were a stranger. Cas no longer cared who heard. "Forgive me," he said quietly, and left.

Cas did not return to the palace that day. Instead, he joined his brother's men on the practice field, where they stayed until the sun dipped low on the horizon.

It was there that they heard the news from travelers leaving the city. The queen was to go south in the coming days, to winter at the palace there. Just the queen and the prince and the servants. King Rayan would visit when time permitted.

Cas knew then that her punishment would not be a public denouncement. It would be a permanent estrangement from the king. It would be exile.

When Cas returned to the barracks, he found a royal messenger waiting impatiently by the quay. Cas was to appear at the palace the following morning. Lena had not forsaken him. He had been granted an audience with the king.

## ✄ 29 ✄

"**D**ID YOU KNOW?**"** King Rayan asked.

Cas stood before his sovereign in the great cavernous throne room of Elvira. No one else was present. "Your Grace, I swear I did not."

King Rayan wore robes of deep blue and a crown that sat heavy on his head. There was nothing of the good cheer and informality he had shown at Palmerin. Today, he looked tired and angry. And sad.

"He said he wanted only to end the war. This is what your brother said to me. What is your opinion? Is this reason enough to betray your king?"

The throne itself was made of silver, the cushions blue. The head of a bull had been carved onto each arm. They looked directly out at the king's audience, at Cas, scowling and furious.

"I have not spoken to Ventillas." Cas chose his words with care. "All I know is that what he did, however misguided" — here, the king snorted — "it was not done in malice, toward you. That is not in him. All his life, he has only ever wanted to serve his king and his kingdom."

Fingers drummed along the arm of the throne. "Instead he has done the opposite."

*Careful. Be silent be silent be silent.* But this was his brother's life, after all. And the time for silence had passed.

Cas bowed his head. "With respect, Your Grace. You have a queen you care for. A son who is healthy. Oliveras is at peace. An enemy would not wish these things for you."

The drumming stopped. "How pleasant you make it sound," King Rayan said in a soft, scary voice. He leaned forward, glaring down the length of the steps that separated them. "Tell me, Lord Cassiapeus, what happens when Brisa sends their ambassadors to our kingdom? They will surely notice something amiss. What happens to my queen then? To my newfound peace?"

Cas had no answer to that nightmare. "Is it why you're sending her away?" Seeing the king's expression, he said hastily, "Forgive me. It's not my place to speak."

"No," King Rayan agreed flatly. "I received your note. You're here to request your boon."

"I am."

"Well, then." King Rayan waved a hand, permission for Cas to continue.

Cas clasped his hands behind his back. "I ask that the punishment levied against Palmerin's soldiers be stopped. That they be allowed to ride home, immediately and without prejudice."

A frown drew the king's brows together. "How are they being punished?"

Cas was startled. Did he not know? "They were removed from the royal barracks nearly two weeks ago. We've been staying by the harbor."

King Rayan's eyes narrowed. "The mercenaries' barracks? That flea pit?"

The same. Cas resisted the urge to scratch his neck. "Yes."

"You've been sleeping there as well?"

"I have."

"I was not aware of this." King Rayan yanked off his crown and tossed it over a bull's head. He shook his hair out with both hands. "The men may leave for Palmerin when they wish, without prejudice."

"Thank you, Your Grace."

"Don't thank me yet. We both know this is not worthy of a boon. You saved my son's life. So let us begin." The king sat back in his throne. "I will go first. Lord Ventillas is to be exiled from Oliveras and all its territories for no fewer than twenty years."

Cas fell back a step, stunned. It was not a beheading, but it was close. "An ambassadorship," he countered, trying to keep his voice from shaking. "Three years."

"What sorts of tutors did you have in Palmerin?" King Rayan asked, incredulous. "An ambassadorship is an honor, not a punishment."

"A punishment this severe will have everyone asking what his crime was," Cas pointed out. "Do you truly wish that question asked?"

King Rayan glared. Half a minute passed before he spoke again. "Fifteen years. An ambassadorship."

*No!* Ventillas would be in his forties by then. An old man, a relic. "Fifteen years is a life gone. I am owed *a life*." His voice trembled on the last two words.

King Rayan resumed drumming his fingers. "This is how you would use your boon?"

"Yes."

Here the silence dragged on even longer. King Rayan turned away, to the tapestries covering the wall. Cas was shocked to see the Palmerin tapestry. Six feet in height, two hundred paces long, it hung in the center. A place of honor.

"My first impulse was to burn it," King Rayan said, seeing Cas' expression. "As you said, I do not want certain questions asked." He propped a hand on his chin, deep in thought. Finally, he stated, "An ambassadorship. Five years. To be funded from his purse, not mine. That is final," he added very quietly, when Cas would have protested.

Five years. Cas closed his eyes. When he opened them again, he said, with difficulty, "Thank you, Your Grace. I'll inform the men they're free to leave. I'll send word to Master Jacomel."

King Rayan regarded him with a frown. "You have not been punished. You may ride with them. Tell Master Jacomel yourself."

Cas looked at the rings on his right hand. The royal emblem, anchored by his father's seal. It was not just for Ventillas that he had come. "I am the queen's man. My first duty is to see her safe. When she rides south, I will too."

King Rayan stared at him. "Your service was requested under false pretenses. I will not hold you to it."

"She's still my queen. That hasn't changed. And Lady Mari . . ." Cas did not know what to call her. "She is still out there."

King Rayan's face tightened in anger. "Do you think I would send my family off without protection?"

"No," Cas said immediately. "Of course I don't. Only . . . she's found a way through our cracks, more than once. I worry she'll try again. Your Grace" — Cas bowed deeply — "I will keep them safe for you."

For one terrible instant, King Rayan's heart lay bare for Cas to see. Pain and rage. A terrible despair. Cas had to look away. "You may go," King Rayan said to him, and Cas bolted.

*** 

"I'm being sent to some godforsaken island called Coronado," Ventillas said.

Cas had never heard of it. "Where is it?"

"West," Ventillas said with a shrug. He was thinner than Cas remembered. His eyes were bloodshot. Like Cas, he wore black. "That's all I know. It's to be a new ambassadorship." His lips quirked. "Death might have been the better choice."

"Don't joke." Cas threw himself into a chair opposite his brother. They were in Ventillas' chamber at the palace, which looked like a room set aside for unwelcome guests. Rickety furnishings, threadbare rugs. The cups on the table were heavily chipped. The fire in the hearth could have been extinguished with one well-aimed glob of spit. It was cold in here. There were bars on the windows and burly guards outside the door. "Why did you do it?"

Ventillas reached for his mug with a sigh. "When we brought Princess Jehan to the hospital, I did not think she would last the night. She had the boils, she was bleeding . . . Every symptom of the pestilence, she had. And I knew then that it was over. With her died any hope for peace." He shifted in his chair. It creaked alarmingly under his weight. "Father died because of the war. Grandfather, too. I have lost countless men, and I was *sick* to death of it. When Princess Jehan asked Mari to take her place —"

Cas bolted upright. "*She* asked Lady Mari?"

"Yes," Ventillas told him. "Princess Jehan was dying. She wanted an end to the war as much as the rest of us. What do you say to a friend's dying wish?"

"You say no."

Ventillas regarded Cas over his cup. "Well, Mari said yes. And so did I. I swore I would keep their secret. I knew it meant lying to Rayan. I did it anyway."

"*Why?* One envoy visiting from Brisa and we are doomed. How did you think you would get away with it?"

"I wasn't thinking," Ventillas said, his expression full of self-disgust. "Clearly. At the time, it felt like a risk worth taking. I would never have done it if I'd known you were alive. I would not have risked your home."

Cas stood up, restless. "Palmerin's still ours."

*For now,* his brother's expression said. "I am sorry, Cassia."

Cas went to stand by the fire. "Faustina and Abril had to stay silent too."

"Yes," Ventillas admitted. "Faustina was no trouble. Abril had a hard time with it."

Cas thought about the sad, quiet artist who had not wanted to share her story with Lena. Now he knew why.

The fire was worthless. Cas fetched his cloak off a hook and put it back on, which amused his brother. Returning to his chair, Cas said, "If this was what Princess Jehan wanted, why is she so angry?" Before the last word was uttered, something occurred to him.

Cas reached into his cloak and pulled out a gold coin. The queen had given him the three coins in Palmerin. She had not asked for them back. He set it on the table so that the two-faced god Zacarias was visible. One face looking forward to the future, the other looking back to the past. The god of doorways and transitions, of new beginnings. Seeing the image now put it in a sinister light. He tapped the coin in wonder. "Two faces," he said.

Ventillas nodded. "She's been terrorizing her friend. Taunting her by leaving these coins for her to find. Her body may have healed, Cassia, but her mind has not."

The rumble of voices outside the door quieted their words for a time. Ventillas held his cup with both hands, not drinking, only looking down into its contents, lost in thought.

Cas had dropped his head into his hands. "Five years, Ventillas. How am I supposed to manage without you here?"

"I was eighteen when Father died and Palmerin became mine. Remember?"

Cas lifted his head. His age now. Could that be? "You seemed older."

A small smile. "Because I had to be. I had a little brother who had lost everything. Except me."

Cas could not speak. His throat felt raw. A great pressure was building behind his eyes. "The king might have agreed to three years if I'd pressed him. I should have pressed."

"Stop," Ventillas ordered him softly. "He might have changed his mind entirely and been within his rights. I have not been a good friend to him. I will regret it always." He set his cup down. "I'm grateful for what you did, don't think I'm not. But I'm glad to go."

Cas scrubbed at his eyes. "Why?"

"I've not felt . . . myself this past year. It feels like someone else is living in my skin and I just . . ." Ventillas pressed a hand against his heart as though he longed to rip it free. "I need to go."

"Kemen." Cas thought of his brother's friend standing outside the plague graveyard at Palmerin. *Don't let Ventillas come again. Please, Cassia. He's here almost every night. It is not good for him.*

"He stayed behind at Palmerin while I traveled to Brisa, and he died before I returned." Ventillas looked into the fire. "We are not promised a long life, Cassia. Just a life. Take what happiness you can. Hold tight to it."

Cas very carefully did not think of Lena. "I just came back. And you'll go."

"I'd take you with me if I could. No," Ventillas added at Cas' look. "I can't. You belong here."

It had only been an idea, briefly considered. "I know it."

Ventillas stood. "Master Jac will watch over Palmerin. Captain Lorenz will take charge of the men. You'll have to go home occasionally. The people need to see you."

"I understand."

Cas helped his brother pack. No servants were sent to assist. A knock on the door brought a wooden box. It contained the king's seal, which Ventillas would need abroad. No gold, though. The king had meant it when he said Ventillas would be paying his own way. A sheaf of parchment relayed information on his new post. Ventillas glanced at it briefly, then set it aside.

Cas, thinking of the queen and the prince, asked, "Do you think he'll keep them away forever?"

"I don't know," Ventillas admitted. "He loves her, anyone can see that. I'm not sure it will be enough."

\*\*\*

Ventillas departed in the predawn hours with only Cas to say farewell. The king had forbidden anything more. Ventillas reached down from his horse and clasped Cas' arm one last time. "I'll be at the harbor in Trastamar five years from today. Today, Cassia. Come and get me."

"I'll be there. Go safely." Cas stepped back. He tucked away his grief for later and sent his brother off with a salute, a smile.

Ventillas glanced upward at a window where a figure stood watching. He bowed his head, a farewell to his king, then turned his horse and was gone.

## ❧ 30 ❧

THE FOLLOWING DAY, once again in the early morning hours, Cas watched as Captain Lorenz led the Palmerin soldiers out of the city. The captain carried a letter to Master Jacomel, one Cas had promised to send if his return would be delayed. It would be. For how long, he did not know. Only when the last man in red had vanished did he turn away. He rode his mare to the central parish where the booksellers kept their shops, and stopped before a house with a green door.

Cas did not knock. Not at this hour. He dismounted and went around to the stables, where he found a young groom carrying a bucket full of oats. Catching sight of Cas, the boy lowered the bucket to the ground.

Cas pressed his face into the mare's neck, heard her nicker in response. She had been a good friend to him. "Goodbye." He offered the boy the reins. "She's for your lady. Tell her . . ."

The groom took the reins and smiled at the horse. He waited.

"Tell her I said thank you. Tell her I said goodbye."

"Will you leave your name, sir?"

Cas gave it, along with a silver stoat that had the boy grinning in surprised delight. Shoulders hunched against the cold, Cas left for the palace on foot.

***

In the palace stables, his ring secured him a handsome bay with a shiny brown coat and an even temperament. The cortege had already begun to depart, a far smaller train of carriages and guards than had left Palmerin. The queen's carriage was near the rear, not yet moving. Cas rode up beside it and looked in the window.

She was alone. Dressed in blue. Her profile revealed someone deep in thought, quite possibly the saddest person he had ever seen, if he did not count himself.

"Your Grace," Cas said.

Her head came up quickly. Shock chased away all signs of misery. "What are you doing here?"

"Riding south. Or so I heard."

The queen took in his traveling clothes, his horse, the ring that proclaimed him the queen's man. "No. This is not a temporary journey for me, Lord Cassiapeus. It is exile."

"I know what it is, Your Grace."

They looked at each other, truly looked, for the first time since he had discovered her secret and said goodbye to his brother for five long years. The queen dropped her gaze first. "You should go home."

Cas wanted nothing more. The rings felt heavy on his hand. "I will if you wish it. But I've already promised the king I would be here."

She looked past Cas to the palace windows, searching for a man who was not there. "He knows you're coming?" At Cas' nod, she asked, "What did he say?"

"He did not tell me to go home."

The queen was quiet. "You've lost your brother because of me. I don't even know where Coronado is."

"West." It would be a simple thing to place the blame on her shoulders alone. "Ventillas isn't a child. You couldn't force him to do anything he didn't want to. I'm his brother. I've tried."

"Nevertheless. I have made such a mess of things."

"Yes," Cas said. "But not only you."

A small crowd had gathered on the palace steps to wave good-bye to the train. Many, Cas saw, were those who had traveled with them from Palmerin. People who had attended the prince's naming ceremony, who had come to know the queen a little. Most appeared baffled, clearly wondering why she was leaving Elvira so soon after she had arrived. High Councilor Amador was there, eyeing Cas with a sour expression. Beside him was his sister, Lady Rondilla, smiling widely as she watched the carriages depart. Seeing them, the queen took a deep breath. She lifted her chin a notch higher.

The nurse Esti approached carrying Prince Ventillas. Seeing her had Cas taking another look at the crowd. He found Bittor off to the side by a potted tree, watching the nurse's departure with a glum look on his face. It occurred to Cas that he had never actually seen them speak.

Before Esti reached the carriage, Queen Jehan said to Cas, "You may stay until we've settled and then you must return home. It's much to ask, Lord Cassiapeus. But I would be grateful for a friendly face on this journey."

Cas looked at her, and the queen smiled suddenly. "A familiar face," she amended. "That will do just as well."

***

It was nearly midday before Cas found himself summoned to the front of the train. Commander Terranova and Ventillas had moved up the ranks together. He was a big man on a big horse, one of the few soldiers who made Cas appear frail in comparison. He rode with a lieutenant to his right, a friendly sort who greeted Cas with a smile.

Commander Terranova had no smiles to spare for Cas. "You were not expected on this journey, Lord Cassia."

The commander did not sit his horse alone. A spirit rode behind him, what had once been a beautiful woman in a dress the deepest shade of purple. Her arms were wrapped around the commander's middle. She had pressed her cheek into his back so that her face was turned to Cas. She looked at him, *through* him, with dark, sorrow-filled eyes.

Cas dragged his attention from her. "No, Commander. It was a recent decision."

"Whose decision?"

"King Rayan's, sir."

Commander Terranova's gaze dropped to the dual rings on Cas' finger. "How long do you plan to remain in the south?"

The queen would have Cas return to Palmerin sooner than later. Still. "As long as I'm needed."

"As long as that?" A black velvet pouch dangled from the commander's wrist, secured by a string. It was small, the size of a chicken egg. "Ventillas is gone. Palmerin must be missing its brothers. It isn't wise to leave a city so unprotected."

"It hasn't been, Commander." Cas held himself stiffly. His presence was not welcome here and he did not know why. He had always been on good terms with the commander.

The friendly lieutenant looked around to smile at Cas. "We'll be in the south a few months only. A new company should relieve us. We'll be glad to get back to our wives, eh, Commander?" For Cas' benefit, he added, "He's only been married a few months."

Cas snuck a glance at the woman in purple. "My congratulations, Commander."

Commander Terranova only grunted. Shrugging, the lieutenant gave Cas a look that said he did not know what had turned the man sour.

Who was this woman in purple? The commander's new wife? Did he know she had died? From the look on his face, blanching at the mention of wives, Cas was almost certain he knew.

"Commander!"

A soldier galloped their way from the road ahead. One of the outriders.

"A problem?" Commander Terranova asked when the man came to a stop before them, slightly winded.

There was. "We're going to have to find another route," the outrider said. "Someone's blown up the bridge."

# 31

THE BRIDGE HAD been built half a millennium ago, spanning a river that bisected the kingdom east to west. The engineers had been skilled, the stone expertly cut and laid. But mortar and stone had proven no match for incendiaries.

A great gaping hole separated one half of the bridge from the other. To Cas, it looked as if someone had loaded a wagon with incendiaries, driven it onto the bridge, and lit the fuses. Nearby villagers said they had heard a terrible booming sound in the early morning hours. Most of the debris had washed away by the time Cas and the others rode up, save for a splintered wagon wheel that had ended up on the riverbank. Stranded travelers gathered on both sides with their horses and carts, looking on in dismay.

Commander Terranova wasted no time issuing orders. The outrider was dispatched to Elvira to report on the damage. Repairs would need to begin immediately. The friendly lieutenant was ordered to turn the train around. They would be taking an alternate route. One that, if Cas remembered correctly, would lead them into the forest. Some of Cas' unease must have shown on his face because, once the other men had ridden off, Commander Terranova said curtly, "You have a concern, Lord Cassia. What is it?"

"This bridge, Commander." Cas had been forced to learn the history of the kingdom's major bridges, a favorite topic of Ventillas'. This bridge was within spitting distance of Elvira. No enemy had ever come close enough to draw a picture of it, let alone inflict damage. "It's been around for five hundred years, but it happens to burn down this morning? Of all mornings?"

At that, the spirit in purple lifted her head and looked at Cas. Not a vacant stare like before. She was listening.

"You think the woman we're searching for blew up the Elvira Bridge?" The look the commander turned on Cas was deeply skeptical. "Do you know what happens when a novice tries their hand with incendiaries?" He pointed to the bridge. "*That* many incendiaries? The outcome is rarely pleasant."

"She could have paid someone to do the work for her."

"You're grasping," Commander Terranova said, unimpressed. "And we're wasting daylight. You're here to play nursemaid to the queen, Lord Cassia. Nothing more. So go," he ordered, "and play nursemaid."

Cas' face turned hot. "Commander," he said as evenly as he could, before riding off.

***

"What is wrong?" the queen asked him when he reined in outside her carriage window. Esti sat opposite her with the prince. "Why have we stopped?"

"We're turning around," Cas informed them, trying to keep his temper in check. He was no one's nursemaid. "We'll take the road through the forest. It shouldn't delay us too long in the end."

The queen frowned. "What has happened?"

"Someone blew up the bridge. This morning," Cas added for good measure.

Two pairs of eyes widened. The queen said, "Do you think . . . ?"

Was this her old friend's doing? "Maybe, Your Grace. I don't know."

"And the commander? What does he think?"

"That it's a coincidence." Which was likely true. But he did not think so. In his heart, in his gut, it felt wrong.

The queen was quiet for the span of five heartbeats. "It is not a coincidence." Cas exchanged a glance with Esti and wondered, fleetingly, how much she knew. Farther down the road, the wagons and carts were being turned around.

Cas said, "We can go back. One word from you, and the commander will —"

"No," the queen said, her tone flat. "That is the one thing we cannot do. The king has sent along his finest soldiers. He's sent you," she added with a smile, there and gone in an instant. "We're as well protected here as we are there. There's nothing in Elvira for us now."

Subdued, Cas answered, "Yes, Your Grace." His heart hurt for her in a way he could not have imagined possible the day they first met. He shifted his attention to the nurse. "Esti . . ."

"I have two daggers," Esti told him brightly.

"Daggers?" Cas repeated.

Esti passed the baby over to a bemused queen. The nurse wore a cloak, unbuttoned, over a white dress. She lifted the hem high enough to show boots that had been well broken in. "Bittor gave them to me. I have one in here," she said, tapping her right boot. "He said to wear boots, not slippers, in case I needed to run. I have another here." She turned her head and lifted her wimple so they could see the hilt of a dagger peeking out by the nape of her neck.

"My goodness," the queen said.

Esti smiled, revealing two large dimples. "He's always been a nitpick for details, ever since we were children. See here?" She tugged open her cloak. "When I told him I was riding with the queen, he added these compartments." A half dozen pockets had been carefully sewn into the lining, holding bits of food, carefully wrapped, flint to start a fire, and two flasks filled with water. "Just in case," she finished, her smile fading.

Cas glanced down at the sleeve that Bittor had expertly mended. "You grew up together," he realized.

Esti nodded. "I moved to Elvira several years ago. I was a nurse for another family. Bittor found me after his family passed on."

The queen held her son closer. "He lost his entire family?"

Cas said, "You mean his sister?"

"Not just Clara," Esti said. "His parents and his three little brothers. The pestilence took them all."

***

The new route would take them west for several days before continuing south. They stopped for a midafternoon meal in an open field. Across the road were woodlands, a pleasant assortment of evergreens and autumn foliage. Before long, brightly colored blankets had been spread about for the queen and her few attendants. The food wagons distributed enough cold chicken to tide everyone over until supper. Cas ate standing up with a group of soldiers; they licked their drumsticks clean and tossed them onto a growing pile of bones.

Commander Terranova strode by without a word. The woman in purple trailed behind him, a hand on his arm. He stopped at a food wagon and spoke briefly with a cook, who reached into a chest and produced a battered serving spoon. The commander tucked the spoon into his belt and headed across the field to the woodlands.

"What's gotten into him?" one of the men asked.

"None of our business," another answered.

"Just a question. He was fine the other day. This morning he's biting everyone's head off."

"Don't be so hard on the man. He had to leave his bride behind. They've been married what? One month? Two?"

"Puh. I have a wife too."

"Yes, but you were happy to leave her."

Cas chuckled with the others, but as he made quick work of his fifth drumstick, his mind was busy. If the spirit was the commander's wife, she was alive no longer. Why hadn't these men heard of her passing? And if her death was recent, why had Commander Terranova accepted this mission? He could have remained behind to mourn. Another would have taken his place.

A baby's cry pierced the air. Cas looked around to see the queen by the blankets, reaching down to take a wailing Prince Ventillas from Esti.

"That's a lonely sight, isn't it?" one of the men said softly.

Cas stopped mid-chew.

"None of our business," another warned, after a look in Cas' direction.

The first soldier turned defensive. "Wasn't going to say anything bad. Queen Jehan's nice for a Brisan. She knows my name."

"Mine, too." There were murmurs of agreement.

The queen was walking the prince in circles around the blanket and patting his back. The baby continued to cry. Esti came up to her, but the queen shook her head and pointed to the food wagons.

"Maybe you should go sing to him, Lord Cassia," a soldier suggested with a grin.

The man nearest Cas eyed him curiously. "You can sing?"

"No," Cas said.

"Puh. You didn't hear him singing the lullabies to little Lady Clara. Made all the women's hearts flutter. My heart fluttered too, a little bit."

Cas felt his lips curve. He tossed a chicken bone at the soldier, who knocked it away, laughing. Cas left to the sounds of good-natured teasing.

***

Cas kept to the edge of the woods, within sight of the guards spread about the road. He had offered to take the prince for a walk so that the queen and Esti could eat in peace. Holding Prince Ventillas was like holding a sack full of feathers. The baby felt almost weightless in his arms. His head bobbed about as he took in his surroundings in wonder: the sky, the trees, the inner workings of Cas' ear. Cas walked the length of the train twice before the prince dropped off into sleep. Cas turned back, intending to return him to his mother, when he heard an odd sound coming from the woods.

A person gasping, choking. Someone was hurt, and without stopping to think, Cas headed into the woods at a fast clip.

Commander Terranova knelt before a tree, shoulders shaking, crying so violently it did indeed sound like a man choking. He had dug a small hole at the base of the tree. The spirit in purple hovered by him, ever fainter. Cas had frozen in horror, terrified the prince would wake and give their presence away. When he glanced behind him, he saw that the two guards who had followed stood as still as frightened deer. Cas turned back to see the commander take the pouch from his wrist and place it in the hole before covering it up with dirt.

The prince yawned, and the small puff of air against Cas' neck jolted him into action. Carefully, he backed away, sliding his boots along the thick woodland carpeting. The two guards did the same. When Cas reached the road, they were waiting for him. All three let out a relieved breath. "Not a word," Cas warned. "Never," one answered. The other nodded vigorously. They went their separate ways. Cas made it back across the field and was handing the prince over to Esti when Commander Terranova emerged. Troubled, Cas watched him return to his horse and converse with several officers. There was no sign of the woman in purple.

As the train prepared to journey on, Cas retraced his footsteps into the woods. A patch of overturned dirt told him it was the right tree. He hunkered down and, using a spoon he had swiped off the queen's tray, started to dig.

It did not take long before he discovered the black velvet pouch. He tugged at the drawstring and looked inside.

And found a little finger.

Cas' mind flew in every direction as he returned the finger to its grave. He searched the woods until the first wagons rolled away, but he never saw Commander Terranova's wife again.

***

That night, the fog came from nowhere. Cas was in the royal carriage because he was the only one who had been able to sing young Ventillas to sleep.

He could not say what woke him. The lantern swaying by his head showed that everyone else slept, the prince in a basket by the queen's feet. Cas lifted a corner of the window covering. A stinging cold struck him in the face. The fog was so thick he could not see beyond the reach of his arm. Not able to use his eyes, he used his ears. A carriage wheel struck a rock, and the queen stirred.

"What is it?" she asked quietly.

Cas pulled his head in, spoke just as softly. "The carriages have left too big a gap. I can't hear the others."

Esti smiled in her sleep, hands tucked beneath her chin like a child.

The queen lifted her window covering and dropped it just as quickly as the cold blew in. Shivering, she pulled her cloak tighter around her shoulders. "Close the window, please."

Cas made to do just that when the fog lifted momentarily, long enough for him to see their immediate surroundings using the driver's meager torchlight.

"Lord Cassiapeus, the window —"

Cas dropped the cover. Whatever showed on his face had her sitting up. She mouthed the question *What is it?*

Cas reached over and shook Esti awake. He held a finger to his lips. "We're not on the main forest road. We've turned off somewhere." How could they have been separated from the others?

Now Esti was wide-awake, listening.

The queen glanced at her child, peacefully asleep. "What should we do?"

Before Cas could answer, the carriage rolled to a stop.

"Good evening."

A female voice. Cas had no trouble recognizing it. Neither did the queen, who froze.

"Step outside, please. You may go first, Lord Cassiapeus."

Esti covered her mouth with both hands. Even so, a whimper emerged. *I have two daggers,* she had said. Quick as he could, Cas took the prince from his basket, blanket and all, and thrust him at the queen. Just before the door opened he slipped one of his daggers into the blanket so that it rested flat against the prince's back. He spoke under his breath. "Courage, Your Grace. You know her better than anyone."

Cas stepped down from the carriage and into the bitter night's cold. He knew this place. In the daylight, he would have been able to see the old aqueduct rising above the trees. These were the ruins at Patalon, a castle abandoned for so long the forest had begun its creep. Vines slithered up walls and into windows. Moss blanketed the castle steps.

At the foot of those steps were four hooded figures. Two held torches; two pointed crossbows directly at Cas. Princess Jehan stood between them, her own hood thrown back despite the cold. When the queen appeared beside Cas, the prince in her arms, he could sense the change in the air. One filled with quiet menace. The stillness before the storm.

Commander Terranova jumped down from the driver's perch. White-faced, he did not look at Cas or the queen, but called out, "I did what you asked. Where is my wife?"

A crossbowman shot him in the throat. The commander fell back onto the dirt, arms and legs splayed wide. Blood everywhere. Esti fainted.

Princess Jehan came closer, smiling slightly at the queen's strangled gasp. Cas had already seen what illness and torture had done to her. Hair turned white, deep grooves carved into her face. The queen had not.

Princess Jehan said, "Hello, Mari."

## ✦ 32 ✦

"HELLO, JEHAN." There was nothing in the queen's voice to suggest terror. It was calm, and it was quiet.

"It's cold out," Princess Jehan said. "Won't you come in? We have a fire." She turned to Cas and in the same pleasant voice said, "If you do anything foolish, we will not shoot you — we will shoot the child. Understood?"

Beside him, the queen did not breathe.

"Yes," Cas said in a stifled voice.

"Good!" Princess Jehan led the queen away. After a helpless glance at Esti, unconscious on the ground, in the cold, Cas followed. How long would it be before the royal guards realized they had lost an entire carriage? The most important one? They must have discovered the queen's absence by now. Which meant that help was on the way.

If they knew where to look.

If others had not been blackmailed.

Cas turned his gaze upward, searching for any sign of the aqueduct, but the moonlight remained hidden by cloud cover. A crossbow prodded him in the back, moving him along.

***

Cas found himself bound hand and foot with rope. He had offered no resistance when the guards had taken his mace, as well as the extra dagger hidden in his boot.

They were in a small room, one of the few that still had a roof. It had likely been used as a steward's work chamber. Master Jacomel would not have approved of the cobwebs and dust. At least the fireplace worked, though Cas had been dumped in a corner far away from its warmth.

Princess Jehan and the queen sat by the fire. A small table separated them. The queen held a cup with her right hand; her other arm cradled the prince against her shoulder. In the hours since they had arrived, she had not let him go once. Cas worried about what would happen when the baby woke, needing to be fed or changed, disturbing the strange peace between the two women.

There had been no mention of poisoned nurses or dead painters. No reference to the prince's near drowning on his naming day. Instead, they sipped at their tea and spoke of the past. Families, friends, childhood adventures and misadventures. More than once, Cas saw the queen's hand spasm from holding the prince up for so long. Neither woman mentioned it.

"We were going to raise our children together, remember?" Princess Jehan said. "And if one of us had a son and the other a daughter . . ."

"We would make sure they married," the queen finished. "Then you and I would be family, truly. I remember, Jehan."

A chill crept along Cas' neck and down his arms.

The guard who had tied him up stood by the door. The three additional guards had not made an appearance, though Cas heard rumblings from other parts of the castle. None of the voices sounded like Esti. This guard had pushed back his hood, revealing a face only a handful of years older than Cas. He was both taller and wider, muscles rippling beneath his tunic. He held a sword. Cas would have thought twice about provoking him even if the prince's life had not been threatened. Cas' mace was on the floor behind the guard, propped against the wall.

Cas had been tossed on his side, bound hands facing the wall. He watched the guard carefully as he tried to free himself. In prison, they had known better than to use rope to bind the men. Rope could be loosened, little by little. It could be chewed through, if one was desperate enough.

"I can't have babies, Mari. He took that from me."

Pausing, Cas looked across the chamber. There were tears in both women's eyes. Someone must have told the queen about their hideous findings at the doctor's house. Chains, cuffs, a womb floating in a jar.

"I know, dear heart." The queen set her cup down. Princess Jehan came around and knelt before her, resting her head against the queen's skirts as she wept, silently, her shoulders shaking. The burly guard stepped forward, a look of concern on his face.

"I should never have left you." The queen stroked her hair, even as the hand cradling the baby shook. "I am so very sorry."

Prince Ventillas stirred. Cas held his breath until the child settled back into sleep, then worked faster on his bindings.

Princess Jehan said, "I woke up and I did not know where I was. You were gone. Faustina, too. Everyone was speaking Oliveran, screaming in Oliveran. The hospital was a nightmare. I was so frightened."

The queen bowed her head. Her tears fell onto her friend's snow-white hair.

Princess Jehan said, "Every time I closed my eyes I thought I would not open them again. I hoped for it. But little by little, I felt better. One of the nurses said a doctor was coming to take me away. He would help me get well."

The queen looked across the chamber at Cas, her face drained of all color. Her expression said she wished the doctor were still alive so she could kill him herself, slowly and painfully.

"What did he do to you, Jehan?" the queen asked. "Will you tell me?"

Princess Jehan brushed aside her tears. "We were not people to him. He wanted us for his experiments. Can a woman live once you remove her womb? The answer is yes. I am proof of it. But having a child of my own? That dream is gone." She glanced over at the guard. "What happens when you cut out a man's tongue? He wanted to know that, too."

The guard had not spoken a word. Cas had not realized until now. Had they been prisoners together? Escaped together? Someone had knocked Cas senseless the night Faustina was killed. Had helped Princess Jehan escape through the mountains. Was this that man?

The queen was also watching the guard. "What happens?"

Princess Jehan smiled. "The man waits for you to make a mistake, to turn your back, and then he kills you."

The guard smiled at Princess Jehan in a way that made Cas think, *Why, he loves her.*

The rope around his ankles had loosened. Cas held himself still as the guard walked over and gave him a halfhearted kick in the side. The pain made Cas' eyes cross. The guard walked away. Cas took several deep breaths before going to work on his hands.

"I have missed you, Mari." Princess Jehan rose to sit beside the queen. "He is lovely. How like you he looks!"

"Do you think so?" The queen sent Cas a desperate glance.

Princess Jehan peered closer, smiling. "Yes, his nose, most certainly. And he has your dear father's eyes. May I hold him?"

"No," the queen said.

That was how quickly pretense vanished and goodwill went away. The guard had turned his back to Cas, intent on the two friends. Cas yanked at his bindings.

Princess Jehan's smile was no more. "Let me hold him, Mari."

"I said no." The queen rose. What control she had left splintered. "You will *never* touch him. How could you, Jehan? Faustina loved you."

"She left me," Princess Jehan said, her voice rising. "Just like you."

"You told me to go!" The queen whisked around the table so that it stood between them. Jolted awake, Prince Ventillas began to cry. "Marry the king, end the war. I did as you begged me to, and now you'll *punish* me for it?"

"And you went, gladly! Without a thought to spare for me."

"That is not true!" the queen protested. "I have wept for you every day since I left Gregoria. I sent men to find you!"

"To make sure I was dead." Princess Jehan held out a palm, stopping the guard from approaching. Her eyes never left the queen's face. "What good would I have done to you alive? What explanation would have offered your dear husband, for me? *My* life, Mari. You stole it. My king. My child. Give him to me."

The guard finally noticed Cas' frantic struggle in the corner. He charged over with his sword just as Cas rolled to his feet. A searing pain tore through him, beneath his arm. Cas lashed out with the rope so that the end struck the guard in the eye. Howling, the man fell to his knees. Cas used his fist, two sharp jabs in the throat, and the guard fell farther, collapsing onto his side and gagging. He looked over in time to see Princess Jehan grab for the prince. Her nails scraped the back of his neck. Like claws.

"No!" The queen slashed wildly with a dagger, Cas' dagger, across the exposed flesh of collarbone.

Princess Jehan stumbled back, too close to the fireplace. Her skirts were set aflame. Shrieking, she swatted and spun like a child's top, then fell against a tattered wall hanging. That, too, caught fire. The queen stared in frozen horror at her friend. While in her arms, Prince Ventillas screamed and screamed.

Cas swept the mace off the floor. He grabbed the queen's hand. "We have to go." He did not know where Esti was. But there were three guards unaccounted for. They would come once they saw the fire and smelled the smoke. Even if they did not, Cas and the queen would have to run fast and run far. If the fire took hold in the forest, it would spare no one.

# 33

THE MOON REAPPEARED, but they no longer needed its light. Behind them, the castle burned.

Commander Terranova had been left where he had fallen. Cas and Queen Jehan raced past him into the forest. There was shouting behind them, too close, and the princess' screams. Of poor Esti, Cas saw nothing.

They stopped once. "Give him to me," Cas said. "It will be faster if I hold him." He slid the prince into his overtunic. Tucked into his trousers, it acted as a sling. The prince's shrieks had quieted to terrified hiccups. Queen Jehan turned back to watch the flames as they spread from the ruins to the trees. She coughed violently, tears streaming down her face. "How do we race fire, Lord Cassiapeus?"

"We don't have to. We just need to find the arches."

"Arches?"

Cas didn't answer. Even at this distance, he could feel the heat from the flames and the heaviness of the smoke. He grabbed her hand and they ran, coughing with every breath.

The aqueduct appeared on their right, white stone in the dark, looming over the trees. It was just as imposing as the aqueduct back home, but this one had been built with triple arches, not double. Queen Jehan stumbled when she saw it. "Arches."

"Yes." When they reached it, Cas dropped to his knees and searched along its base.

Queen Jehan crouched beside him. "What are you looking for?"

"A ladder. Hopefully it hasn't crumbled . . . Here. Do you see these?" He found the rungs. Ancient slats that led up to the second arch. "You go first. Test each one." His voice had turned ragged. It was hard to catch his breath.

Queen Jehan said suddenly, "You sound strange. Are you hurt? Where?" She clutched at his shoulders, trying to see him through red, watering eyes.

"It's nothing. Please, Your Grace. We must hurry."

She went, tugging gingerly on each rung before placing her full weight on it. Even so, one broke off under her step. At her muffled shriek, quickly cut off, Cas knew a moment of hair-raising terror. He heard her scrabbling about before she found solid footing. Once she reached the top and called to him, Cas followed. Halfway up, the prince squeaked indignantly in his ear. "What?" Cas said with a laugh that even to him sounded a little crazed. "You had a different evening planned? So did I, little prince. So did I."

Cas had seen this aqueduct at a distance many times before, traveling with Ventillas. It had not been used for at least a century. Water no longer coursed through it, which meant they could walk safely through the empty pipes. It would keep them high above the flames. Eventually, it would cross a river where, if good fortune smiled upon them, the fire would not follow.

***

They walked through miles of pipe, wending their way past the lime deposits, or sinter, that had built up over the decades. The incrustation grew along the floor and walls, sometimes so thick they could not pass through. Cas had to chip away at the deposits with his mace.

It could have been worse. At least they had the warmth of their cloaks. They had been allowed to keep them on at the castle, though they were both searched. Not the baby, however. No one had thought to inspect his blankets for weapons.

It was morning when the river appeared below. They crossed over and kept walking until they came to an opening where the aqueduct crumbled away. After that there was nothing to do but sit and wait.

"Here, let me take him." The queen knelt before Cas and lifted the prince free of his overtunic. "He's . . . oh, he's wet all over you!" Her eyes met Cas'. Seconds passed before they both began to snicker.

"How are we laughing?" She tucked her son inside her cloak and sat beside Cas. Dirt smudged her cheek. There was a scratch on her chin, likely from a tree branch. "You're hurt. We're trapped. It's a disaster. And Jehan. Oh, Jehan." She buried her face in her son's hair. Her laughter turned abruptly to tears.

Cas let her be. Much later, when she had cried herself out, he spoke. "I'm sorry."

"I am always leaving her." She sounded exhausted. "I did not even try to help her."

"There was no time —" The look in her eyes stopped him. Grief and guilt. A terrible understanding.

"There was. We had time to try. I left her there on purpose. What sort of person does that make me?"

Cas was quiet. He was remembering Princess Jehan's words. *My life, Mari. You stole it. My king. My child. Give him to me.* He was sorry for her. He would not wish what had happened to her on anyone. Seeing Princess Jehan, he knew there was a part of her that loved her friend and the life they had shared. But there was a terrible rage in her too, and as long as she lived, she would be a threat to the queen and her family.

Cas said, "The sort that protects her child. The good sort." He leaned his head against the stone and closed his eyes. "I'm glad you're both safe."

"Yes," she agreed quietly. "Because of you. The histories will be kind to you, Lord Cassiapeus of Palmerin."

"Cas," he said without opening his eyes. "Or Cassia, that one is bearable too. Just not Cassiapeus. Please."

He heard the smile in her voice when she said, "Cas, then."

Cas turned his head, looked at her. "It does me no good now, being in the histories. I would give it up for a bath, and supper, and . . ." The queen's face grew blurry.

Frowning, she reached over, lifted his arm. A gasp. "Cas."

He tried to focus. There was something in her eyes, a different sort of fear. "Your Grace?"

"And what else?" the queen prompted.

"Supper."

"Yes," she said patiently. "You mentioned supper. What else? *No.* Do not sleep just yet. You told me your injury was nothing. This is far from nothing."

Cas looked down at his arm. The guard's sword had cut deep. But . . . "It doesn't hurt anymore. Do you think she'll keep the horse?"

"What?" he heard the queen say. And then, more urgently, "Cas!"

That was all he understood, all he heard. *So tired,* he thought, and closed his eyes.

***

For the rest of his life, Cas would remember the sound of hoofbeats. The approach of many soldiers, including King Rayan, who had come to his senses and gone racing to bring his family home. And Lena. She was there too, riding her mare. They heard a baby crying and stopped their horses, looking round and round, and then up, their expressions incredulous, at the crumbling upper tier of an aqueduct.

## 34

"HOW DID YOU find us?" Cas asked.

He was at the palace in Elvira, in a bedchamber he remembered from years past. The rugs and tapestries were decorated in forest greens and deep golds. An uncovered window revealed the dark of night. He had woken to find little Clara asleep at his side. Thankfully, the side that was not injured. Her face was buried in the pit of his arm.

Lena sat cross-legged on the enormous canopied bed, looking down at him. Her dress was a shade of red that reminded him of the flame trees back home. At his question, she held up a piece of cream-colored fabric. The sleeve of a dress, made of silk rakematiz. "You remember Bittor's family are wool merchants?"

A cheerful fire blazed across the chamber. In front of it, Bittor worked through a set of intricate moves with Cas' mace. Bittor's family were no longer wool merchants. They were gone. If Bittor chose not to speak of it, then neither would Cas. He answered, "In the north. I remember."

"Well, Bittor suggested bringing the sleeve to the clothing guilds. If anyone would know who worked with silk rakematiz, it would be one of them."

Bittor pointed the mace at him with a flourish. "And I was right."

"Every guild master I spoke with mentioned the same person," Lena continued. "A dressmaker in one of the southern parishes. She recognized the sleeve right away. She said that a woman brought the silk to her shop months ago and asked that a wedding dress be made from it. The dressmaker said that the woman's hair was a pure white even though she didn't *sound* old. She said her name was—"

"Faustina," Cas said.

"Yes."

Clara stirred. She wore a white ruffled nightgown. Someone had also dressed Cas in a white ruffled nightshirt that reached his knees. Bittor had burst out laughing when he first saw it.

Lena leaned over and brushed the hair from Clara's face. "She wouldn't tell the dressmaker where she lived, but she paid extra to have the dress delivered to a village inn in Patalon. She had made arrangements to have it picked up from there."

Patalon.

"I went right away to tell Rayan," Lena said. "He was in the stables already, in a *frantic* state. He didn't know what he'd been thinking. He was going to bring back his family. We met up with the cortege, and they had to tell him that they had lost the queen's carriage."

"That was unpleasant to watch," Bittor added.

Lena shuddered in agreement. "That's when we saw it. A fire burning in the forest, just outside Patalon."

Cas eased his arm out from beneath Clara and sat up against the pillows. The pain beneath his arm had been reduced to a dull throbbing. He touched the stitches behind his ear. Nothing leaked. It was all he could ask for. He said with difficulty, "Bittor. We lost Esti."

"We found her." Bittor waved the mace at the door. "She was just here a moment ago."

"What?" Cas said, astonished. *"How?"*

Lena smiled at him. "She found her way to the road. It's difficult for her to speak. The smoke damaged her throat and lungs, but the doctor says he doesn't think it will be permanent."

The relief made his head spin. "Where was she?"

Lena said, "She fainted by the carriage and woke up in the exact same place. Those wretched guards!" she added indignantly. "They just left her there in the cold. She said she heard voices coming from the castle and ran in the opposite direction. Into the forest."

"Did you find anyone else?" Princess Jehan, her guards?

Lena and Bittor shook their heads, solemn. Parts of the forest were still on fire. It was too dangerous to search for others.

Cas did not know what to say to either of them, except "Thank you."

"You're welcome." Bittor held up the mace. "Can I have this?"

"No."

Bittor turned away, grumbling.

Cas said to Lena, very quietly, "I am sorry."

"You already said so." Her lips curved. "In front of the history guild masters, no less. My grandfather's friends. It's all right, Cas. You didn't have to give up your horse."

"I'll take her back if you want."

"No."

They smiled at each other. Lena took one of the bed's many pillows and wrapped her arms around it, chin propped on one end. "You'll go home soon."

His hand strayed to the wound at his side. Home was very far away from her. "Yes."

"I'm glad."

He did not want her to be glad about him leaving. "You don't look it, Lena."

"But I feel it. Most of the time," she insisted, hugging the pillow tighter. "Ever since you returned to Palmerin, there's been one disaster after another. You haven't had a chance to just *be*. To enjoy being home. I wish that for you." She set the pillow aside, intending to swing off the bed, stopping when he took her hand in his and brought it to his lips.

Seconds only. Long enough for her eyes to fill with tears, before she slipped her hand free and jumped off the bed. "I have to take Clara to her room." Lena hurried across the chamber and out the door, leaving the little girl behind.

For once, Bittor offered no comment. He set the mace against a chair and came over to gather Clara in his arms. "Good night," Bittor said, and took himself off, closing the door behind him.

# 35

WHENEVER CAS TRIED to leave Elvira, Queen Jehan found a way to delay him. First, she insisted he stay until he had healed sufficiently. Once that happened, she insisted he be formally named a queen's man. There was no escaping the pomp and fuss. He found himself kneeling before the king and queen in Elvira's great throne room, dressed in Palmerin red.

Cas wore his family's seal on his left hand. The queen had taken the other back days ago. She returned it now, to his right ring finger, where it was no longer loose. It fit perfectly.

"We are grateful for your service, Lord Cassiapeus of Palmerin." Queen Jehan wore blue and silver and a diamond crown. "We wish you a safe journey home and ask only that if you are called upon for aid, you will answer."

Warmth filled the crowded chamber. He could hear the rhythmic snapping of fans against collarbones as he made the formal response. "Your Grace, you have only to send word and I will answer. I am grateful for this honor. I am humbled by the faith you have placed in me, and in my house."

The formal applause was drowned out by the cheering and whistling behind him, the king's soldiers who had become his friends on the journey to Elvira. Cas stood and kissed the queen's hand. He bowed to the king, who said, "Cas. Be sure to leave your mark." He tipped his crown toward a cluster of soldiers, including Bittor, who carried Clara on his shoulders. Bittor stepped to one side. Cas saw a table with an open ledger and a pot of ink. Lena sat behind the table, watching him.

Like the queen, she wore blue and silver. No diamonds or circlets, though. She was here in an official capacity, in the role her grandfather once held. She pointed to a page in the ledger. "Your name and seal for the histories, Lord Cassiapeus."

Few paid them any attention. Others were coming forward for their share of glory. Receiving knighthoods and boons, or paying homage to the queen.

"Lena," Cas said. He had not seen her since that night in his chamber. She had been avoiding him. When he turned up at her green door, she was not home. When the king and queen held a supper, her seat was taken up by others. He needed to say a thousand things and he did not know how. The weight of the words pressed against his heart.

Lena met his eyes, then looked away. She held the quill out to him. "I wish you a safe journey home. I wish you dreamless nights. Goodbye, Cas."

It was not meant to be. This was her home. He needed to return to his, far away in the mountains. Cas took up the quill, dipped it in ink, and signed his name. He pressed his rings into the wax. First his family's, then his queen's, and made his mark beneath his name.

He stepped away from her. "Goodbye," he said.

Cas went straight to his chamber. He opened his trunks and threw in his clothes. He counted the hours until morning.

\*\*\*

Before Cas left the following day, he received a final summons from King Rayan, who was alone in his private chamber, looking out a window. Beside him was a table and on that table was a box Cas had seen once before.

"It was delivered by messenger this morning." King Rayan watched him closely. "From Trastamar. Did you know what he intended?"

It was Ventillas' box. It held the papers for his ambassadorship. He had not taken it with him. "No, Your Grace."

"But you are not surprised."

*I've not felt . . . myself this past year. It feels like someone else is living in my skin and I just . . . I need to go.*

"I am not."

"Where would he go?" At Cas' wary look, King Rayan said with annoyance, "I'm not going to send the hounds after him. Once upon a time, he was my friend."

Chastised, Cas said, "I don't know. Truly I don't."

King Rayan studied him, then waved him off with a sigh. "You may go. Safe travels, Cas."

The door opened and High Councilor Amador walked in. There was no mistaking the amused glint in the king's eyes when he said, "Amador. It seems you'll have to find another ambassador to that hell kingdom in the west. Coronado, was it?"

Lord Amador stopped, outraged. "Your Grace?" he said, glaring at Cas.

Cas left the chamber. He was not his brother's keeper. He had told the king the truth. Where Ventillas had gone he could not begin to guess. But he took comfort in knowing his brother would keep his word, that he would be at the harbor in Trastamar in five years' time. Waiting for Cas. Ready to come home.

# ❦ 36 ❦

WHEN CAS LEFT Elvira, he took a shovel with him.

They had found no sign of the strange, unnamed woman who had kidnapped the queen, or her accomplices. It had been too dangerous to search the forest until now, when days of autumn rains had finally doused the most persistent sparks.

From Patalon, Cas led his horse through the charred, blackened forest. The palfrey, a gift from the queen, did not like the smell of smoke. Neither did Cas. It clung to his clothing and saddlebag. It layered his skin like dirt. He patted the horse's neck in apology and continued on.

If it had not been for the aqueduct, now partially burned, he would not have been able to find the castle. All that was left were bits and pieces of crumbling foundation.

A skeleton lay in front of the ruins, what remained of Commander Terranova. The authorities had searched his home in Elvira and discovered a household in mourning and disarray, for the commander's wife had been pulled from the harbor, drowned, a finger severed cleanly from her left hand. For his actions against the queen, his estates had been forfeited, everything he had once owned returned to the crown.

Cas left the horse and went to search what was left of the castle. He found them together. Two skeletons on blackened earth, one large, the other small, their arms around each other. Princess Jehan and the man who had loved her, suffered with her. Cas had never learned his name.

Cas turned slowly, looking for a spirit with white hair and a face older than her years. He said, "Princess Jehan?"

His words were met with silence. Over and over he tried, calling out her name. No one answered. Even the birds had gone.

Cas searched the rest of the castle and then the outlying areas. He located three more skeletons a quarter of a mile away. Princess Jehan and the men who had done her bidding were all accounted for. Cas could not say what the future held, but for now, the queen's secret was safe.

He dug two graves beside the castle. In the first, he buried the men, save one. In the second, he laid Princess Jehan with her guard, taking care to bury them as they had died. Arms around each other. Cas did not know why he could not see her spirit. He hoped her absence meant she had found some measure of peace.

Before he departed, he retrieved three gold coins from his saddlebag — Zacarias, god of beginnings and endings — and left them on her grave.

C AS PASSED THE winter at Palmerin Keep. Five months of snow and solitude. He no longer woke in the night, and he rarely jumped at shadows. His own or others, living or dead. He felt himself growing stronger, and he wondered if Lena would recognize him now, or if she had forgotten him completely, the strange, quiet lord from the mountains.

The city kept him busy. He met with the city inspector, funded repairs for the streets, the aqueduct, the bridges, the baths. He oversaw the addition to the amphitheater. And he spent as much time as he could training with Captain Lorenz. In the library he studied maps, imagining where his brother could be.

At the first signs of spring, he asked Father Emil to ride with him beyond the city gates. The priest, who had never been invited anywhere by Cas before, readily agreed. The journey took them to a single-arch bridge where a toll keeper's cottage stood desolate and abandoned. Since Cas had last seen it, the thatched roof had fallen in completely. The priest shook his head at the sight. After tethering their horses to a tree, Cas untied the wooden cross strapped to his saddlebag. He led the priest to the small clearing where he had buried Izaro last autumn. "I buried him there." Cas pointed. "But I wanted to leave a marker. And I thought you might say a prayer."

"Certainly I will." Father Emil waited until Cas had pounded the cross into the dirt and grass before asking, "Will you join me?"

Cas hesitated. That he even considered prayer surprised him. "Not today, Father."

Cas waited for him by the bridge. He leaned against a post, watching the water go by, listening to the birds in the trees.

"I didn't think you'd come back." Izaro stood beside Cas. Nearly solid one moment, barely visible the next.

Cas glanced at him, then turned back to the river. "Yes, well. I felt sorry for you."

A rumble of laughter. "Not sorry enough. Who is that infant priest you've brought to pray over me?"

"The only one I have." From where Cas stood, he could just make out the priest kneeling before the cross. "He isn't bad."

"What infant is?" Izaro rested his elbows on the railing. "Did you ever find that horse thief of yours? The girl?"

"I did." Just thinking of Lena hurt his heart.

"What happened to her? Sent her to the dungeon, hm? The gallows?"

"I gave her the horse."

Izaro turned to Cas, appalled, before looking past him. "Who's this, then?"

Riders came through the trees. Ten men in black, along with a boy, about twelve. Cas did not recognize them. They stopped at the far end of the bridge. One called out, "You're on private lands, stranger. State your name and business at once."

Cas, eyebrows raised, looked at Izaro, who shrugged.

Cas stepped away from the post. "My name is Cas, second lord of Palmerin. My lands are just there."

"Oh!" The boy broke into a smile. He started toward Cas on horseback even as the man who had first spoken called him back in exasperation. The boy ignored him, stopping several feet away from Cas before jumping off his horse. He beamed up at him. "You're Lord Cassia! The queen's man!" Two men came to stand beside him.

Cas smiled down at the boy. "I am. And who are you?"

"Ferrer, sir. Lord Ruben was my uncle. Well, my uncle six times removed. I never met him. I'm here to claim my inheritance." His sunny smile faded as he regarded the dilapidated cottage. He added dispiritedly, "Such as it is."

The man who had spoken bowed. "My name is Cosme, Lord Cassia. I'm Lord Ferrer's guardian and steward. Forgive my wariness earlier. We've been on the road many days now and have learned to be cautious of strangers."

"Understood. This is Father Emil," Cas said as the priest navigated the slope and joined them. "Your toll keeper, Izaro, was buried here last autumn. We came to add a cross by his grave and to say final prayers."

The newcomers thanked them. Young Lord Ferrer crossed himself, which earned him an approving smile from Izaro.

Cas said, "It's not as bad as this." He indicated the cottage. "Your estate has been looted, like many others, rather severely. But the buildings themselves are sound. You're welcome to stay at Palmerin Keep until the repairs are done."

Both the boy's and the steward's faces flooded with relief. Lord Ferrer said, "We're very grateful. Lady Analena said you would welcome us, but we didn't want to presume."

Cas stared at him. "You've spoken to Lena?"

"She traveled with us from Elvira," the boy informed him, and for the first time in five months, Cas felt his heart beat in his chest. "She told us all about your adventures, and how you saved the queen and the prince. Twice! She said you were handsome and brave and tall as a tree. I know everything about you! You're exactly as I pictured."

"My lord," the steward said ruefully to the boy. "I'm not certain the lady will appreciate your candor."

"Handsome, eh?" Izaro said. "I don't see it."

"Where is she?" Cas asked.

"Riding to Palmerin," the steward answered. "She went off on her own by the aqueduct. She said she knew the way."

Cas looked at Father Emil, who smiled and said, "Go. I will show them the way back."

Cas could have kissed him. Izaro raised a hand in farewell. Cas told his new neighbors he would see them very soon, and then he ran for his horse and rode off.

***

Not long after, he found his old mare. She stood off to the side of the road near a copse, one he knew well. He had killed a lynx here many months ago. He had rescued a girl from a tree.

The same girl who knelt before the mare, inspecting a hoof. Lena wore a deep red cloak. The color of his city. Her hair had grown to her shoulders. She looked up at his approach and set the hoof down.

"Hello, Cas."

"Lena." Cas dismounted. He tried to think of something else to say that did not sound too foolish. "Is she hurt?"

"Some stones in her shoe. This last one is stubborn."

"Let me see." Cas ran a hand along the mare's side. "Hello, girl." She wore red ribbons in her mane. Dozens of them. He thought they might be silk.

Lena smiled at his sigh, shifting to give him room by the hoof. "She enjoys them. Don't you, Clara?"

"Clara?" Cas knelt beside her. Their shoulders nearly touched.

"I told Clara she could name her. She named her Clara."

Smiling, Cas inspected the horseshoe. The stone was lodged tight. "She's better, then? The queen said she was, in her letters."

Lena plucked several blades of grass before answering. "There are fewer nightmares, and she speaks more each day. Especially to Bittor. He's become a favorite." Cas snorted at that. "But she still hoards her food. The servants find it under the bed or in her slippers. They complain about the bugs."

Cas tugged at the stone. It barely gave way. "That should stop too. In time." He no longer felt the need to keep food in his chambers or saddlebag. Or to eat more than he needed, worried that the meals would end.

Lena said quietly, "I'm glad it stopped, for you."

The mare's breath was warm on their faces, pleasant against the coolness of spring.

Why had she come? "You're a long way from home, Lena."

A blade of grass was tied into a knot. She did not look at him. "The guild masters received your letter."

Cas felt the heat spreading up his neck. He ducked his head, busying himself with the stone. "Oh yes?" he muttered.

"Yes. The one where you reminded them there has not been a historian in the mountains for many years now, and that one is sorely needed. That letter."

Cas had written and rewritten that cursed letter more times than he cared to count, agonizing over every word. Master Jacomel had scolded him about the wasted parchment. Cas had been afraid she would not come. Or worse, that some ancient historian would show up in her place. He had not wanted that.

"You're the one who said there are stories here you've never heard of and food you've never tasted. Every region needs its own history. That is what you said." Cas worked the stone free and tossed it aside. He snuck a glance at her, confessing, "I had Master Jac sign it too, for more authenticity."

Lena smiled. "I saw. The guild masters said no."

"What? Then . . . how are you here?"

Lena rose, shaking bits of grass from her dress. "Guild master Hipolito said he remembered you, and he did not trust young, handsome men who made such requests. Those were his words. I had to offer a compromise."

"What comp—?" Cas felt it then, beneath his boots. The thundering of hooves. He stood, dusting his hands on his trousers, and looked down the empty road in the direction from which he had just come. "Feels like a large party."

"It is. They are the compromise. My family," Lena explained with a rueful shrug. "And everyone else. Chaperones. I rode ahead because they were moving far too slowly."

Cas started to smile. "How long can you stay?"

"Until the work is done," she answered before speaking in a rush. "There's Palmerin, of course, but I'd also like to visit the outlying villages and towns. See what I can gather from there. I want to see where your jumping beans grow. Palmerin can be my base. Jehan has promised to stay through the summer and as long as others take her place afterward . . ."

His smile grew. "You can stay awhile."

"Yes. It was all decided rather suddenly. There was no time to send word to Master Jacomel. That poor, poor man."

Master Jacomel was going to have an apoplexy. All the food to ready, the chambers to prepare. But if anyone could do it, it would be Palmerin's master steward.

"Let's go tell him. I just met your Lord Ferrer. We'll have to find room for him, too." Clara the mare had wandered off to greet Cas' horse. "We should rest her foot." Cas held out a hand to Lena. "Will you ride with me?"

Instead of taking his hand, Lena walked straight into him, burying her face in his chest. He wrapped his arms around her, breathing in her hair. And that was how they stood, for a long time, until the thundering hoofbeats warned them they would not be alone for long.

"I should have written sooner," Cas said. "I should have written to you directly."

Lena shook her head, her nose still pressed against his heart. "You needed to be here on your own. That is what Rayan said. You needed time to get better. You look different, Cas. Happier."

Cas pulled away slightly, looked down into her beautiful face that he had missed for five long months. He would not pretend he did not know what she spoke of. More than anyone, she had seen the darkness in him. "I still feel it sometimes," he admitted. "Around the edges. It's less each day." Each week, each month. Better. A thought struck him. "You'll write Palmerin's history. What about your grandfather's?"

Her eyes shadowed. "There won't be one. The notes have been lost."

"Lost how?" She had never been careless with her grandfather's work.

"Burned. With Rayan as witness."

Cas was quiet. "I'm sorry, Lena."

One shoulder lifted. "My grandfather used to say that history is written by the historians, and we are all of us flawed. They're my family, Cas."

"You don't have to tell me about family." Cas whistled the horses over. Lena shared the palfrey with Cas, sitting in front of him. Clara would walk by their side.

Lena twisted around to smile up at him. "Do you remember the last time we were here?"

"I remember you stole my horse, and I saved your life anyway."

"I remember I fell out of a tree, and you dropped me."

Smiling, Cas kissed her. On a bright spring day, without a cloud on the horizon. "I like my memory better."

She laughed. That was the sound Cas took with him as he led both horses onto the road, the ancient aqueduct to their left, his family's legacy, guiding them home to Palmerin.

# AUTHOR'S NOTE

I have always been fascinated by plague. I think it stems from not having cable television as a kid. CBS was one of the few channels we *did* have, which meant that whenever *Ben-Hur* was on, I watched it. All three and a half hours of it. Seeing Judah Ben-Hur and Esther in the Valley of the Lepers was something I never forgot.

Because plague does not play favorites. Whether it's leprosy, cholera, yellow fever, Spanish flu, or the coronavirus, it does not care if someone is rich or poor, kind or wicked, religious or an atheist. Plague can happen to anyone.

I began writing *Year of the Reaper* in 2018, long before the coronavirus arrived in the United States. But even then I found myself curious about the aftermath of plague, specifically the Black Death of the fourteenth century, which wiped out a third of Europe's population. As I read history book after history book, trying to figure out what sort of story to tell, I realized that the past held all the inspiration I needed.

A feral child found alone in a village. Crowded hospitals. Abandoned homes. Mass flight from the cities.

Most curious of all was a reference to Princess Joan, teenage daughter of England's Edward III. In 1348, Joan set sail from England to Spain to marry Pedro, heir to the kingdom of Castile. But Joan never reached Spain. She died en route, in France, of plague. There are differing accounts as to where in France she was buried, and there is no record of her body being returned to London for burial. She left behind an unworn wedding dress made of fine silk rakematiz.

I grew up on the U.S. territory (and former Spanish colony) of Guam, an island three hours away from Japan and seven hours away from Hawaii. When I was seventeen, I flew across the Pacific to attend the University of Oregon. It's not difficult to imagine the nervousness and excitement Princess Joan must have felt leaving home and heading off into the unknown. I have been there myself.

As I'm writing this, it is early in 2021. I'm at home with my family and a vaccine appointment is still months away. I worried that it might not be the right time to tell this story. But I also thought it important to show young readers a glimpse of the past when, even in the most trying of times, people carried on. At its heart, *Year of the Reaper* is a hopeful tale, a story of friendship and family and the resilience of the human spirit. Cassia's spirit in particular. I love this character, bruised and battered though he is, and I very much hope you enjoyed his story.

Discover Thrilling YA
Fantasy from